Where Was God

A Contemporary Christian Romance

Novel by

Sheila L. Jackson

Virtuous Books

ALSO BY SHEILA L. JACKSON

Non-Fiction

The Enemy Within

Perfectly Normal

Contemporary Christian Romance

Joi and Payne

Coming in January 2018, Where Was God, Book II

Where Was God
Virtuous Books
Copyright ©2015 Sheila L. Jackson
http://www.sheilaljackson2.com
SJ@comcast.net

Cover Photo by Asha

ISBN -10:0692583106
ISBN: 13:978-0692583104
For Worldwide Distribution
Printed in the USA

Dedication

To my husband, Timothy, you have given me words of wisdom throughout my spiritual journey. I love you for always taking care of our girls and my well-being. You are truly the definition of a real man.

Acknowledgements

Thank you, Lord, for without Your anointing, penning this novel would have been impossible.

To my husband, Timothy, and daughters, Brittany and Amber, thanks so much for listening to my constant rambling about writing. Also, thanks to my family and friends who have continued to encourage and pray for me, your support means a lot.

I am grateful to Debra Kavanaugh and Ivy Woodard at the Shreve Memorial Library in Shreveport, Louisiana. Whenever there is an event in the area, you ladies make sure that I am a part of it.

To the bookstores, who never failed to house and set-up my book signing events, thank you so much for your hard work.

I am humbled and grateful to the many readers who purchased my books throughout the years. Your e-mails and posts on social media have inspired me to continue to write uplifting material.

Many thanks to those in the ministry, who prayed and encouraged me along the way; this has indeed been a long, hard, and lonely journey. But through your intercession, I was strengthened to persevere.

Prologue

Augusta, Louisiana
Fifteen years earlier

Twelve-year-old Fayth Angelica Hope sat motionless next to her aunt as the mourners flooded the Saint Gabriel Baptist Church fellowship hall. She rolled her red, puffy eyes heavenwards as she tried to make sense of her father's death. Bursts of laughter jolted her senses. *What is so funny?* she thought. The grieving faces she had seen earlier now beamed with excitement. Stories and jokes about her father's life filtered throughout the small, stuffy room, which sent flames shooting from her nostrils.

"My father is dead, and these people are celebrating," Fayth cried as anger continued to well up inside her petite frame. Shaking her head in disbelief, she collapsed onto her aunt's broad shoulder, giving in to the tears that tugged at her heartstrings.

"That's what people do after funerals, baby. They remember the dead," Beatrice said, cuddling her arm around her distraught niece. "Your dad was a good man."

"I don't want to be here, Auntie," she pouted, wishing she could wiggle her nose and disappear into thin air, like the character, Samantha Stevens, in *Bewitched*.

"None of us want to be here, sweetie." Beatrice brushed the curls from her niece's moist face. "I miss my brother, too. But he'll always live on in our hearts."

She was angry with everyone, especially God, for taking her father away from her. "My dad was all I had," she sniffed as she lifted her head to survey the room.

Fayth frowned and thumbed her nose up at those who were laughing and stuffing their greedy faces with free food and drinks, while she mourned the loss of her father. "Vultures," she muttered through clenched teeth.

"Sweetie, you have me, your mom, and baby sister. You're not alone." Beatrice leaned down and planted a kiss on her brow.

"My mother doesn't care about me, Auntie." Her lips quivered, but she managed to steady them for fear that her secret would escape. Who would believe her anyway? No, it was best to keep her lips zipped or face the consequences that were sure to come.

She'd noticed the sparkle in her aunt's brown; her oval-shaped eyes had darkened when they became fixated on the brazen woman across the room.

"Shh. Don't talk like that, baby. Your mother is grieving too," Aunt B whispered, never taking her eyes off the woman.

Her aunt's smile faded from her chubby, round face. Beatrice's body stiffened in her seat after she watched the woman pressed one of her alluring fingers to a man's lips.

Fayth craned her neck to get a better view of the woman her mother, the new widow, flirting with a strange man. Her stomach did somersaults. The sight was enough to make her want to barf. Her father hasn't been in the ground for an hour, and her mother was already shamelessly flaunting her curvaceous body.

Wise beyond her twelve years, she knew exactly the types of games her mother played to get what she wanted from the opposite sex. And love wasn't one of them. When she and her mother locked eyes, Fayth knew that it meant trouble, with a capital "T." Wearing a provocative, low-cut, hip-hugging black dress that left nothing to the imagination, her mother sashayed in their direction.

"Beatrice, why are yhu babyin' this gal?" Gladys yelled, yanking her daughter from her sister-in-law.

Like a rocket, her aunt flew from her seat. Standing eye-to-eye, the two faced off. "I'm not babyin' her," she snapped. "If yhu weren't so busy throwin' yourself on that man over there," Beatrice pointed in the man's direction, "yhu would know that yhur child is grievin'."

"Mind-yhur-own-business," Gladys growled with one hand propped on her curvy hip. "At least I can get a man... unlike yhu."

"I swear Gladys Hope, I don't know what my brother ever saw in yhu," she said, pointing one of her plump fingers in her face.

"All of this." Gladys seductively slid her smooth, caramel hands down the length of her hourglass figure.

Fayth wanted to find a rock and crawl under it, as she gawked up at the battling women from her seat, mortified by their actions. It wasn't the place or time for a standoff. It was a home going for her father. Or had they forgotten?

"Gladys, yhu can give Cruella Deville a run for her money as the Queen of Mean," Beatrice barked.
"And just in case yhu don't know the difference, this is the house of God, not a whorehouse."

Shocked by her aunt's foul language, Fayth's hair stood on end, especially as the crowd began to stare at the women going back and forth with insults.

"Well, at least I don't look like Cruella," Gladys raised an evil brow at her sister-in-law. "And for the record, yes, I know this is a church, yhu old saddlebag."

Fayth heard snickering from some of the onlookers.

"This old saddlebag," Beatrice quipped, "has been tendin' to yhur grievin' daughter."

At that moment, Gladys realized that her daughter's prying eyes were watching them. "Fayth, don't yhu see grown folks are talkin'? Gon' over there where them kids are." She shooed her off in their direction. "I have some unfinished business to tend to." She turned, rolling her eyes at Beatrice.

The crazed look in her mother's eyes scared the bejesus out of Fayth. "Yes, ma'am." She leaped from her seat to escape the feuding women. As she straightened her black pleated, knee-length dress, she noticed one boy, in particular, trying to get her attention. His fresh-cut fade, average height, and smooth, bronze skin gave him an edge and maturity over the other boys in the room. Saint Gabriel Baptist Church had only fifty or so members, and he wasn't one of them. She would have remembered a cutie like him.

Thankful the battle scene between her mother and aunt didn't scare him off; she walked over and introduced herself.

"Hi. I'm Fayth." She wasn't shy when it came to meeting people. "I haven't seen you around here before."

"I'm JC... and no, I don't live here in Augusta. I'm spending the summer with my aunt and uncle," he grinned, sliding his hands into his pants pockets. "I'm sorry that your father died."

Her heart sank in her stomach. She used every muscle in her tiny body to keep from breaking down in front of the stranger. "Thank you," she managed to get out.

"I tried to get your attention at the funeral, but your mother seems to have a tight leash on you," he said, giving her a puzzled look.

She didn't respond, and instead, faked a smile. *You don't know how tight of a leash,* she grumbled inwardly.

Closing the distance between them, he took his handkerchief from his jacket pocket and wiped a tear from her cheek. "You're just as beautiful as your name," he said with confidence.

His gentle touch sent goose bumps up her arms. She never knew such feelings existed between a boy and a girl until now. "You don't mean that," she said, blushing. "My mother doesn't think so." She lowered her head in shame at the hurtful admission spilling from her lips.

"All mothers think their kids are beautiful," he said, furrowing his brow.

She'd noticed the weird look he'd given her. It was the truth. Her mother never once told her that she was beautiful. "Not mine." She debated telling him why, but decided against it. She feared the repercussions if word got back to her mother.

For some unexplained reason, she was completely comfortable in his presence but not comfortable enough to share her terrible secret.

"Well, it's the God's honest truth. I think you're beautiful, no matter what your mother says. When I grow up and get married, my wife is going to look just like you," he admitted, smiling from ear to ear like the Cheshire Cat.

"Marry," Fayth gulped. "My mother says I'm too black for anyone to love me. And you know y'all boys only want them light skin girls." The spunk in her voice returned as she placed a hand on one of her narrow hips.

"Girl, don't you know black is beautiful. Your mother is wrong. I like what I see," he said, eyeing Fayth from head to toe. "You remind me of my older sister's Barbie dolls... the African American ones."

"Nobody ever complimented me with such nice words before, but my daddy." Her lips trembled, and her voice was caught in her throat at the mention of her father. She managed to force back the tears that threatened to spill. Things were going well between them, and she didn't want her crying to scare him off.

"Really?" he asked in disbelief.

"Really."

"So you expect me to believe that no boy has ever told you how pretty you are?"

"My mother is strict. And it will be over her dead body before any boy comes near me." She wrung her hands together as she glanced around the crowded room for her mother. The last she'd seen or heard of her mother, she was about to go fisticuffs with her aunt. "I'm surprised she hasn't caught me talking to you."

5

"Well, let's sneak outside before she does." He gently pulled her clasped hands apart and cupped them in his.

"I don't know," she said, fidgeting with the charm bracelet dangling from her wrist. Her heart was racing a mile a minute. After all, she'd just met him.

"I really like you, Fay Fay. And I want to get to know you better," he said, looking down at her with his big, brown, puppy-dog eyes.

She liked the fact that he'd already given her a nickname, which made the butterflies in her stomach fluttered, but the fear of Gladys' wrath lingered in the back of her mind. Fayth hesitated for a second and then dismissed the voice of reason. She figured her mother was probably too busy preying on an unsuspecting pair of britches to stick her claws into to notice her absence. "Okay, but only for a few minutes, though."

The hot, sticky, August heat did little to deter the new friends as they found shade under an oak tree. Underneath was an inviting old wooden bench. The scorching heat intensified the stench coming from a nearby cow pasture, but it wasn't strong enough to chase them back inside.
The six-foot-tall corn stalks surrounding the fellowship hall blocked the summer breeze. However, the two hardly noticed.

"I feel as though I've known you all my life." JC broke the silence with a more mature and serious tone to his voice.

"I know," she agreed, staring down at the withered grass beneath her feet. Now that they were alone, she became a bundle of nerves under his intense stare.

"Are you nervous? Your hands are trembling," he asked, gently rubbing them.

"A little. I've never been alone with a boy before." Her heart leaped with excitement, but fear trailed closely behind.

"Fayth, I want to give you something to remember our friendship." Taking a tiny gold cross from around his neck, he swept her locks aside and draped it around hers.

"It's beautiful," she said, with her back facing him. Her trembling hands enveloped the tiny cross.

"Do you believe in love at first sight?" he asked, turning her around to face him.

"Yeah. I guess. I don't know," she said, trying to make sense out of what was happening between them. *My father is dead. I should be grieving, not talking about love, feelings, and stuff with a boy I hardly know.*

As evening approached, they talked and learned more about one another. The crickets and all the country critters sang their evening songs as the two made plans to meet somehow at Augusta's Annual Youth Revival and Vacation Bible School over the next two weeks. She knew it would take an act of God to pull it off, but she was determined to see him again.

Later, JC surprised her when he pulled a pack of Strawberry Twizzlers from his pants pocket. He tore open the plastic wrapping and pulled out one of the red, chewy candies. They nibbled from opposite ends, stopping when their lips met. They held each other's gaze for what seemed like an eternity. Neither knew what to do next until an infuriated woman broke their trance when she came galloping in their direction, kicking up dust with each step she took. The two became fearful because the woman's visage mimicked a possessed person. She and JC jumped at the sound of her mother's thunderous voice as she spewed brimstone and fire with each word she spoke.

"Gal, brang yhur lil' fast tail here. And boyyyyyyy, yhu betta get your mannish behind away from that Jezebel daughter of mine," Gladys barked, with fire in her eyes that could sear through flesh.

Gladys snatched her by the arm, like a rag doll, and then turned on her heels and unleashed a mouthful of expletives on the young boy who'd shown Fayth nothing but respect. Fayth's young face was rushed with heat. She glanced over her shoulder and saw JC scared stiff from her mother's antics.

7

Hauled away like a common criminal in front of the remaining mourners, who'd now migrated outside because of all the commotion, Fayth braced herself for the beating that was sure to follow. The floodgate opened, and the tears erupted down her flushed cheeks with a vengeance. At that pivotal moment, her faith in God died. With a strike to the face, she believed God had abandoned her to the harsh brutality of her mother's iron fist.

Chapter One

Fifteen years later
Port City, Louisiana

"Sorry I'm late," Angelica said, rushing into her therapist's office, tastefully adorned with African paintings and figurines. "But the traffic was bumper to bumper."

Twenty-seven-year-old Angelica Hope decided to sever ties with her first name, Fayth, after moving from the country town of Augusta, Louisiana. Parting ways with a name that had more curses attached to it than blessings had given her the fresh start she craved. Unfortunately, it was short-lived. The nightmares had finally gotten the best of her. She found herself crying the blues over a life that had more baggage than she could carry.

"No problem, my next patient called and canceled just moments before you arrived. So, you're in luck... have a seat," Dr. Hawthorne gestured towards the beige leather sofa adjacent to her. She slid her glasses down her narrow, brown nose while flipping through some medical files. "Last week, Angelica, we ended with you talking about your father. Today, I want to discuss your mother, since she's the source of the nightmares. Tell me about her and the abuse you suffered after the death of your father."

Angelica settled back on the comfy sofa, caught her breath, and hoped she didn't sound like a blubbering fool at the end of her session. She hated crying, and she hated sharing her feelings even more. It made her feel weak. Investigative reporters were supposed to be tough. She asked all the hard questions not the other way around. But here, she sat across from a shrink, opening up about a past that she'd rather forget.

"My mother demoralized me every chance she got. I still have nightmares about the evil things she'd done to me." She wrung her hands together, fighting hard to control her voice. "I remember coming home late from Vacation Bible School. The church van had a flat tire. And Gladys—"

"Who is Gladys?" Dr. Hawthorne interrupted, looking confused.

"My mother," she said in a deadpan tone.

"Why do you call her Gladys?" she asked, peering over the rim of her bifocal glasses.

"Because she said demons don't have mothers." Angelica squeezed her eyes shut as the humiliating words slid off her tongue like hot lava.

She opened her eyes and focused on the soft, soothing, neutral paintings on the wall. It helped her to relax. The office walls of Angelica's previous therapist had been bland and overly decorated with certificates and plaques, displaying only medical achievements. There was no doctor-patient connection, so she ended her sessions. Dr. Hawthorne's office had the comforts of home, which allowed her to open up more than she had expected.

"Why would she say something so cruel?" she asked, scribbling in the folder.

"Now that's the million dollar question both you and I would like to know," Angelica retorted.

When the nightmares and sudden crying spells invaded the new life Angelica was trying to live, she sought professional help. The anger and hatred she'd suppressed over the years for her mother had proven to be more than she could handle. Gladys continued to control her every thought, in spite of her resistance.

"Okay. Continue with what happened when you arrived home." Dr. Hawthorne insisted.

"When the church van finally pulled up in front of my house two hours late, Gladys was fuming. She accused me of sleeping around. Actually, I had a boyfriend... JC, which I kept a secret, but nothing happened. My explanation about the flat tire went ignored. She made me undress and started sniffing me from head to toe." Wiping the perspiration from her upper lip, she continued the horrid details. "Gladys made me stand against the bathroom wall, spreading my legs apart. She took her index and middle fingers and inserted them into my private parts, to see if I'd lost my virginity." She crossed her legs as spikes of pain shot through the lower part of her body. Her pelvic muscles tightened at the thought of her mother's probing fingers inside her. "Gladys said the police used the technique on whores who were strip-searched in prison." Fayth stopped, took a deep breath, and resurrected the memories she'd tried to bury more than fifteen years ago.

"Gladys always thought the worst of me. She once threatened me, saying, before she became a grandmother, she'd rip the little bastard out of my womb and feed the fetus to the town's stray dogs." Remembering the past was taking its toll. She buried her face in her hands and sobbed bitterly.

Unfazed by the sordid details, Dr. Hawthorne chimed in and handed her a box of Kleenex. "I know it's painful, revisiting your abusive childhood. But it's all a part of the healing process." She sat back in her chair and continued. "If you don't release the anger and hatred you have for your mother, it will destroy you."

"I'll never understand how she could love one child and hate the other." Her words were caught in her throat as the pain welled up inside. "What did I do that was so wrong? I was only a child," she cried, throwing both hands up in defeat.

"Your mother could possibly have some unresolved issues herself. Do you know anything about her childhood?" Dr. Hawthorne asked stoically.

"Ha! She would rather have a root canal than discuss her personal life with me," she said, wiping her eyes and nose.

"In order to make progress and heal mentally and spiritually, you must talk to yo—"

"No. I will never speak to that woman, even after my sister informed me that Gladys is dying from ovarian cancer." She declared adamantly, cutting her therapist off. "The day Gladys lost custody of me to my Aunt Beatrice, she told me never to return to Augusta. And you know what? I've done just that."

"Angelica, this anger you're holding on to will destroy you. Getting the answers to your mother's past could possibly give you some insight to your own abuse. Allow God to help you. Give your problems over to Him. It's the only way you can move forward." Dr. Hawthorne advised, taking her glasses off and placing them on the table beside her.

"Where was God when I was beaten black and blue, huh?" she yelled out in anguish. "He sure wasn't rushing down from heaven to rescue me."

"Please hear me out," she stressed, moving closer to the edge of her seat.

Angelica tuned Dr. Hawthorne out when an image of her strapped to a bedpost, naked and beaten relentlessly by her mother with an extension cord, entered her thoughts. That day wasn't how she'd imagined spending her sixteenth birthday, but it turned out to be one of the best days of her life. Her aunt Beatrice Hope, who'd come to town to surprise her on her birthday, saved her life when she walked in on the beating and caught Gladys red-handed. Unfortunately, the psychological damage had already taken root, when the Child Protection Agency came to remove her from the home she referred to as, "Hell."

Dr. Hawthorne's voice jolted her back to the present. "I'm leaving," Angelica blurted out. She leaped from the sofa, grabbed her purse, and like the speed of lightening, bolted towards the door.

"Wait! Hold on! What's wrong?" Dr. Hawthorn shouted, chasing behind her.

She stopped in her tracks. "I know you incorporate Christian principles into your counseling sessions, but this head shrinking and God stuff just isn't working for me," she said with her therapist in pursuit. "This will be my last session. If God really loves me, He has a funny way of showing it."

"You haven't given Him or counseling a chance, Angelica. You need help. And quitting is not the answer. I suggest—"

She left, slamming the door shut, before Dr. Hawthorne could utter another word.

Chapter Two

Jasion McCoy trod with caution when it came to the opposite sex. The twenty-eight-year-old financial advisor had met his fair share of gold diggers, enough to last a lifetime. As one of Port City's most eligible bachelors, he attracted women, who were more interested in his six-figure income, than him; a God-fearing man.

Nicole Swaggart, his ex-fiancée, was one of those women. She loved what he represented in the public eye. Her bossy and conniving ways caused their relationship to sour, so Jasion broke off their engagement. His reputation was at stake if he continued dealing with her.

He had the magic touch for making shrewd financial decisions that most men in his line of work envied. Investing in real estate properties and small businesses had earned him a very impressive bank account. He lived in one of the most desirable neighborhoods in Port City, but material possessions with no one to share them with had become unfulfilling.

His life had turned topsy-turvy overnight. The stress of possible prison time because his clients' retirement investments had come up missing weighed heavily on his mind. Embezzlement charges threatened to claim all he had accomplished.

"Son, what's troubling you?" Evelyn asked Jasion, picking over the food she'd placed before him. "You haven't eaten a crumb off your plate. It's your favorite."

The mouthwatering aroma of his mother's roast beef, mashed potatoes, and corn, usually left him salivating for seconds. Today, the sight of it turned his stomach.

"Uhuh. I'm sorry, Mom. My mind is somewhere else. Next time I come over for dinner, I promise to leave my problems outside the door," Jasion said, sliding his plate aside.

14

"Baby, I pray you're not letting this investigation get you down. I know you are innocent. Your father and I didn't raise a thief. God will see you through this."

Jasion studied the worry lines that had formed across his mom's face. She was just as concerned as he was.

"I love you, Mom. You're always the optimist. No matter how bad things seem, you always see the good."

Pushing from the table, he walked over to the stove where she stood and planted a kiss on her brow. Petite, with a salt and pepper topknot bun, his mother was always his rock, especially after the death of his father. He'd followed in his father's footsteps as a financial advisor. Being taught at an early age how to make wise business decisions made him one of the most sought-after consultants after graduating from college.

"That's what mothers do," she said, reaching up to caress the sides of his fatigued face.

"Mama, the case isn't the only thing weighing on me. I'm almost thirty and still single." He took her hands from the sides of his face and held them inside his. He wanted more than a mother's love or touch. He wanted intimacy. The kind that only a wife, a lover could give.

"I've prayed and prayed for a mate. I've done what God asked of me. I've traveled from city to city, evangelizing His Word since the age of thirteen. When will He honor my request for a wife?"

"God hears your prayers, but you're tying His hands. You're expecting the women you meet to be Fayth. They're not her. Baby, you've got to move on with your life," she pleaded in a motherly tone. "You're stuck in the past. Let her go."

"I know they're not her, Mother. And I don't want you to think I'm pining away over the past either," he said with a reassuring smile, but his heart said differently. The girl he'd left somewhere in Augusta more than fifteen years ago consumed his every waking thought. Knowing that his mother would never understand, he decided to keep quiet on the matter. He didn't understand it himself. Why was God torturing him with a woman he would never see again?

"Good. You were beginning to worry your dear old mother there for a second." An uneasy look danced across her face as she gently brushed his cheeks with the back of her hand. "You'll find that special someone. Be patient, love will come."

"What? You think your baby boy is losing it?" he teased, pulling her into his embrace. Thoughts of him and Fayth managing to steal two weeks together after their chance meeting at her father's funeral brought a smile to his face. Thank God for Augusta's Annual Youth Revival and Vacation Bible School that brought the surrounding communities' youth together.

Each year, he returned to his aunt and uncle's home in Claysville, Louisiana for the summer, hoping to rekindle their summer romance, but it seemed as if she'd dropped off the face of the earth. Heartbroken, he ended his search. He regretted to this day, never knowing or asking Fayth, her last name. The two were so overjoyed to be together that it didn't seem to matter at that time. She'd begged him to keep their friendship a secret. If her mother ever found out about them, she feared the consequences, so he never asked anyone in town about her, which made his search impossible.

"No, you're not losing it, son," she withdrew from his embrace. "It's called being lonely. And lonely people tend to make hasty decisions when it comes to love. I don't want you to miss finding the right woman by chasing after a memory. That's all, baby. No one wants to see you happy and settled down more than I. Shoots; I want some grandbabies." Laughing, she grabbed her son and planted a big, wet kiss on his cheek.

The love radiating from his mother's face gave Jasion the added courage he needed to face his troubles head on.

As a young boy, afraid of the dark, he would search his closet and underneath his bed for monsters. He wished she could protect him now, but he had to be a man and fight his

16

own battles. With possible criminal charges forming against him, only God knew how things would play out.

"I love you, Mom and I hear you loud and clear," he said as she removed her arms from around him.

"That's my boy." She looked up at him and smiled.

"It's getting late, Mom. I better get going. But, I promise to keep you posted. Corporate office scheduled for CBN News investigative reporter Angelica Hope to work on the case alongside Port City detectives. I have a meeting with her tomorrow. I found a couple of articles about her from the newspaper. She has a compassionate heart from what I read, but she can be tough. One of the articles stated how she visited the hospital daily to check on a little girl, whose stepfather had beaten and left for dead."

"She sounds like the type of person you need in your corner."

"Indeed she does," Jasion agreed, preparing to leave. He kissed his mother goodbye and headed out of the door to an uncertain future.

Chapter Three

Angelica stepped inside the vacant elevator at Spitzer Financial Firm. She pressed the button for the twelfth floor where her new assignment awaited her. She leaned her tired body against the steel guardrails as the doors closed. Even the smooth, melodic sounds of jazz bellowing from overhead couldn't drown out the voice of her high-strung, over-the-top boss, Lance Swann as it invaded her thoughts on the ride up.

The last thing she wanted was to take on a new assignment. But Lance barged into her office more than a week ago with what he deemed another big story that needed her undivided attention. She could hear his flamboyant voice ringing clearly in her head. *"Hope, CBN News didn't earn Best Broadcasting Station of the year by sitting on our butts."* Then he'd pour on the flattery with, *"you're the best reporter this station has. The others are just too darned soft. I can trust you to get down and dirty to find the truth."* He was right about that. She took her job seriously, sometimes a little too seriously, and often leaving enemies in the aftermath.

She was blindsided when her overzealous boss assigned her to investigate Jasion McCoy without consulting her first. She had planned to take a long overdue vacation, which Lance knew she deserved, after uncovering the teacher's sex scandal that rocked the Port City school system last month. She had her own problems to sort out. As usual, Lance had thrown a monkey wrench into those plans when he'd handed her a folder containing Mr. McCoy's profile.

She pulled a photo from the folder of a strikingly handsome young man; she'd remembered seeing that face on an infomercial. After the Procter Investment Firm scandal, people had begun withdrawing their investments from local financial firms in Port City. He had encouraged the public that it was safe to reinvest in their future and not allow one company's mistake to scare them away.

Angelica studied the photo of Jasion McCoy with awareness. She brushed her hands across the glossy image toward his eyes and then down to the most perfect set of lips she'd ever seen. He didn't look like a crook, but neither did the rest of those high corporate thieves who'd scammed billions from their clients. *Well, Mr. McCoy, I hope you're ready for me. I don't take kindly to those who take advantage of the innocent, no matter how handsome they are,* she thought, trying to convince herself that his good looks wouldn't interfere with her doing her job.

Ding. The elevator alerted that she'd reached her destination. The sound pulled her back to the present. While exiting, she tried, refocusing on her purpose for being there. She proceeded down a narrow hallway in search of the man whose photo had her counting down the seconds until their meeting. She arrived at his office door, where a gold plate bore his name in bold black letters. Before she could knock, a tall, handsome, and immaculately dressed man charged out of the door, nearly knocking her over.

The gorgeous creature leaned into her, quick reflexes and a strong masculine hold around her waist broke her fall. The last thing she needed was a concussion from landing on the hard ceramic floor beneath her.

"Ma'am, are you alright? I'm sorry. I didn't see you," he apologized, holding her securely in his arms.

Seconds ticked before Angelica could speak. There was a sense of familiarity about the man holding her in his arms. She'd seen those soft, brown, caring eyes before, but where? The only placed she'd seen him was in the photo and on television.

"You need to watch where you're going, Sir," she scolded, breaking out of his firm grip. Straightening her oversized, black blazer, she sported an annoyed look. "I could've been seriously hurt."

19

She was more than okay. It wasn't every day that a handsome, six-foot-three — give or take an inch—hunk, stormed out of an office and held her in his arms. Too bad, the hardnosed reporter inside her wouldn't allow her vulnerability or gratitude to show.

"You're right. I should've been more careful." He peered over her shoulders at his secretary's empty desk. "May I help you?"

"Yes. I am looking for a Mr. Jasion McCoy." She knew exactly who he was. The sight of him had taken what breath she had left. She tried to gather her composure in light of the awkward moment they'd just shared. *Focus. Focus. Focus.* She screamed within herself.

His photo and television infomercials didn't do him justice. Live and in living color was much better. His bronze, chiseled face, and beautiful full lips surrounded by a neatly trimmed goatee were enough to make her want to fall again, just so he'd catch her. There wasn't a flaw to be found, and if there were, he hid them well.

Dateless for more than two years hadn't diminished her womanly abilities to scan a man from head to toe in a matter of seconds. Her skills were still on high alert. His tan designer suit complemented his toned body, drawing attention to all the right places.

"I'm your man. Sorry... my apologies, that didn't come out the right way." Stumbling on his words, he extended his hand to her for a formal introduction. "I'm Jasion McCoy. And you are?"

"Angelica Hope, from CBN News. The station's secretary scheduled me to meet with you at ten-thirty this morning."

"Come into my office and let me check my schedule for today."

She followed closely behind, checking out the full view of his masculine physique. *Not too bad. Not too bad. His wife is one lucky woman to have a man like him to come home to. I thought Idris Elba was the only man who oozed sex appeal, but I was wrong.*

"Have a seat while I verify the time with my secretary. I hope she's returned from her morning break." He turned, gesturing towards a black leather chair near his desk. "Ms. Kennedy is good at keeping me on track." He dialed her extension and placed the phone on loudspeaker. "Ms. Kennedy."

"Yes, Mr. McCoy," she responded in a high-spirited voice.

"Do you have me scheduled to meet with Mrs.—"

"It's Ms.," Angelica interrupted. *Why did I do that? I could slap myself. I hope he doesn't get the wrong impression.*

"I'm sorry. Do you have me scheduled to meet with Ms. Angelica Hope from CBN News at ten-thirty this morning? I could've sworn it was for tomorrow."

"Hold, please, while I check." She returned, "yes, Mr. McCoy, I reminded you of the appointment first thing this morning."

"Thanks, Ms. Kennedy. That will be all for now." He disconnected the call. "I apologize for my oversight, Ms. Hope. It's been chaos around here ever since detectives stormed into my office, confiscating my clients' portfolios."

"Your boss, Mr. Lexington, contacted the station and briefed us on the matter."

"If you don't mind, can we discuss this over a late breakfast?" he asked, slipping on his suit jacket. "I'm famished."

"I have lunch plans in a couple of hours. We could reschedule for tomorrow if you'd like." She couldn't believe those words had escaped her lips. Postponing a meeting of this nature wasn't in her vocabulary. She had to be insane or weak to the magnetic powers transmitting from the handsome man standing before her.

"No, I prefer to get this over with as quickly as possible," he snapped.

"I don't know about quickly, Mr. McCoy. We're stuck together like Siamese twins. After the case, we can both go our separate ways. Where I come from, stealing is a serious crime." No one used that type of tone with her, even if he did look as if he'd stepped off the pages of GQ magazine.

"Whoa. Hold on; Ms. don't come in here making false accusations. I know Mr. Lexington prefers that CBN News cover the story because of their network's reputation for accuracy. However, I won't hesitate to boot you up out of here," he shot back.

"Look. I apologize for making false assumptions. In my business, you're innocent until proven guilty." Her reporter instincts warned that things were going to get worse before the case was over, and sticking her foot in her mouth wasn't helping. "Okay, let's go and discuss the events leading up to the disappearance of your clients' assets. Maybe we can put our heads together and figure it out before the news get out to the public. After the Procter Investment Firm closed its doors due to money laundering schemes, the last thing you need is for Spitzer's investors to begin panicking."

*****

The company's cafeteria rush hour was over and now had dwindled to a handful of employees, allowing Jasion to speak free from prying eyes. Turning his attention to the beautiful, feisty reporter sitting across the table from him, he made a mental note to switch from watching BCB News to CBN News. She was stunning.

Feelings of déjà vu crept up his spine as he locked eyes with her from across the table. Her creamy, mocha skin and hypnotizing, brown eyes were enough to paralyze any man who looked into them, but her attitude needed a major overhaul

"Is there anything else you need to know, Ms. Hope?" he asked impatiently.

"For now," she said emphatically. "I don't want to overload you with questions today."

Not that he'd mind. He could sit and gaze at her all morning. It was her tongue lashing that he could do without. "Good, because my brain is fried," he laughed.

She kept a stone face.

If we're going to be working closely together, I pray she loosens up, or communication will be like pulling teeth out of a lion's mouth.

"We've only scratched the surface, Mr. McCoy. I will be working directly with Port City detectives." She took a sip of her coffee. "If you cooperate with me, I'll do all I can to help prove your innocence. But, if not, I'll do everything in my power to see that you end up behind bars."

"Ouch. That cut and dry, huh?" Jasion asked, steadying the cup of coffee in his shaky hand. The last place he wanted to end up was jail, especially for a crime he didn't commit.

"Yes. So, do we have an understanding?"

"Yes, ma'am, we do."

Jasion could tell by the tone of her voice that she meant business. He hoped as time passed that the five-foot-six beauty would ease up on the threats. His nerves were already working in overdrive, and her straight-to-the-point attitude wasn't helping matters.

The reputation he'd spent years building was crashing down around him. God had promised in His word, never to leave him or forsake him. However, he had never felt more forsaken than now and questioned how he was going to get out of the mess.

Chapter Four

The medicated odor of Ben-Gay alerted Angelica's nostrils that her frisky, seventy-five-year-old neighbor, Mr. Nate, was on the prowl. Reaching the top of her apartment stairwell, his frail body came into view. When his beady, brown eyes spotted her, he immediately strutted in her direction, giving her no time to escape into her living quarters. The tattered, dingy bathrobe he wore revealed more than she cared to see or know about a man of his advanced age. She assessed; hiding behind the sea of wrinkles and loose skin, was once an attractive and muscular man. Too bad, he believed he still possessed those qualities.

"Lawd have mercy, woman. When yhu gon' accept the fact, yhu are my Angel, signed, sealed, and shipped straight from heaven to my doorstep."

He deemed himself a self-proclaimed ladies' man and used the same tired lines on the other female tenants, young and old. It didn't matter to him if they were blind, crazy, or crippled. He loved women.

"Hi, Mr. Nate," Angelica said, wearing a facial expression that read, approach with caution. Today she was not in a playful mood, not after the confrontation she had earlier in Jasion McCoy's office. She just wanted to wash her troubles away in a hot, soothing bath. However, Mr. Nate was persistent. Like a stray cat, getting rid of him would not be easy.

"Gal… don't yhu know all that workin' gon' kill yhu. The Bible says, 'A woman shall not live by work alone,'" he said, adding his own interpretation to the scriptures. "What yhu need is a strong, virile man to keep yhu warm."

Angelica watched as he paraded around like a black stallion coming in first place at the Kentucky Derby. Instead of a smooth stride, he wobbled around like an animal ready to be put out to pasture, ready to meet his fate. She shook her head in disbelief at her naughty neighbor and replied, "Thanks, I'll pass." She could never bring herself to hurt his feelings.

A recent widower, Mr. Nate, was just as lonely for companionship as she. His days consisted of pretending to be the apartment's neighborhood watchman. When in reality, tenants had to watch out for him, especially the females. They never knew what to expect from him.

"Don't keep me waitin' too long, cus I gots women lined up to take a peek at all this." He opened and closed his robe, giving her a peep show.

"Bye Mr. Nate." Nausea settled in the pit of her stomach at the sight of his shriveled body. His tattoos had gone down south along with everything else. Bashful, he was not. "I've had a long day." Angelica cringed, charging past him towards her apartment. She fought to keep the contents of her stomach from ending up on the breezeway. Against her will, a giggle escaped her lips at Mr. Nate's outlandish antics. Each day proved to be a new adventure with her elderly neighbor.

Once inside, her somber mood returned. The dead silence from within her small living quarters reminded her that she would be spending another evening alone. Flipping on the light switch and throwing her keys on the coffee table out of sheer habit, she sighed because of the hand that life had dealt her. She collapsed on the sofa, drained by the pressures of the day; she vented her frustrations into the empty room.

"Who does Dr. Hawthorne think she is? Contact Gladys? Never. To add insult to injury, she wants me to take my problems to God. For what? He's the reason for all my troubles in the first place. I'm not feeling all of that gibberish nonsense. God doesn't care about me. Look at how my life has turned out since the death of my father. He died, leaving me with a woman who called herself a mother. A Taskmaster seemed more befitting. Thanks, but no thanks, Doc. Shove that advice down someone else's throat." The venomous words oozed off her tongue as she tried to find a comfortable spot on the sofa.

The tears stung the back of her eyelids as she continued to lament. "Daddy, it's been fifteen long years since you were taken from me. I miss you so much." After her pity party, Angelica laid the back of her head against the sofa, allowing the couch's headrest to alleviate the pressures from her exhausting day. Overwhelmed by years of grief and self-pity, sleep rescued her from further misery.

Temporarily. On cue, her painful past entered her dreams and threatened to disrupt her peaceful rest.

"Fayth. Bring yo' behind here, gal. Where yhu at? I know yhu hear me callin' yhu."

In Fayth's young mind, the house seemed to shake from Gladys' thunderous voice.

Never having enough to eat, Fayth stashed food to fill the emptiness in her constantly growling stomach. Gladys counted and measured the food stored in the refrigerator and pantry, which meant she was busted.

Out of breath from hurrying into the kitchen, she answered, *"Yes, Gladys."*

"Did yhu eat a slice out of my chocolate cake? I had six, and there's only five on this hea' plate." Gladys shoved the cake-dish in front of Fayth's terrified face.

Afraid to lie, she confessed, *"yes, ma'am. I... I was hungry. I haven't eaten since lunch. I'm sorry, Gladys. I promise I'll make you another one, please don..."* Before she could utter another word, Gladys knocked her into a chair and forced her to eat the remaining slices without water. Cramming chunk after chunk into her small mouth, she fought the urge to gag.

"This will teach yo' lil' thievin' behind a lesson about eatin' anythang else without gettin' pro-miss-ion. And yhu betta not leave this table until every crumb is gon' or I will beat yhur behind black and blue."

Terrified of the giant hovering over her with clenched fists, Fayth swallowed every particle in sight, knowing her mother meant every word. After consuming five slices of cake, the last thing she needed or wanted was to have it beaten out of her.

"Gon' over thera' and wash that cake-dish out in the sink and when yhu finish, go get yo' butt ready for bed," Gladys demanded and stormed out of the kitchen.

"Yes, ma'am."

She made sure Hurricane Gladys had cleared the room. She cupped her hands underneath the running faucet and filled them with water to quench her thirst. She continued to drink until her stomach began to ache.

Hours later, Angelica awoke, drenched in sweat and paralyzed with fear, to the sound of her own familiar gut-wrenching screams. She yelled out into the darkness. "God, why are you tormenting me?" Raising her head off the sofa, hoping that someone, anyone would answer her plea. But as usual, dead silence. The vindictive words of her mother continued to resonate in her mind. Tired of hearing the negative voices of the past, she curled her body up into a ball on the sofa and cried herself back to sleep.

I'm a curse, which explains why God doesn't love or answer me. Gladys was right. If God doesn't love me, how can I expect any man to love me? I might as well accept the hand that life has dealt me and expect to live the rest of my miserable life alone, she cried.

The night turned into morning, and she awakened, finding herself in the same spot as the day before.

Angelica had to get her act together before going back to Jasion's office. And wallowing over an unfulfilled life didn't pay the bills. She had an investigation that needed her undivided attention. She wasn't going to allow self-pity get in the way of stopping Mr. McCoy from walking away with millions of his clients' life savings. His smooth talk and pretty boy good looks had no effect on her. She prided herself on doing an effective job and planned on standing her ground with the handsome financial advisor.

She sprang up from the sofa with a new surge of energy that only work could provide. "I'm going to lick my wounds and press forward. Today will be better," Angelica professed. "I will not allow Mr. McCoy to call the shots. Lance chose me to investigate the case because of my experience. That's exactly what I'm going to do." She rushed to the shower, determined to stay focused. Love and relationships worked for others, not her. The sooner she realized it, the better off she'd be.

Chapter Five

Despite her tough girl act, Jasion sensed Angelica's insecurities. He'd encountered women in her position who came off as aggressive in a world dominated by males. But on the inside, they were gentle and caring. He prayed that somewhere deep inside the woman who'd invaded his office yesterday like a whirlwind had a tender spot.

He watched as she cautiously pushed her chair in front of his desk. He couldn't help but noticed her natural beauty. From tucking her wealth, of course, black hair behind her earlobes to the way she sat up straight in her chair, he inhaled it all in. But he thought she needed to fast forward her wardrobe to the twenty-first century. The black, baggy slacks, white dress shirt, and oversized, black blazer took away from her figure. He wasn't much of an expert in women's attire, but that look went out with the eighties female detectives, Cagney and Lacey.

Discreetly, he watched her full, glossed lips envelop the rim of the Styrofoam cup filled with coffee, wishing he could trade places with it. He tried to come up with a reason as to why a woman as beautiful as she, was so brutally mean. But he couldn't think of one. There was no excuse for her behavior, and today he was determined more than ever to stand his ground.

"Ms. Hope, I know your time is valuable, so I won't prolong it any further. And please do accept my apology for my short-term memory on yesterday."

"Apology accepted, Mr. McCoy." She placed her coffee on his desk to retrieve a notepad and pen from her handbag.

"No need for the formalities. Call me Jasion since we'll be seeing a lot of each other as you stated," he said, smiling to lighten the tension in the room. But she showed no interest in his niceties.

"Are you ready to get started, Mr. McCoy?" she asked with raised brows.

Her nonchalant demeanor took him aback. Here he was trying to be cordial about their working arrangement, and she dismissed it as nothing.

"Yes," he replied dryly. What other choice did she leave him? She was as frigid as the North Pole. An Eskimo could find more warmth in the middle of sub-zero temperatures than he received from her in his office.

"You can start, Mr. McCoy, from when you first noticed that your clients' funds had been depleted from their accounts." She gave him a cold stare.

"I've gone over most of the files, but what I can't understand is how millions disappeared from a highly secure company without raising any red flags?"

The last thing Jasion needed or wanted was a nosey, smart aleck reporter, snooping around, causing further panic among his clients and employees at Spritzer Financial Firm. But it was in his best interest to comply. From her brash tone, she'd already placed his head on the chopping block. "Two weeks ago," he shrugged. "It's possible that the original files could have been replaced with phony ones to throw us off."

Resting her chin on her balled fist, she asked, "and you came up with that brilliant idea all by yourself?"

Caught off guard by her rude comment, Jasion jumped to his defense. "Ma'am, I'm not going to sit here and allow you insult me." The tension in the room had gone from a scale of five to ten in a matter of seconds. "I may not be a computer guru, but I have some knowledge concerning them."

"I'm not trying to insult you, Mr. McCoy. The documents that I received from detectives appear to be authentic, but I will make a note of it," she said as she wrote on her notepad. "The person involved would have to know an awful lot about computers. No amateur can embezzle large amounts of money without leaving incriminating clues behind. Does Spitzer have an IT person?"

He settled back into his chair. "Yes. Caleb Michaels is the firm's information technologist. He's good at fixing minor problems. I doubt he's smart enough to create a program that duplicates a client investment portfolio."

"Never underestimate people, Mr. McCoy. You don't need a college degree in computer science to develop a program. Heck, babies come out of the womb nowadays computer literate."

"Yeah, I guess you're right." Jasion never cared for Caleb ever since he started working at SFF a year ago. He was a young, cocky know-it-all who tried throwing his weight around the office whenever employees needed their computers serviced. But Jasion wouldn't accuse him of being a thief, a pain in the butt, yes, a thief— no.

"My job here is to find out why your clients' files were the only ones targeted." Leaning back in her chair, she asked, "do you have any enemies here at Spitzer, Mr. McCoy?"

He sensed the reels spinning in that pretty little head of hers. She was determined to find holes in his statement to crucify him. "No. Not that I'm aware of," he paused. "Wait. I don't know why I didn't think of this sooner. Mr. Lexington asked me about taking over as CEO of his company when he retires next year."

"And why would that cause a problem?"

"He has a son, Ian Lexington, who works here at the firm."

"Well, Mr. McCoy that gives me three persons of interest, Caleb Michaels, Ian Lexington, and you."

Not liking her brusque tone and accusing stare, Jasion asked, "is there anything else you need to know, Ms. Hope?"

"No, that would be all for today. I have to get going."

"Another lunch date?" The words spilled from his lips without thought. For some weird reason, he wanted to know, despite her candor. She was mysterious, beautiful, and smart, which intrigued Jasion. Or maybe it was his pledge of celibacy that had him delirious. Never in a million years would he have given a woman as arrogant as she a second glance or cared what she was doing and whom she was doing it with.

"Excuse me, Sir, but that's none of your business," she replied, cocking her head to the side.

Jasion watched in amusement, knowing he'd struck a nerve as he watched her stuff the notepad into her handbag. He wanted to give her a taste of her own medicine and put her in the hot seat for a change.

"Are you married, Ms. Hope?" he asked to agitate her further. He wanted to know if his opinion of her was right, tough on the outside but soft and sensual on the inside. Unfortunately, for him, she wasn't cracking under pressure.

"My, my, my, aren't you the nosey type?" She stood to face him, appearing unfazed by his questions.

"My mother taught me that the only way to get your questions answered is to ask."

She stood and leaned forward over his desk, giving him a don't-try-me look. "I'm not here to play games with you, Mr. McCoy. But for your FYI, no, I'm not married."

"A boyfriend?" he persisted.

"No, Mr. McCoy," she snarled, standing upright from his desk. "What does my personal life matter to you?"

"You asked me questions; now I'm asking you questions. Fair is fair." He stepped from behind his desk.

"I'm not the one under investigation. You are." She snatched up her purse and handbag from the chair.

"Am I making you nervous, Ms. Hope?" he asked, laughing on the inside as she fidgeted with the hair draped behind her ear. "I don't want to cause any potential problems in your relationship since we'll be working closely together. That's all."

"There will be no problems. I assure you. Let's not get off track as to why I'm here. We'll talk more tomorrow, and please, don't forget." She gave him a piercing stare as she headed towards the door.

"Those are important questions in order to establish a good working relationship," he said facetiously. "I don't want any jealous boyfriends storming into my office, doing me bodily harm." He followed her to the door, waiting for her to react, but like steel, she didn't bend.

"You got your questions answered. I'll see you tomorrow afternoon at four." She snatched the door open and left.

"See you then, Ms. Hope and I promise to be on time," he said, smiling, and closed the door behind her. His words made her uncomfortable. He could tell by her body language, although her face remained stern. Today, he wasn't going to let her get the upper hand. If she wanted to play the hard- nosed reporter role, then she had better come well prepared for their next meeting.

Chapter Six

"Girl, you better have a good excuse for showing up late. I'm sitting here wasting away from hunger," Marissa teased, scooting out of her seat to hug her best friend since college. "I was beginning to think you weren't coming, Fay."

Marissa was one of the few people who continued to call Angelica by her first name, Fayth. She had been her rock throughout college. Without Marissa, who knows what would have become of her. She was a good listener and never turned a deaf ear when Fayth needed someone to tell the horrid stories of her abusive childhood.

The tantalizing whiff of home cooking slapped them both in their hungry faces. The Mom and Pop's Diner was one of their favorite eateries in Port City.

"You know how the lunch hour traffic is downtown. It's like watching a snail inch across the street." Angelica laughed as they settled into their favorite booth.

"So tell me, what's been going in the life of Port City's top reporter?" The look of excitement filled Marissa's sparkling marbled blue eyes.

"Lance assigned me to a new story," Angelica moaned.

"I thought you were going to take some time off?" Marissa inquired, sweeping her long blonde mane off her shoulders. "At least that's what you hinted the last time we spoke."

"Yes, I was. But Lance wouldn't take no for an answer." The high profile story at Spitzer Financial Firm might perhaps put her in the same league with some of the top anchors and reporters across the country. She wanted to refuse, but the adrenaline rushing through her workaholic veins wouldn't allow her to. Her interest in the case, and the man who was at the center of it aroused her curiosity. "This one is challenging, and you know how I like a good story."

"Isn't that what you say about them all?" Marissa huffed with a disapproving look. "And what's so interesting about this one?"

"I can't explain it."

"There's more to life than work, Fay. What about a relationship, marriage, and kids?" Concern etched her tanned face. "Work can't take the place of those things. We've all been hurt before, but the key is to learn from your mistakes and move on."

"Girl, my head is so screwed up. I don't need to bring my baggage of abuse and trust issues into new relationship," she said, playing with her silverware, and dismissing her friend's concerns. "Besides, I'll end up running a man off with all my drama."

"You're not the only woman, Fay, who's been sweet talked out of her virginity and dumped after he'd gotten what he wanted. Remember, I was stalked and conned by a no-good, lazy, free-loading bum. It's enough to make any woman want to throw in the towel. But there are still some good men out there."

"Look, we came here to have lunch and good conversation. Don't turn this into one of your woe is Fay lectures." Whenever her love life or lack of love life came into question, Angelica went into defense mode. Feeling stupid for choosing the wrong men, she'd rather throw herself into her work than to have her heart trampled over by another man's lies.

As they scanned their menus, a Spitzer Financial Firm commercial came on the television mounted on the diner's wall in front of them. A well-spoken, male voice caused both women to turn their heads in the direction of the screen.

"Greetings, my name is Jasion McCoy, and I would like to assure our investors that we will handle your investments with the greatest of care. Our company has faced much criticism over the past weeks due to the declining economy. But we at Spitzer will do all we can to calm those fears. If you have

any questions or concerns, please feel free to call our representatives at the number at the bottom of your television screen. Our lines will remain open twenty-four hours a day. Again, your investments are in good hands with Spitzer Financial Firm."

Angelica piped in when the commercial ended, "he's my new assignment."

"Get out of here. Everything is becoming so much clearer now. That's why you can't explain why you decided to take this case. It's because of him."

"No. No. No… don't go reading the wrong thing into this, Marissa," she stressed, trying to convince her friend that it was strictly business.

Angelica was mesmerized by how poised and convincing Jasion seemed in the commercial. She watched in amazement as the gorgeous man, whom she'd been with just hours earlier, was showing concern for his investors. But her, interested in him? Never, she lied to herself.

"He's not my type."

"Why not, Fay? A man like him is every woman's type. Girl, the man is F-I-N-E," Marissa spelled it out. "Your eyes were glued to that television set, and it wasn't your reporter look either, but the look of a woman who is interested in a man."

"Who, me?" Shocked by her friend's comment, she took a sip of iced tea to quench the fire igniting inside her. "I'm hired to investigate his clients' missing funds, not to find a love connection." *I wish she'd drop the subject, a man as striking as he would never be attractive to me. Men like him are only interested in the legally dumb type with nice bodies.* After two failed relationships, she'd learned her lesson. No slick-talking financial advisor was going to take advantage of her.

"That's what your lips say, honey; I'm a married woman and even I can appreciate a piece of eye candy every now and then. And Mr. McCoy is most definitely eye candy."

"Enough about that man, okay," she snapped, changing the subject. "I've been meaning to tell you that I stopped seeing Dr. Hawthorne."

"Fay, you were doing so well. What happened?" she asked, resting her salad fork on a napkin beside her plate. Marissa's humorous behavior had turned more serious.

"Alycee informed me that Gladys is terminally ill. She wants me to return to Augusta, immediately. Just the thought of going back to that place brought on my panic attacks and nightmares again. I promised myself that I would never step foot in that town again."

"That doesn't explain why you decided to end your sessions with Dr. Hawthorne."

"I'm tired of people blaming the devil for Gladys' actions. She is responsible for what she did to me." Her palms began to sweat as they always had at the mention of her mother's name. "It wasn't Satan who kicked and beat me for no reason. It was my mother. How can that holier-than-thou doctor tell me to forgive and move on when she hasn't experienced my hell?"

"I'm not trying to lessen the abuse, Fay. Lord knows I'm not. But you have to turn this issue over to God," she pleaded. "This is too heavy for you to bear alone."

"Don't go ruining my appetite with that religious talk. I'm not in the mood, Marissa." She gave her a dismissive wave, cocking her head to the side. "If God wanted to help me, He would've done it a long time ago."

"I promise not to preach at you, but I'll never stop telling you about God's saving grace," she stated.

"And I'll never stop letting it go in one ear and out of the other one," Angelica mouthed, her head mimicking a bobble head doll. She hated when her friend brought God into their conversation when what she was going through had nothing to do with Him. Or, so she thought.

They ate their lunch in silence, which was fine with Angelica. But she noticed Marissa's disapproving eyes staring at her. It didn't intimidate her or change her mind about going back to Dr. Hawthorne for counseling.

She believed that her mother's sudden illness was karma for all the mean and rotten things she'd done to her as a child. Until Marissa and Dr. Hawthorne walked in her shoes, she thought it best they keep their opinions and advice to themselves. She was the one who'd lived the abuse, not them or their God.

Chapter Seven

"I know we made plans to meet at my office around four o'clock, but Spitzer's video conference ran longer than I'd expected," Jasion said, as the maître d' escorted him and Angelica to their table.

A month had passed since the reporter from Hell came blazing into his life with a pitchfork in hand. Jasion hoped a change in the atmosphere might smother the flames and ease the tension that combusted between them in his office. And what better way for the two to get acquainted than over a friendly business dinner. Jasion hoped Angelica would see him as harmless and not some eight-armed sea creature, ready to grope and take advantage of her. He was tired of their constant bickering and wanted to call a truce.

"I'll let you off the hook this time," she said, warning him with her big, beautiful, almond-shaped eyes.

"Whew! That went over well, considering." Smiling, he playfully took one of his hands, wiped it across his forehead, and used the other to pull out her chair. "I didn't know how you were going to react. My lateness was out of my control. Scout's honor," he said, giving her the three-finger salute.

"Come on, now. I'm not made of stone. I do have a sensitive side." She scooted her chair up to the table. "Did you bring the files I requested?"

"You don't waste any time getting to business, do you? I thought we'd order drinks first and satisfy our palates with some fine cuisine before discussing the case."

"For the record, this is business and not pleasure. Let's not get this confused with a date,

Sir." Her face was so tight that it would have taken several jackhammers to break it apart.

"And what if it was a date, ma'am?" he teased, just to see her reaction.

"Well, get those thoughts out of your head. You have more to worry about than a date."

"Can I ask you a question?" Taking a more serious tone, he prayed she wouldn't dash her glass of water in his face afterward.

"Sure, if it will move things along faster." She waved a dismissing hand gesture in the air.

"Why are you so mean and uptight?" he asked, as delicately as possible. He didn't understand his physical attraction to Angelica. He'd dated women more refined and sophisticated than she. But something about her, the day she'd stormed into his office had caused his heart to skip a beat. Maybe his two-year hiatus from dating had affected his ability to see or think straight. Or was God testing him, to see if he'd keep his vow of celibacy? Whatever the case, he didn't like the way Angelica was making him feel. After all, the woman had a whip for a tongue.

"Mean? Uptight? Humph." She folded her arms in shock at his frankness.

"I'm not trying to offend you or hurt your feelings," he said, trying to calm her down before people began staring at them from the neighboring tables.

"Well, you did, Mr. McCoy."

"I apologize if you took it that way, but that's how you come across. We have been working together for over a month now, and we're still referring to each other as Sir, Ma'am, Mr., and Ms." Jasion could feel the dampness underneath his armpits. He had reason to sweat from the look she was giving him.

He watched as she fidgeted with a gold chain peeking from under her shirt, and hoped, what he had finally admitted, had sunk in. He was tired of her cold, impersonal attitude, and knew the problem had to be addressed sooner rather than later.

"I'm not uptight, Mr.... sorry, Jasion," she acknowledged, giving him a disquieting look.

Her first attempt to be civil and he was impressed. She did have a heart after all.

"Now was that so hard to say?" He gave her a friendly smile. The last thing he wanted was for her to walk out, leaving him to dine alone as he'd done so many nights before. "Let's enjoy dinner. Afterward, I promise to answer whatever questions you may have," he said, pleading with his eyes. "I'm starving, and I can't function on an empty stomach as you know from our first encounter."

"Yes, I remember." Her lips curled into a smile.

For the first time since their meeting, Jasion had finally seen her smile. Correction, a half-smile draped across her beautiful, mocha face.

As the evening wore on, Jasion actually couldn't believe how well they were getting along. He really enjoyed her company, although he could sense she hadn't let her guard down completely. But halfway was better than dodging the bullets from her gun slinging tongue. She used more tact when questioning him about the missing money, and that made him relax. The only problem he had the entire night with Angelica was that she didn't bless her meal before eating, but decided to keep silent about it for now.

The smooth sounds of jazz played in the background. And out of nowhere, he asked, "may I have this dance?" He glanced across the table at his dinner companion, praying she didn't shoot him down.

"Excuse me. We are in the middle of an important discussion about your future, and you're asking me to dance?" She scrunched up her nose at him.

"Would you like to dance? You do dance, don't you?" He ignored her question, for fear of ruining a perfect evening. "The music is really good tonight. And besides, that's all we've talked about since we arrived." Walking over to her seat, he reached for her hand before she could protest. There was no way she'd refuse him in a room full of people, he hoped. "I'm not trying to make a move on you. I just want to dance, nothing more." To ease her suspicious mind, he rolled up his sleeves in a gesture to prove he wasn't hiding anything up them.

"Seriously, how can you think about dancing when you're in the fight of your life, Jasion?" she craned her neck to look up at him.

"It's in God's hand. I learned a long time ago that an innocent man doesn't have to plead his case. My faith will see me through this. Now don't get me wrong, I am concerned, but I still have to live my life."

He extended his hand again for her to take. "So, are you going to dance with me or not?" He hoped she'd just go with the flow and loosen up.

Reluctantly, she took his hand.

He'd noticed a slight frown on her face when he'd mentioned God, but he didn't want to read much into it, just yet.

Jasion was in heaven as he danced with the most beautiful woman in the room; despite the black, outdated power suit, she wore. He held her in his arms as the music played, but she felt as tense as a mouse cornered by a roomful of bloodthirsty cats.

Even with a woman as beautiful as Angelica in his arms, memories of Fayth, his first love, invaded his thoughts. He'd asked himself the same
haunting questions a million times over. Was she married with children? Was she happy? Was she still the same feisty young girl he'd fallen in love with at the age of thirteen?

The soft skin and long, coarse hair of the woman he now held in his arms triggered so many unresolved emotions about the love he'd lost. Emotions he wished would stay buried. Fayth and Angelica shared so many similarities.

The music stopped, but they continued to dance in the middle of the empty dance floor. The sound of applause broke their trance. And there they stood, wrapped in each other's arms, at a loss for words. Jasion knew why he'd zoned out, but why had she?

"I'm so embarrassed," Angelica broke the silence. She jerked out of his arms and scurried past the onlookers to her seat.

"Why? It was nice to forget about work, if only for a short time," Jasion admitted, trailing closely behind her.

"It's getting late, and I have to get up early in the morning." She gathered up her purse and jacket.

"Yes... it is late. I had a wonderful time." He wanted to add, with a beautiful woman, but didn't want to push his luck. "Too bad it had to end so soon. I really enjoyed your company once I got pass your interrogation," he smiled.

"I see you still have jokes?" Standing with her arms folded and a serious look on her face, she asked, "Jasion, are you married?"

"Huh... uh, no." Her question caught him off guard. "Do you think I would be out in public, dancing with the most beautiful woman in this establishment, if I were?" There, he'd said it. She was beautiful and needed to hear it. Maybe her gentle side would show more now than the bad girl image she'd tried to portray.

"Like you, I don't want any drama between you and your girlfriends, either."

"Well, you can ease your pretty little mind. I'm not married with children nor do I have any girlfriends as you stated."

"Uh huh... that's what they all say."

Jasion escorted Angelica out of the restaurant into the parking lot. To their surprise, someone had slashed the tires on his BMW. Scared that the perpetrator might still be lurking nearby, they rushed back inside the restaurant and called the police.

Jasion was speechless.

"This has jealous lover written all over it," Angelica remarked, switching back into her investigator from Hell mode. "A crime like this is personal, Mr. McCoy." She put emphasis on

43

his name, letting him know it was back to business. "I've covered enough stories on the subject to know."

"I'm just as shocked as you are. And despite your comments, I have never hurt a woman to the point she'd do something this evil." He rubbed the sides of his temples to alleviate the headache caused by her sarcastic comments.

"Please inform your women that what's between us is business. And business only. I don't want to be involved in any drama." If looks could kill, Jasion would have been dead from the lasers shooting from her eyes. "Now come to think of it, I did notice a woman staring at us from the back of the restaurant, but I blew it off as nothing. Do you still want to stick to your story about being single? "

Feeling the veins bulging in the sides of his neck, ready to erupt, he snapped," Ms. Hope, I'll be all right until the police arrive. I think it's best if you leave. I'm not in the mood for any more of your cynical remarks."

"Trust me, I would love to leave but I can't, Mr. McCoy. Detectives will want to question me as well. We discovered the crime together. Remember?"

"Well, I'd appreciate it if you would keep your rude comments to yourself." He walked off, leaving her in the restaurant's lobby. Baffled by what had just transpired, Jasion tried to understand how what started out as a wonderful evening, had ended on such a sour note.

Chapter Eight

Angelica lay in bed, staring aimlessly at the closed wooden Venetian blinds that blocked any source of light from entering her small bedroom. She replayed the previous night's events over in her head. Her negative opinion of Jasion weighed heavily on her mind. *He must think I'm heartless. Why do I always think the worst of people? Stick it to them first before they can stick it to me has always been my safety net. But where has it gotten me over the years? Alone, bitter, and depressed,* she thought.

Tired of making scathing remarks, and then, having to apologize for them later was getting a bit old. But her abused childhood made her that way. Strike first, or she would be the one hurt in the end. Her way of thinking worked for years, until now. Jasion wasn't backing down the way other men had in the past. They just left, instead of confronting her as he had.

Angelica promised to keep her negative comments to herself during their next meeting. She wanted nothing more than to wrap up the case and get Mr. McCoy out of her life for good. He was making her feel and think about things she'd tried to suppress after two failed relationships. How did she allow her boss to sweet talk her into investigating a man who was proving to be more of a challenge than she had anticipated? She'd finally met her match.

She had to keep her wits about her without allowing his rugged good looks and flirtatious words lead her down a road of emotional destruction. She'd been there a time or two and had no plans of returning. No gamer was going to add her to his scorebook. Even with a smile that could bring the strongest of women to their knees. She wasn't going to be one of them.

I've fallen for his type time and time again. It's important to stay focused on the job at hand and get out of this man's life as quickly as possible. I refuse to allow his seductive brown eyes and slick words pull me in. She tried to convince herself.

Still unable to pull herself out of bed, Angelica's daydreaming ran rampant with thoughts of JC. Thoughts such as, what type of man he'd become? Was he as good looking as Jasion? She quickly tossed that image out of her head. Comparing her first love to a possible thief was insane. *Mr. McCoy could never hold a candle to JC, who is perfect in every sense of the word.*

After wallowing in self-pity the entire morning, Angelica decided to crawl out of her bed of defeat. The digital clock on the nightstand read, twelve-thirty p.m., which meant she'd wasted away half of her day off. She slipped on her robe and moped into her kitchen that barely seated one. Reaching into the tiny cabinet, she pulled out her favorite mug, which read "The World's Greatest Big Sister." Alycee, her baby sister, had given it to her as a house-warming gift. She brewed a cup of pomegranate tea. The slight citrus aroma always seemed to help relieve the stress of a bad day, or in her case, night.

Before she could remove the piping hot beverage from the microwave, the telephone rang.

Longing to hear another human voice, she rushed to answer it. "Hello," she greeted cheerfully to hide her sadness.

"Fayth." Her younger sister Alycee chimed in. Like Marissa, she also refused to call her big sister, Angelica.

"Hey, Sis. It's good to hear from you, especially right now."

"Are you having another woe is me moment?" she asked. "Don't bother lying. Cause I can hear it in your voice."

"You think you know me so well, don't you?" Her lips curled into a weak smile at how keen her sister senses were, even miles away in Augusta. She didn't want to get into the details of last night, especially her dancing with the man she was supposed to be investigating, but she did. "I had a business dinner with a male client yesterday, and I may have offended him."

"You never cared about rubbing anyone the wrong way in the past. Why would that concern you now?" she asked and then paused. "Wait a minute, unless you're falling for him. Are you falling for him, Fay?"

Angelica didn't want her sister fishing for something that wasn't there. She quickly answered, "no."

"Well, what's the problem? Why are you so down in the dumps over someone you're not interested in?"

"Forget it; you wouldn't understand. You've had a perfect life ever since we were little." Angelica always hit below the belt when she felt trapped in a corner. She'd always turned a minor disagreement with her sister into a fight.

"I'm not going down that road with you, Fay. You need to stop living in the past. What's done is done."

"Down what road, Alycee?" Angelica's voice was now rising with anger. "Until you've walked in my shoes, you can't tell me when I should be over what happened to me or how long it should take."

"Hold on one minute. You're trying to bring Mama up indirectly as you always do. I remember.

And for the record, she gave me away to the Louis' or did you forget? So don't you go trying to act as if you were the only one hurt," Alycee snapped. "Granted, she didn't abuse me. But, she abandoned me. It took years of therapy and prayer to deal with it, but I got over it. I survived."

She knew her sister had been hurt just as much as she. Angelica heard the rumors circulating in their small town about her mother sleeping with Deacon Louis, a married man. But to conceive a child with him was a disgrace. Angelica was thankful in a sense that her father had passed away a year earlier before the scandal had hit. Knowing that his wife had an adulterous fling would have killed him for sure.

"People like you act as if it's easy to go to therapy and poof, you're healed." She flung her hand up in the air and changed the subject. "Look, what did you call me for anyway, Alycee?"

47

Ignoring her sister's tirade, she said, "I know you don't want to hear what I am about to say, but God saw me through it. I never lost my faith and trust in Him as you have. Fayth, you need Him. And you need Him, bad. I love you, and you can get angry with me, but I will never stop talking about God's love just to spare your feelings."

"Well, on that note, bye," she hung up the telephone. Her heart had hardened against God, and she rejected any topic concerning Him.

The telephone rang as quickly as she'd hung it up. Reluctantly, Angelica answered.

"Why did you do that? Ooooooh... I swear. I wish I could slap some darn sense into that hard head of yours!" Alycee yelled through the receiver. "The reason I called in the first place is to tell you that I don't know how much longer Mother has, Fay."

"And what does that have to do with me?" she said without any trace of compassion.

"Girl, did you hear what I just said? Our mother is dying."

"No. Your mother is dying. To me, she is Gladys. She never wanted me to call her mother, mama, or any words close to being maternal."

"You need closure, and coming to see her will give you just that before, it's too late."

"I can't. I haven't seen that woman—"

Alycee interrupted, "she's not some woman off the streets, but your mother."

"Just because she gave me life doesn't make her a mother," she growled back. "I haven't laid eyes on her since I went to live with my Aunt Beatrice. And I have no plans of returning."

"Please, Fayth. Please do this for yourself, I am begging you."

"No, Alycee."

"Pray about it, Sis. I love you, and you're not alone in this. I got your back."

"I love you, too." She rested her back against the kitchen wall and turned up her nose and said, "prayer hasn't worked for me in the past, so why start now?"

Chapter Nine

"Man, what's wrong with you today? I thought we were playing a friendly game of basketball. You're pushin' and shovin' as if you're 'bout to sign a multi-million dollar contract with the NBA or somethin'." Rico complained in his thick Latino accent about the brutal blows Jasion was laying on him.

"Sorry man for hammering you. I'm under a lot of stress these days." Huffing and puffing, he confided to his friends, "I think someone is trying to frame me at work. I didn't want to believe it at first." He continued to breathe heavily. "And to make matters worse, I am falling for the investigative reporter the company assigned to the case."

"Whaaaaaaaaaaaaat?" Brandon, Rico, and John sang in unison.

"Man. I wouldn't want to be in your shoes," Brandon admitted, shaking his head in disbelief.

John and Rico agreed.

"I don't know what to do. It's been a while since I've shown any real interest in dating. Most women seem to have a motive for wanting to date me. But Angelica is different. She hasn't tried to use her feminine wiles to seduce or chase after me," Jasion explained, panting. He rested his back against the brick wall and then sat on the basketball. "The lady is all business."

"Maybe she's gay," John added.

"I seriously doubt it," Jasion said, furrowing his brows at his friend.

"Man, I haven't seen you this worked up over a female since you broke up with that crazed chick, what's her face?" Rico asked, tapping his finger on the side of his face as if in deep thought. "Now I remember, Nicole Swaggart, that's her name."

"Man, pleasssse. Don't go there. I almost lost my position as youth pastor behind all the drama she caused." Jasion used his shirt as a makeshift towel to wipe the sweat from his face. The mention of the woman, who'd almost destroyed him, caused him to perspire even more.

Jasion had broken off their engagement because he'd grown tired of Nicole's possessive behavior. Her jealous escalated when he'd socialized with the female parishioners. Her paranoia about someone stealing him away from her became a bit overbearing. He'd explained to no avail that the women were parents of the kids who attended his youth center.

Jasion finally became fed-up when Nicole gave him an ultimatum that things had to change once they were married. He could no longer hang out with the other ministers after church service or play basketball with his hoodlum friends. She'd even had the audacity to order him to stop trying to save those ghetto hoodrats at his youth center, as she referred to them.

When he informed her the engagement was off, she'd vowed to destroy his career and his ministry. And Nicole Swaggart always kept her promises.

To ruin Jasion's chances of taking over leadership of the youth ministry, Nicole had barged into the senior office at Bountiful Blessing Ministry with her dress ripped and hair tossed all over her head. She lied, claiming that Jasion had forced her into an empty classroom and physically assaulted her. If it hadn't been for the security cameras placed throughout the church, she might have gotten away with it.

"Of all the people in the world, Rico, why did you have to remind J about that demented chick?" Brandon piped in.

"I didn't mean to bring you down, bro," Rico apologized.

"I'm praying when the investigation is over, Angelica will loosen up and let me take her out on a real date," Jasion said, rising to his feet and shooting the basketball into the goal. "I can't seem to focus on anything else, much less this case since she walked through my office door."

51

"Dang Minister McCoy, som' female got you all twisted."

Darius, one of the inner city kids benefiting from the youth center, appeared out of nowhere, sticking his nose into their conversation.

"Darius, it's not polite sticking your nose into grown folks' business," Jasion scolded. "Shouldn't you be in your tutoring class and not out here adding your two cents into our discussion?"

"Okay. Okay. I'm going. I just came out here to give you this," Darius said, handing Jasion a letter. "But on the real, though, Minister J, ain't no woman worth gettin' yo' head all messed up over," The teenager advised.

"Kids today," Jasion laughed, opening the letter with all eyes glued to it.

"That looks like a check!" Rico shouted.

Each of them focused on the one hundred thousand dollar check Jasion pulled from the envelope. Someone had endorsed it to the youth center, but the handwriting was illegible.

"This goes to show that God still works miracles, dude," Brandon rejoiced.

"Darius, who gave you this envelope?" Jasion inquired with excitement and curiosity.

"Some weird-looking guy came into the center earlier and said to give it to you and you only."

"Huh... that's strange. Did he leave a name?" Jasion asked, puzzled. "Because he didn't bother to put a return address on this letter, so we can send him a receipt for a tax write-off."

"Nope. He was sort of creepy."

"Creepy how, Darius?" Jasion lifted a brow as the other men discussed the mysterious money in the background.

"He appeared to be wearing some type of disguise," the boy explained.

"Okay son, go on inside before you miss your class," Jasion ordered. He patted the envelope in the palm of his hand, alarmed by Darius' description of the Good Samaritan.

Chapter Ten

Angelica and Jasion avoided each other like the plague. She requested that his secretary should bring another desk and chair into his office, knowing that tension would flare if they continued to share his. They worked in silence and spoke only when each had pertinent information to discuss. When finished, they withdrew back into their private corners of the room. Stealing glances when the other wasn't watching became the norm. Since the slashing of Jasion's tires, and Angelica making rude comments about it, the two had hardly spoken.

She felt ridiculous and childish about how they were behaving, and decided to call a truce and reopen the lines of communication. "I'm starting to sound like a broken record, Jasion."

Angelica noticed the surprised look on Jasion's drop dead gorgeous face when she addressed him. He gave her his undivided attention. It had been so quiet in his office over the past week that her voice sounded foreign to her.

The knot in her throat loosened, allowing her to speak freely as she rubbed her sweaty palms together underneath her desk. "I shouldn't have said that it was one of your girlfriends who damaged your tires. It was insensitive and out of line. We have a serious crime to solve, and I behaved unprofessionally. I'm sorry." She blew out a deep breath, thankful she hadn't hyperventilated.

"Thank you. I accept your apology." He walked over to where she sat and gave her a friendly handshake. "Angelica, I don't play games with a woman's heart," he said, towering over her. "I might be a lot of things, but a man who'd intentionally hurt a woman isn't one of them."

"Good for you." She smiled halfheartedly and removed her hand from his endearing grip. He had the type of hands that a woman would love touching. But she was no fool. Most men had perfected the art of lying, by saying all the right things, and she planned to avoid his web of deceit.

"I don't know how much longer we'll be working together, but I would like it to be as pleasant as possible."

"Sure," she agreed, nervously staring up into his hypnotizing brown eyes. His closeness caused her heart to race. The only other person who had made her heart beat at rapid speed was JC. Yes, she'd been with other men but none that made her insides smile, and that was exactly the way she didn't want to feel about a man she could never have. "I'll keep my opinions to myself for the remainder of the investigation. I promise." She smiled, this time much wider.

Happy they were back on speaking terms for now; Angelica moved her paperwork and chair back to Jasion's desk. It had become a hassle walking back and forth to collaborate on the case. She'd never admit it, but part of her wanted to believe Jasion was a good-hearted person. After years of investigating bad ones, she wasn't going to be distracted by him. He was sexy and mysteriously dangerous, too risky for her.

An hour later, she was beginning to think that moving back to Jasion's desk had been a bad idea. His alluring stare made her uncomfortable, and she hoped that she hadn't sent the wrong message when she'd called a truce. She thought it would make for a pleasant working atmosphere if they communicated.

"May I ask you a question Angelica?" he asked, resting both hands on top of his desk.

She rolled her eyes in her head, bracing herself for the battle that was sure to erupt. "A question? What kind of question?"

"You are a beautiful, smart, and intelligent woman. Why do you feel the need to   assert yourself?"

"What?" she gasped, slapping both hands to her chest.

"It hides the real you," he said, never taking his eyes off of hers. "What man hurt you, Angelica?"

"Jasion, we've just called a truce. Don't make me regret it."

Angelica's heart was pounding out of control. She didn't know where his question was going, and too terrified to find out.

"I read people well, and I know when they're pretending to be someone they are not." Jasion came from behind his desk to where she sat, closing the distance between them.

No, he didn't. Pretending? Your clients' money is missing, and you're the prime suspect, and you're trying to say I'm pretending? she screamed inwardly. "I think you have a lot of nerve insinuating that I'm pretending. You don't know me," she retorted.

"Then help me to know you."

"Jasion, in case you haven't noticed, I was hired here to gather information to prove your innocence or guilt. Not to become one of your women." She tried to remain in control, but the handsome man standing over her was about to make her throw caution to the wind. As quickly as the thought had entered her mind, she knew she was in trouble. Every story she'd covered in the past was an open and shut case, no attachments but this one was working on her heart.

"Would that be so bad?"

"Are you listening to yourself? I'm not interested in you." *Liar!* She stood, retrieving her purse and briefcase off the empty desk.

"I'm interested in you."

He stopped her dead in her tracks, grabbed her in his arms, and planted a passionate kiss she'd never forget on her lips. Her arms seemed to have a mind of their own. She wrapped them around his strong, thick neck and kissed him with a sense of urgency. Whatever reservations she had swirling around in her head earlier about him quickly disappeared. He deepened the kiss and pulled her closer into his embrace. And she didn't resist.

When their lips parted, she stood speechless and disoriented. Angelica was afraid she had opened the door to a

55

world of passion that would be hard to close. She had seen the moon, the stars, and the whole nine yards with that explosive kiss. She tried to make sense of it. Sparks like that only happened in the movies, not in real life. It was everything she'd hoped it would be and more. Like a frightened child not knowing what to do next, she collected her belongings and ran out of his office.

Is he trying to run some sort of game on me? He's only known me for a month, how can he be interested in me? Yeah, right, I might be lonely, but I'm not desperate or naïve. She rested her back against the outside of his office door. Her head continued to spin from his electrifying kiss.

*****

Jasion stood on the opposite side of the door. He was happy that he'd put all his cards on the table concerning his feelings for her. Now the ball was in her court. It wasn't going to be easy to win her heart, but he trusted that God would work things out.

Angelica's eyes and demeanor reminded him of Fayth. Her big, brown, almond-shaped eyes, smooth, dark brown skin, thick, jet-black, shoulder-length hair, and full, voluptuous lips, mirrored his first love's features. He'd wanted to kiss and touch her since their first meeting and couldn't hide his feelings from her any longer. The only obstacles that stood in their way were the investigation and her lack of belief in a higher power. There was no way Angelica would compromise the investigation to go out with him. She played by the rules and convincing her to trust him would be even harder.

He'd held out for as long as he could, in hopes of finding Fayth and rekindling their friendship. Now he had to move on with his life and leave the memories of her in the past. The Lord had promised him years earlier that his soulmate would come to him physically and spiritually broken. He didn't know much about Angelica's situation, but he was aware that someone had hurt her deeply.

"Lord, I know you work in mysterious ways. And I will never question You or Your decisions.

But please give me a sign that Angelica is the one. I am falling for her and hard. You know I don't have the best track record when it comes to women. Open my spiritual eyes that I may choose wisely."

Chapter Eleven

"*This is easier than taking candy from a baby. No one will ever suspect me of milking millions from Spitzer Financial Firm clients' accounts. Mr. Lexington and his board members will regret the day they ever fired my father. He gave his blood, sweat, and best years to help build this company. And for what? To be hauled away like some common criminal off the streets. They destroyed and embarrassed my family; now it's time for me to return the favor. Because of them, I had to settle for a smaller college, while Mr. Lexington's imbecile son, Ian, attended one of the most prestigious colleges money could buy.*

I can waltz in and out of any office I choose and take whatever I want, no questions asked. Soon, I'll have Ms. 'Star Reporter' Angelica Hope, wrapped around my little finger. She will never know what hit her until it's too late. When she does put all the pieces of the puzzle together, the money and I will be long gone. Top reporter, my butt. She and those Keystone Cops are chasing false leads that I purposely planted in those files. And they call themselves experts. Ha!

Hooking up with Nicole Swaggart is the best move I could've ever made. She is a loony tune for sure. But the criminal expertise she contributes to the heist has proven to be a valuable asset. Her desperate need for cash will help me pull off one of the biggest embezzlement heists ever. Life can't get any sweeter than this.

I hate to break Nicole's heart after the job is finished. But, I'll have to kick her crazy behind to the curb. Wait… better yet, I'll call Forest Oaks mental facility and turn her in. She's a loose cannon, and her constant nagging and threats will cost me my freedom. If she tries to rat me out, hopefully, the police will just think she's delusional from drug withdrawal."

He pushed the send button from one of corporate office computers, transferring money into his overseas account. When he finished transferring the money, he infected the remaining computers with viruses and encryption codes to throw the authorities off his trail. Once the computers were up and running again, the original documents would be lost in cyberspace.

Revenge had made him heartless, and he wasn't concerned that hundreds of innocent employees could lose their jobs or that hundreds of investors stood to lose millions because of his plot to avenge his father's death.

He marveled at what his actions would bring to the people he'd grown to hate at the SFF. *"God, I know that you said vengeance is Yours. But today, it belongs to me."* He anticipated the day he would see their shocked faces, when the multi-million dollar company would come crumbling down to the ground. *"I will be standing among them to witness it all and loving every minute of it. I'll do as always in times of trouble, offer words of encouragement and pretend to care."*

Slithering from one office to the next, he planted viruses on each computer. When the employees logged into their PCs the following morning, they would continue to reboot their systems until it eventually crashed.

A wicked grinned crept onto his face at the thought of his evil works.

Spooked, he jumped at what sounded like footsteps approaching the door. He ducked behind a desk until security had passed. When he'd finished the last of his dirty deeds, he slipped out of the office door, making his way down an emergency stairwell. The disguise he wore altered his appearance just in case security spotted him in the building.

"Letting their guard down is a costly mistake. When the pallbearers threw the last shovel of dirt on your grave, Dad, I promised to get justice. I'm close to completing my mission. Mr. Lexington and all his flunkies will hate the day they ever laid

eyes on me. I'm going to make their lives a living nightmare like they did ours."

Chapter Twelve

"The next time you put your lips on me, I will file harassment charges against you," Angelica threatened, trying to sound convincing, with no such luck. Jasion's kiss awakened parts of her that she'd forgotten existed until now. She loved it, needed it, and welcomed it. But it would be over her dead body before she'd ever admit it to him. *It was best to let sleeping dogs lie. No use in acknowledging such feelings*, she supposed. Feelings, she knew would only lead to heartache.

"You kissed me back, so it's considered consensual," Jasion said, smugly.

"Humph." Angelica rolled her eyes at him, knowing it was the truth. She wasn't going to win that battle. Instead of arguing the facts, she went straight into work mode as usual when she felt challenged. "From this point on, we'll work at separate desks." She began removing her files and documents from his desk.

"I'll try," he smiled, leaning back in his chair.

"No. You will do more than just try, Jasion. This is not a game." Angelica could sense he was getting a kick out of watching her squirm by the smirk on his clean-shaven, ultra-sexy face.

"You don't have to move back to the empty desk. Stay. I promise to be on my best behavior."

Angelica hesitated and then returned the papers to his desk. She hoped he'd keep his word because his closeness became more intoxicating and too powerful to ignore. Trusting herself around him had proven to be harder than she'd expected. All she could think about was *that kiss*. The kiss that had her wanting more but more came with a price. A price she wasn't willing to pay.

The last man she fell head over heels for, wined and dined her, reeling her in, hook, line, and sinker. Then, he'd shot an arrow straight through her heart with his lying and cheating ways.

"Jasion, I spoke with Spitzer's IT guy, Caleb Michaels, earlier. He's working on the infected computers on the fourth floor. The receptionists' PC's are the only ones up and running."

"The receptionists' computers aren't considered high risk. So, it would be a waste of time for someone to tamper with them. Let's just pray Mr. Michaels knows what he's doing since he's regarded as the technology guru around here."

"He didn't give me the impression that he thought someone had tampered with them." She raised an inquisitive brow at the fact that Jasion would imply someone had infected the computers. She made a mental note of it. "From your tone, you don't seem too fond of the guy."

"He's arrogant and very flirtatious with the female employees, which he's been reprimanded for on several occasions." With a hint of irritation in his voice, Jasion leaned forward in his chair, locking eyes with her.

Feeling uncomfortable because of his penetrating stare, Angelica flipped through the documents sprawled across his desk to avoid it. Was intimidation his way of getting what he wanted? She just couldn't figure him out. Why flirt with her? The only answer that came to mind was the investigation. He probably wanted to woo her in hopes of throwing her off his tracks. No such luck, she wasn't biting. He had no reason to be interested in her. A man like him could have his choice of women. There had to be an ulterior motive behind his interest in her. And rest assured, she planned to find out what he had swimming around in that gorgeous head of his.

"He seems nice enough. A real gentleman."

Jasion frowned, "have detectives questioned him concerning the computer problems?"

"Yes. He's clear for now, but everyone here at Spitzer is a suspect." Glancing up from the papers she pretended to read in an attempt to escape his gaze; she warned, "just to give you a heads up, you will be brought in for questioning later today."

"Fine with me. I have nothing to hide."

She watched his demeanor, but Jasion was cool as a cucumber. Not even a flinch. Either he was calling her bluff or he was truly innocent. Whatever the reason, she would be keeping a close eye on him.

"Then you have nothing to worry about."

"We've been thumbing through backlogs all morning. Let's ditch this stuffy office and grab a bite to eat, on me."

"I don't think that's a good idea," she said with reservation.

"I promise to behave. Besides, you made yourself perfectly clear. The last thing I need is harassment charges brought against me. I have enough to worry about as it is," he said with a wink.

"In that case, let's go before I begin grazing on these folders." She gave him a guarded smile.

Men preyed on women who they thought were weak and insecure. It was a lesson she'd learned all too well and wasn't going to repeat. *Mr. McCoy, you have another thing coming if you think all you have to do is flash that beautiful smile of yours, and I'll be under your spell. Well, think again,* she mused.

"Let me get the door for you," he said, reaching for the doorknob.

"Thank you." She quickly brushed passed him, hoping he wouldn't get any more bright ideas.

Angelica breathed a sigh of relief once she was out of his office. But before they could reach the elevator, Jasion's secretary stopped them.

"Mr. McCoy, before you and Ms. Hope leave for lunch, I have a letter that reads, urgent. Someone dropped it off when I was away from my desk." She handed him the sealed envelope.

Out of curiosity, Angelica craned her neck to see what pertinent information his secretary had for him that could not wait until they returned.

"Put it on my desk. I'll get it after lunch Ms. Kennedy," Jasion ordered.

"It reads urgent, Mr. McCoy," Ms. Kennedy replied.

"Okay. I'll read it at lunch."

She handed him the envelope and returned to her desk. Jasion stuffed it into his suit's jacket pocket, and then he and Angelica stepped inside the elevator.

When the elevator door closed, Angelica asked, "well, are you going to open it?"

"Aren't we nosey?"

"It reads urgent. I think you need to see what it is."

Retrieving the letter from his pocket, he ripped it open to appease her reporter appetite and read it aloud. *"Your days as a free man are numbered, McCoy."*

Chapter Thirteen

Jasion read the disturbing letter for the umpteenth time. Without a shadow of a doubt, someone was setting him up. But who? A question he'd asked a million times. Things were heating up, and he didn't like where the flames were spreading. He had no plans on taking the rap for a crime he did not commit. Proving his innocence had become his top priority.

Believing his eyes were playing tricks on him, Jasion read the letter again. Angelica listened from across the table. "Your days as a free man are numbered." He took a sip of his black coffee to take the edge off. If he were a drinking man, Jasion would have asked for something much stronger. "Why would someone target me at the firm when there are other major financial players earning billions on real estate properties for their clients? What's so fascinating about my clients and me?"

"Jasion, you will have to turn this letter over to the authorities," Angelica advised.

"I just pray they catch the person or persons involved," he stressed. "I can go to prison… for life, if they don't." The reality of his possible fate had begun to sink in. He must fight the good fight of faith or be swallowed up by someone's devilish scheme to make him the fall guy. Justice would prevail. He just had to believe it.

"The detectives that Mr. Lexington has working on the case are good. I promise they will get to the bottom of it and scan it for any possible signs of fingerprints."

"Do I detect a hint of concern in your voice, Angelica?"

"Let's not go there… okay," she said, twisting her napkin in her hand.

The waiter placed their food before them. Jasion bowed his head and blessed his food. Angelica tore into hers. He'd noticed during their last business dinner that she had done the same.

"I don't mean to come across as rude, but do you believe in God?" he asked.

"What does my believing or not believing in God have to do with anything?"

"Everything, at least for me. So, do you?" God had revealed to Jasion's spirit that his prayers for a wife would come to pass, but the only woman he'd been around lately was Angelica. Surely, God would not send him a woman who didn't reverence Him?

"I did, once," she pursed her lips, cocking her head to the side.

His heart dropped to the bottom of his stomach at her admission. How could a woman as intelligent as she not believe? He just couldn't digest it. True, he could be going to prison, but in his opinion, Angelica was already there, spiritually.

"What made you walk away from Him, Angelica?"

"It's a long story that I prefer not to discuss it," she answered sharply.

"I pray in time, you'll come to trust me enough to share what it is that made you lose your faith," he encouraged, his voice softening. "I probably would have lost my mind by now if I didn't have a higher power guiding me through this investigation."

"We can't all be as fortunate," she uttered, smugly.

"But we are."

"Yeah... right."

Jasion wasn't about to allow the distracting noise level at the small diner drown out their conversation. She was hurting, and it concerned him. He blocked out the disruptive chitchat and prayed inwardly that God would restore her faith. Angelica had been a thorn in his side ever since she'd landed in his office, but he genuinely cared about her spiritual state. Now that he had a glimpse into her personal life, he felt compelled to help her.

"Angelica, I have an important question to ask you."

She blew out a deep breath, placing her chicken sandwich on her plate. "It's not about God again, is it?"

"No, it's not," he hesitated, although he'd love for it to be. "Once this investigation is over, granted that I don't go to jail, I would like to get to know you on a more personal level."

"Why? So, you can lay hands on me and save my soul, Brother McCoy? She batted her eyelashes at him, waving both hands in the air, mocking church worshippers.

"Wow." Was all he could say and he signaled for the waiter to pour him another round of black coffee. "Someone must have hurt you really bad?" He was more determined than ever to break through that tough exterior to find the real Angelica.

"My personal life is off limits. You should be more concern with who is trying to sabotage your career," she countered.

"Yea, though I walk through the valley of the shadow of death, I will fear no evil: for thou art with me." He recited the twenty-third number of Psalms with assurance. "God will declare my innocence, not man."

"I think we'd better head back to the office." She signaled for the waitress to bring her a to-go box for her half-eaten sandwich.

"What are you running from Angelica?" he asked, puzzled. Refusing to drop the subject, he put his problems aside to help the beautiful woman across the table with hers.

"You need to mind your business, Jasion. You will never understand my pa—"

She stopped, choking on her words.

"Pain," Jasion said what she could not admit.

When a lone, solitary tear trickled down one of her flawless mocha cheeks, he immediately left his seat to comfort her.

"No," she said, pulling away from him. "Don't touch me."

"I'm not trying to make a move on you, Angelica." With the news she'd just laid on him about her faith or lack of it, he thought it was best to keep quiet about him being a minister. Instead, he pulled a couple of napkins from the napkin-holder and handed them to her. "I would never try to take advantage of you."

"I'm not weak if that's what you think," she sniffed.

"I didn't imply that you were." The tough girl act wasn't working anymore. She was hurting and too stubborn to ask for help. No one breaks down into tears for no reason. He'd counseled enough parishioners to know. "Trust me; you're anything but weak. I have the scars to prove it," he joked, trying to lighten the mood.

"Please," she begged, now in a more humbled tone. "Let's just go. I've lost my appetite."

"Angelica, I know you've formed your opinions about me, but if you ever need a friend to talk to, I'm here. No strings attached. I promise," he said.

She wiped the corner of her eyes with her napkin. "A friend would be nice." A faint smile spread across her perplexed face. "But, I'm not interested in anything outside of friendship."

"I will never disrespect your wishes. But whatever it is you're holding inside; you really need to talk to someone about it."

"It's nothing I can't handle."

"When my father died, Angelica, I shut down emotionally. I withdrew from family and friends. My mom and sister were worried about my mental health. I had to pray to release the hurt and anger before it destroyed me." He rested his hands on top of hers, giving them a gentle squeeze. To his surprise, she didn't protest. "Seeking help doesn't mean you're weak. It means you're human."

As they headed back to his office, he hoped that she'd received his advice. Learning to let go of past hurts wasn't easy, but God made it possible for him. It was a bitter pill to swallow when the company his father worked for fired him after years of dedicated service. Their thirst for blood and unwarranted justice, Jasion believed, killed his father and nearly bankrupted his family.

Chapter Fourteen

Angelica charged through her office door at CNB News, annoyed by the moment of weakness she had displayed in front Jasion earlier at lunch. Slamming the door shut, she marched over to her cluttered desk, flopped down in her chair, and sulked.

"Ughhhhhhhhhh! I was a blubbering fool in front of Jasion," she ranted, burying her face inside the palms of her hands.

She tried focusing on her work but Jasion wanting to see her exclusively weighed heavily on her mind. Was it a ploy to get inside her head or was he truly interested in her? Jasion's sincerity seemed real, but so did her last boyfriend who'd ripped out her heart. This time she'd made the decision to think with her head and not her heart. She wasn't ready to jump in headfirst at his offer of friendship. She still had reservations concerning him.

Angelica sat at her desk, trying to piece the puzzles of the case together. After hours of flipping through file after file and coming up with no clues, she decided to call it a night.

She gathered up her belongings to leave the station when thoughts of Jasion entered her mind. A warm, tingling sensation flowed through her insides. How could she face him after today? She felt foolish. *A relationship… with me? What is he up to?*

A knock at the door startled Angelica, ruining the fantasy of what could never be with Mr. Perfect. Apparently, she wasn't alone at the station. "Come in," she yelled, thinking it was one of the cleaning crew.

The door pushed open and in came Jasion McCoy.

"Good. I caught you just in time. I apologize for showing up at your place of business unannounced. But, I think it's time we stop dancing around each other and talk like mature adults.

Something is happening between us, and it goes far beyond this investigation," he admitted.

Are my eyes playing tricks on me? This has to be a mirage. Jasion McCoy, standing in my office.

She was scared to blink for fear she might be hallucinating. If her mouth were a flytrap, she would have caught plenty of flies. She stood paralyzed, trying to process his words, but Angelica had to play it cool, or she would melt at his feet.

"Nothing is happening between us, Jasion." It took all her strength to force those untruthful words from her mouth. Something was happening between them, but she'd never admit to it. She rushed to her desk before her knees buckled underneath her. The sight of him standing in her office made her want to collapse in his arms, but she wasn't going down that road again. She has been there, done that, and she wasn't going back to being a puppet on a string for no man. Not even for the delicious one standing before her, though he was getting harder to resist.

Without responding, Jasion followed suit. He sat in the vacant seat adjacent to her desk. She'd made a mental note to kill Lance — her boss — later for not taking the extra chair back to his office. Feeling like a deflated balloon, she waited to hear what hot air he had to fill her head with next.

"Do you mind?" he queried, scooting closer.

"It seems you've already made yourself comfortable," she responded. Trying to remain calm, cool, and composed, proved to be a hard task. The fresh minty smell of his breath had her nerves on end, but she was determined to keep her hormone level under control. She had to protect her heart. The small, still voice in her head encouraged her to go for it, but common sense screamed, *Don't be a fool.*

Angelica knew that he had no problem when it came to women. She'd witnessed his magnetic powers attracting the opposite sex at SFF. Female employees would pass his office, flirting and practically drooling at the sight of him. No, she didn't want to come off as some desperate chick. She thought it was in her best interest not to get involved with a man who had other women vying for his affection. She was there to do a job, and she wasn't going to deviate from those plans for any man. Not even for Mr. Universe himself.

"I admit, I'm a little rusty at this because I haven't dated a wo—"

He stopped.

She asked, jokingly, "what? You dated men before?"

"I see you have jokes, but no, to answer your question. I love everything God created on a woman." He took hold of her hand and placed it inside his. "From her full delectable lips all the way down to her curvaceous hips."

She sighed, becoming putty in his hands.

"We started out on the wrong foot. And I want a chance to rectify our working relationship; with hopes that it can lead to a beautiful friendship. My spirit is telling me this is right, which is why I'm here tonight."

Her voice cracked at his unadulterated honesty. "A non-hostile environment sounds nice. But I have a job to do, and friendship will only complicate things." In her heart, she wanted to scream at the top of her lungs, *Yes, yes!*

She knew the types of games men played and had no plans of being a participant in his. Jasion's seductive words charmed every part of her weak, affection-starved ego. She must remain strong until the completion of the investigation, and then get Jasion McCoy out of her life, for good.

"I don't know what you've been through, Angelica, as far as men go, but please don't lump us all in the same category."

"A friendship will affect the investigation. I don't want people thinking I can't do my job because of our involvement."

"I don't care about this case. Heck, let someone else take it. I want you… uh, mm, uh," he admitted, stammering over his words. "I mean I want to get to know you better."

Angelica's eyebrows rose at his slip of the tongue.

Removing her hand from his, she scooted her chair to the side, giving them some distance. The passion in his eyes scared her. Jasion was taking her to a place she wasn't ready to go. There were demons in her past she needed to face before allowing another person to enter into her dysfunctional life.

"Look, Jasion, I know you said your God would work things out, but you need to be realistic. This is serious. You can go to jail if you're proven guilty. This case is bigger than just reporting a story. It's a crime, and the Port City Police Department is looking to throw the book at the guilty party or parties involved. No ifs, ands, or buts about it," she stressed.

"I'm not taking this lightly."

"I just don't think this is the time to be talking about a friendship or whatever you want to call this."

"'This,' as you call it, is a man who wants to get to know a beautiful and intelligent woman." He confessed, moving his chair closer to hers. "I don't care how it may look to people. I can't just sit back and not live my life. Women complain about how hard it is to find a good man. Well, it's just as equally hard for a man to find a good woman. I'm not going to let you slip through my fingers."

They sat in silence, trying to process what had been said.

Finally, she asked, "why me, Jasion?"

"I'm obedient to the Spirit of God."

"Right. And you expect me to believe that?" she asked. "People make things happen, not God. Look, I've had a long day, so have yourself a good night." She jumped up from her seat and headed for the door with Jasion on her heels.

Chapter Fifteen

"Hold up," Jasion shouted, sprinting down the hallway of CBN News, trying desperately to keep up with Angelica's quick steps. "Let me walk you to your car. This part of downtown is swarming with shady characters." *Why on God's green Earth is this woman so darn stubborn and distrusting of others, especially men?* He asked himself.

"I can take care of myself," Angelica yelled over her shoulders.

Finally catching up with her, Jasion realized that he needed to hit the gym more. She moved like lightening. "I have no doubt that you can," he huffed.

"Jasion, I don't know what kind of game you're trying to play."

She stopped when he gently grabbed her by the arm, turning her around to face him. "Angelica, talk to me. Why are you so angry?"

"Men use Christianity to prey on women and once they've gotten what they were after," she gestured with her hands, "Poof. They're gone."

"Is that what you think of me?" He opened the door leading out into the dimly lit parking lot and escorted her to her car.

"I'm not naïve." She spun around with her car remote in hand. "I've been around the block a couple of times. All men want something."

"Wow!" Here, he'd been thinking he was a nice guy, but all she saw in him was a predator looking to score.

"Well?" With raised brows, she patted her foot on the pavement, waiting for his rebuttal. "Don't you?"

"I want to know you as a person. My parents raised me to respect women," he explained. "I don't mistreat or abuse God's most precious gift. And I surely don't use God's name in vain for sex, if that's what you're implying." *Lord, this woman has some serious trust issues.*

"Kudos to you," she gestured with a handclap. "I don't need a knight in shining armor to rescue me." She plopped down in the driver's seat of her car and closed the door. Her windows partially lowered. She turned the key in the ignition, and it refused to start

"That isn't good," Jasion said. "Step out and let me try." He checked the gas and battery gauges, and then he jumped out of the car, lifted the hood, and discovered the problem.

"What's wrong?" she shouted frantically.

Alarm stretched across the contours of his face. "Someone has stolen your battery."

"WHAT?" Her screams were loud enough to wake the dead in downtown Lincoln Memorial Cemetery. "How? Why?" she asked, shaking like a leaf on a tree.

Without thinking, the fear in her voice caused Jasion to pull her into his arms to calm her down. They went back inside the news station and called the police and a tow truck company. Port City's downtown area wasn't the best place to leave a car overnight, especially after someone had stolen Angelica's battery from her car in plain sight. He'd thought it best to have it removed from CBN's property.

The police had taken both their statements and searched the area and car for evidence before allowing Big Bubba's tow truck to haul it away. Jasion offered Angelica a ride home. She hesitated for a second and then accepted.

Within minutes, thirty to be exact, Jasion pulled into Angelica's apartment complex. The two had hardly spoken during the entire ride. It was hard to believe that someone was after them. First, with his car at the restaurant, now hers, things were definitely heating up and fast. He jumped out of his car and ran to the passenger's side to open her door. Jasion thought it best to see her safely inside her apartment. Before they could climb the last flight of stairs, an unshaven, elderly man appeared out of nowhere, nearly sending Jasion into cardiac arrest.

"Whatchu' doin' with my woman, son?" The man questioned while positioning his frail body in a battle stance.

"Excuse me, Sir," Jasion tried acting unfazed by the elderly man's antics.

Quickly coming to his defense, Angelica stepped between the two men. "Mr. Nate, meet Jasion. Jasion, this is Mr. Nate, my overly protective neighbor."

For a split second, Jasion thought Angelica was into older men. "How are you doing, Sir?" He couldn't lie and say it was a pleasure. The seasoned gentleman almost caused his heart to leap from his chest.

"Whatchu sniffin' roun hea fo', youn' buck?" Mr. Nate remained in his battled stance, without taking his eyes off Jasion.

Angelica gave Jasion a wink to play along with the old-timer.

"Oh. I'm just making sure this beautiful, young lady arrives home safe and sound. That's all, Sir," he explained, winking and mouthing thank you to her. Jasion didn't have a clue as to what he'd stumbled into. "It's not what you think, Mr. Nate."

"It's Mr. Nathaniel to yhu," he corrected. "Don't nobody call me Mr. Nate but the ladies."

Mr. Nate wore a dingy bathrobe, black knee-high socks, and worn, brown slippers, revealing his ashy legs and corned pinky toe.

"Yes, Sir. Mr. Nathaniel, it is." Jasion laughed within himself. The old man reminded him of his Uncle Pete, and he thought, surely, there couldn't be two of them roaming around, pretending to be the original Casanova.

"Since wee-ee-ave gotten that straight, let me clue yhu in on somethin' else. If yhu harm one hair on this pretty lil' thang's head. Oh, yhu gon' have to deal with me," he scolded, giving Jasion the evil eye. "Do we have an understandin'?"

"Yes, Sir." Jasion saluted him like a soldier being reprimanded by his superior officer.

"A'aight then." He strolled down the corridor to his apartment, leaving the two alone.

"Whew." Jasion blew out a sigh of relief once Mr. Nate had disappeared. "That guy is nuts."

"He's harmless. Mr. Nate is a lonely widower. He flirts with all the female tenants. He wouldn't hurt a fly," she assured Jasion.

"That's good to know," he added. "For a second, I was beginning to think you were into old men."

"Oooooo— don't even go there," she laughed, slapping him on the arm.

"I'm glad he's not your man." Without waiting for an invitation, Jasion reacted on impulse. He slid to where she stood, pulled her into his arms, and kissed her with a passion he didn't know existed inside him. He'd worry about the repercussions later. He was falling hard for the woman who could end his career with the stroke of her pen.

To his surprise, Angelica didn't resist. He held her in his arms for what seemed like an eternity. The silence was deafening when their lips parted. Neither knew what to say or do. Instead, Jasion took her hand, and being the gentleman he was, he walked her to her apartment door. Once there, he broke the silence with one last plea before she retreated inside. "I pray you don't close your heart to God, Angelica. I really do like you."

"I ca—"

"Shhhhhhhh," he interrupted. "Let's just end tonight on a good note, especially after the car incident and your whacky neighbor." They both burst into laughter. "Good night, beautiful lady."

Heat rushed to her face from his sentiments. "Would you like to come inside for a cup of coffee? That's the least I can do to show my appreciation."

"No, thank you," he declined, noticing the look of surprise on her face. He wanted to gain her trust and going inside wasn't the way to do it, at least not yet.

"N...No," she stuttered.

"Angelica, I have been celibate for over two years. I asked God for the strength to abstain from sex until He sends me my soul mate. And I don't want an invitation into your apartment to cause me to break my vow to God."

"I was just inviting you in for coffee. Nothing more," she said, defensively.

"But that's how the enemy sets you up, with a potentially innocent invitation."

"Since you're not coming inside, I guess this is good night."

"Good night." He wanted to kiss her again but decided against it.

Jasion stood outside her door until he heard the last lock clicked. He headed down the stairwell to leave but not before having a final stand-off with Mr. Nate.

"Ha, Ha, Ha," Mr. Nate laughed. "Yhu thought all that sweet talk was going to get yhu inside her apartment. Didn't yhu?"

Jasion jumped, knowing that someone was following him and Angelica caused paranoia to settle in, and like magic, the old man had appeared out of nowhere, causing him further anxiety.

"No, Mr. Na— Nathaniel. It's not what you think."

"Yhu ain't smooth, youn' buck. Game recognizes game, remember that the next time yhu show yo' face round' hea uhgin," he warned and wobbled off.

"I hear you loud and clear, Sir." Jasion chuckled as he dashed down the stairs to his car before the cantankerous old man struck again.

Driving off into the night, he couldn't help but smile at how God was slowly, but surely filling the empty void in his heart. With a possible new love interest, memories of Fayth had begun to diminish as each day passed, which no women he'd dated before had been able to do. Why now? What was it about Angelica that caused him to forget the girl he'd been pining over for years?

Chapter Sixteen

"Stupid! Stupid! Stupid!" Angelica shouted, slapping her forehead with the palm of her hand. With her back pressed against the locked door, the same door where Jasion had stood just seconds ago. She couldn't help feeling like a complete idiot. "The word 'desperate' had to be written across my forehead." She was angry with herself for allowing Jasion to kiss her, not once, but twice. And to make matters worse, she invited him inside her apartment for coffee. She'd hoped the friendly gesture didn't give him the wrong impression. What was she thinking?

Celibate. Yeah, right. If he was practicing abstinence, then she was Mother Theresa. She wasn't a gambling woman, but if so, she'd bet he was on his way right now to sow his wild oats with another willing participant.

Play the gentleman role. Decline the invitation to come inside my apartment. Reel me in with everything a woman wants to hear, then lower the boom and crush my heart. He'd better come up with a better plan than that. The celibate line didn't work. You're not made of steel Mr. McCoy, but flesh and blood. No twenty-something-year-old man, full of raging hormones would decline a woman's offer to come inside her home.

No. I have something more valuable to offer you than a one-night stand. I have the inside track on your case. And you're probably trying to ease your way into my good graces to sift information out of me. Yes, that has to be it. What other reason could Jasion have for playing the, let's take it slow routine? she thought.

The kiss they'd shared outside her apartment door still had her lips tingling. No man had ever touched, looked, or even kissed her the way Jasion had. Making her feel things she'd fought so desperately to suppress over the years. It left her confused. Why play with her emotions, knowing full well he didn't truly care about her? He was the master of deception and manipulation. If she were the gullible type, he probably would have lured her into his little web by now. His concern was only for himself. He would charm the skin off a snake to keep from going to prison.

True, she wasn't a bad looking woman, but a man of his stature had no use for her. He rubbed elbows with the cream of the crop among Port City's elite. A man such as he had no need or reason to be in a serious relationship with her. She'd convinced herself; it had to be information he was after.

"I'm so angry with myself. Why did I allow him to kiss me? As soon as he played his tune, there I went, a hypnotized fool, dancing to his music," she mused, propping her tired feet upon the ottoman that sat in front of her black leather sofa. "Get cozy with the reporter. Make her fall for you and find out what she knows. Not this time, though. I plan on being much smarter in the men department. I'm not falling for some smooth-talking financial advisor with a million dollar smile. No matter how good his strong hands feel caressing my face." Shivers of pleasure shot through her body at the thought. She had to get her hormones under control.

Thinking of the man she was investigating, in any other way than professionally, would be her downfall.

She pulled a tarnished necklace bearing a small cross from underneath her blouse. Not a day had passed that she hadn't worn it. JC, her first love, had placed it around her neck at the age of twelve. It was a gift from his heart, signifying their new friendship. To Angelica, the necklace represented the meaning of true love, which she hasn't experienced since. She'd been with other men, but none came close to the young boy who was wise beyond his thirteen years. With no trace of him after fifteen years, Angelica decided it was time to get JC out of her system. Finding him was like searching for a needle in a haystack. She was sure he had moved on with his life. He hadn't come searching for her, so why put needless energy and thoughts into what would never be.

The telephone rang, jolting Angelica from her trip down memory lane. Wondering who could be calling her at this godforsaken hour— eleven p.m. to be exact, she answered with reservation. "Hello."

"Good evening, CBN News star reporter. Have you figured out who's responsible for embezzling millions from Spitzer Financial Firm?" The cryptic computerized voice asked.

"Who is this?" Panic erased the sleep from her eyes. The caller sounded like something straight out of a horror movie, which caused further terror.

"Awwwwwwww… now." Smugly, the caller slurred his words. "You disappoint me, beautiful lady. If anyone can crack this case wide open, surely it's you. Or I may be wrong, seeing that you're falling for Mr. McCoy."

"How did you get my number?" She tried to hide the fear in her voice, in order to press him for information. "Who are you and what do you want?

"Uh-uh-uh, sweetie. You play by my rules. I ask you questions, not the other way around," the caller said arrogantly. "Question number one. Did you
know that Mr. Richard Lexington, owner of Spitzer Financial Firm, asked Mr. Jasion McCoy to run his company when he retires next year and not his heir, Ian?" A pause. "No, you didn't. Question number two. Did you ask that pretty boy, McCoy, where he's getting the money to keep his youth center open when other centers have closed their doors? No, you didn't, because you are too busy trying to lure him into your apartment."

"Are you following us?" she asked. Now terrified, the telephone shook in her hand. "If I were you, I would stop playing this whodunit game and come forward with what you know. Hardworking people are losing their life savings. They don't deserve what's happening to them."

"What's happening to them? We all have to lose something valuable in our lives sometimes," the anonymous caller said with a sinister laugh. "You just ask Mr. McCoy where he got the one hundred thousand dollars for his youth center from, and what did he do to get offered that prestigious job. Looks to me, he or Ian has motive... wouldn't you say? I would consider it a slap in the face if my father asked another employee, instead of his biological son to take the helm of his empire. Now run along and crack this case. I'll be watching from a distance to see how it all plays out. That's if you're not too busy trying to crawl into McCoy's bed instead of doing your job."

"Don't you dare insult me with your— Hello? Hello?" Angelica yelled into the receiver. She heard nothing but silence. The caller had hung up. His words haunted her long after they'd disconnected. She knew about the promotion Jasion was offered, but what shocked her was that he'd received money for his youth center, a center she knew nothing about. Why did he felt the need to keep it a secret? Ian also had a motive. It would be an insult among his peers to have an outsider, especially an African American run his father's business. "Maybe the caller is right," she admitted to herself. "What if I'm slipping? Jasion knows exactly what he's doing. He's trying to take my focus off the case by getting romantically involved with me."

Chapter Seventeen

"And the Academy Award goes to J for the best male actor of the year," Nicole Swaggart teased, rolling off her partner in crime. She snuggled next to him, panting from the intimate moment they'd just shared. "Shame on you, lying about practicing abstinence."

"I had to tell her I was celibate in order to bait her in, babe. I need to stay two steps ahead of the Feds, even if that means I have to lie and manipulate the Pope of Rome," he quipped, wrapping his arms around Nicole's silky, soft peach skin. "Ole girl has too many issues. Humph, I have my own demons to contend with."

He caressed her nude body as he contemplated his next move in his mind. He had no long-term plans for Nicole. She was just some chick he'd met at a bar that had a similar ax to grind. He needed her to help do his dirty work.

"Yeah, she does have some major issues if what you say about her is true."

"I like a woman who doesn't mind taking risks. A woman who lives life on the edge. A woman like you." He gave her a squeeze and placed a kiss on the side of her head.

"'Well, you're with the right woman," she boasted, rubbing a slender finger up and down his bare chest. "I love taking risks, almost as much as I love money."

And that had scared him the most — her greed.

"That you do, sweetie. That you do."

He loved her company. Nicole was fun, exciting, and sexy, but her attitude and constant whining drove him insane. She wanted to know his whereabouts at all times. Calling his cellphone incessantly frustrated him. He'd tolerate her antics for now. Transferring the money out of SFF clients' accounts took precedence over her little diva tantrums. He wasn't going to allow some overwrought female to ruin the plans he'd devised for nearly a year. No. Everything was going according to schedule, and that was how he intended to keep it. He'd pacify her for now and then cut her loose later.

Hiring a hit man to rid himself of her after she'd served her purpose was out of the question. He could never bring himself to murder another human being, good thing for Nicole. He'd already broken two of the Ten Commandments. Thou shalt not steal, and thou shalt not lie. He didn't want to add murder to his mounting sins. Spitzer Financial Firm would pay for putting him in this predicament. They'd fired his father, kicking him out on the streets like a vagabond. And now, vengeance belonged to him.

"J... J." Nicole crooned, nudging against his still body. "Have you been listening to a word I've said?"

The blur of spinning blades from the ceiling fan came into focus. He'd dozed off.

"I'm awake, babe. Just thinking about all that money we'll be coming into soon." He lied to keep from listening to another one of her, 'taking me for granted speeches.'

What had he gotten himself into, fooling around with an escaped mental patient? Then, involving himself in a workplace romance at the same time, thank goodness he'd only had to sleep with one of them. He'd quickly learned that one woman with issues was a handful. But two with issues was enough to cause a man to drink himself into an alcohol-induced coma. He couldn't believe his string of bad luck when it came to women.

Once he left the country for good as a rich man, he would have women at his disposal. Golddiggers could sniff out a man with money like a bloodhound looking for an escaped convict. If a woman acted, looked, or talked crazy, he'd kick her to the curb and find another one. For now, women were the least of his concerns. He had a job to do.

J cocked his head to see if Nicole had fallen asleep. To his surprise, she hadn't uttered a word in over ten minutes, which was a record for her. *Thank goodness.* He'd been waiting for the opportunity to search her purse for any signs that she was trying to double-cross him. She was street smart, so he thought it best to keep a close tab on her. A woman as cunning as Nicole might have something brewing in the back of that twisted little head of hers. He wasn't taking any chances of one of her razor sharp schemes, cutting him in the end.

He methodically tried moving her arms from around his waist. To his dismay, even in her unconscious state, she wouldn't release her hold on him. He stopped, for fear of waking her. Lord knows he didn't want that to happen. He'd never met anyone that slept as light as she did. Frustrated, he lay on his back, eyes fixated on the spinning blades of the ceiling fan, praying that REM sleep would overpower Nicole, but instead it claimed him.

The next morning, he awoke to the sound of running water and humming coming from his bathroom. He was furious with himself for falling asleep without searching through Nicole's purse last night. Tossing the covers aside, he leaped out of bed on a mission to find her handbag. A woman like Nicole didn't carry a suitcase for a purse for nothing.

Kicking the sea of garments aside, a reminder of the intimate night they'd shared, he got down onto the carpeted floor where he'd fished a large black leather handbag from underneath the bed. *Let's see what she's hiding in here.* He dug and dug in the bottomless bag. His heart pounding out of control, beads of sweat formed across his forehead. The fear of Nicole catching him made him a nervous wreck.

"Ta-Dah," he hummed. He held a flash drive labeled, SFF Confidential in his hand. She'd hidden it between a tube of ruby red lipstick and other cosmetics.

Got you. My instincts were right. Never trust a female.

Chapter Eighteen

"Good morning, McCoy. Have you made a decision concerning my father's offer to run his most prized possession?" Ian questioned, pushing past Jasion.

Barging into Jasion's office unannounced had become the norm for Ian and today was no exception. The thirty-year-old financial advisor spent the bulk of his day chasing skirts rather than building his repertoire as a competitive consultant for SFF. Women flocked to Ian like leeches to the smell of blood. Being often mistaken for Aaron Eckhart made him a tad egotistical. He had the total package, money and lots of it, golden blonde, cropped hair, square chin with a dimple, and eyes bluer than the heavens that drove most women crazy with lust. The female attention had sidetracked him from his responsibilities at SFF. Jasion tried warning his friend that the women were only after his inheritance. But Ian saw it as jealousy, which caused Jasion to back off, leaving his friend to learn from the School of Hard Knocks. Unlike his father, an older look-a-like, Mr. Lexington had a heart for people, especially his employees. He was one of the founders of Spitzer Financial Firm. Mr. Lexington ran his company by the Christian principle, "*do unto others as you would have them to do unto you.*" He swore it was the sole reason for his company's success, but on more than one occasion, he had to reprimand his son for going against those fundamentals when he'd mistreated SFF employees. However, his father did look the other way when it came to Ian's extravagant spending and playboy ways.

Even with a soft spot in his heart for his heir, Mr. Lexington would never allow his son to run his company. Ian had zero business sense. His father knew that within months, his business would go bankrupt. He had built his business from nothing, and was often overheard saying to fellow board members that it would be over his dead body before he'd permit his only son to extinguish his legacy.

Over the past five years, Mr. Lexington had observed Jasion's impeccable investing skills, which brought top-notch clients and fresh ideas to the firm. Jasion also sat in on important corporate meetings, just to see how he'd respond and react to the board members' opinions on how to better run the company. Mr. Lexington was impressed with Jasion's ideas to move the firm into the next generation. He believed that Jasion was the right man to take the helm of Spitzer Financial Firm after his departure.

"Good morning to you, too. And to answer your question, no, I haven't decided. You can't make a hasty decision about something as important as heading a company," Jasion responded, sounding as if he'd just rolled out of bed. He couldn't sleep a wink last night. Thoughts of the woman that stepped into his office more than a month ago controlled his mind, which left little room to concentrate on anything else. He never was one to believe in the previous life theory or déjà vu, but that was how he'd felt around Angelica. It was as if they'd met, touched, and kissed before. She had one of those faces a man never forgets. If only he could jog his memory to recall where. "You are his son. Shouldn't he have asked you?" Jasion knew the answer but decided to pose the question anyway. It was common knowledge around SFF that Ian's father paid for his degree. Mr. Lexington donated millions to Calvary University, his alma mater. Ian often joked about how the chancellor would look the other way when professors gave him grades he didn't earn. The University was more concerned about losing their cash cow than Ian's education.

"I was thinking the same, but my dad feels differently, saying that I don't have what it takes to run his baby. One of these days, I'll show him," he replied disparagingly, walking to one of the chairs in Jasion's office and then flopping down into it.

Jasion followed close behind him but remained standing. "It's a great opportunity, but my kids come first. They depend on me down at the center where I volunteer. To run a company this size will take up what little free time I have. Plus, I'm the youth minister at my church."

"Man, what gives? You get a golden egg laid in your lap. And you're talking about kids that are not yours and ministry. Are you in the running for the saint of the year, McCoy?" Ian mocked.

"Look. I'm not trying to come between you and your father. You and I have been good friends ever since I can remember. I value that, Ian, but business is business. And at some point and time, we're going to have to learn to separate the two," Jasion shot back, dismissing his sarcastic sense of humor. "I don't expect you to understand the calling that is on my life. But preaching God's Word gives me great joy. Why don't you come down to the center or church? You might learn something, my friend. Many of these kids would never have gone to college or trade school if it weren't for people sacrificing their time. Not all of us were fortunate to be born with a silver spoon in our mouths." Jasion gave Ian a sidelong glance.

"No, thank you, I'll leave that religious, and, *We Are The World, We Are The Children*, stuff to you. I'm too busy living it up in the fast lane right now. Maybe when I'm old and gray and can't do anything else, then I'll consider it. For now, my money and my women are supplying me with all my wants and needs." Ian gloated with a devilish grin plastered across his face, crossing his legs.

Jasion shook his head at his poor misguided friend.

"Now back to why I came into your office in the first place. I need to use your computer again. I don't know what's going on with mine, but I need to check my e-mails. Who knows what I've missed, waiting on that so-called slacker computer tech, Michaels. He seems to be disappearing a lot lately. "

"Help yourself, bro. I need to step out for a moment. Nature calls, and besides, I have a meeting in twenty minutes. Don't forget to log off when you're done." Jasion yelled over his shoulders. He then turned and appealed to his friend and co-worker one last time. "Don't stay in the fast lane too long, Ian.

Old age isn't promised to any of us. For what shall it profit a man, if he shall gain the whole world, and lose his own soul?"

"Huh," Ian grunted. He never took his eyes off the computer monitor.

"Never mind." Jasion left, closing the door behind him. His heart broke for his lost friend.

Chapter Nineteen

Angelica stormed into Jasion's office, eyes lit with anger, demanding answers. "Why didn't you tell me about the youth center and the one hundred thousand dollars donation you received, Jasion?"

"Where is my secretary? I swear that woman takes more breaks than anyone I know. She and I are going to have a serious talk about leaving her desk unattended. People assume that they can just waltz into my office unannounced," Jasion snapped. "And where do you get off barging in here spitting out demands?" he asked, raising his baritone voice to another octave.

"I received a call last night after you left my apartment from the person I believe is following us. I'm trying to be understanding about the problems this company is facing. But the caller scared the crap out of me, saying things he had no way of knowing. The person knew when you left my apartment. Now, how do you expect me to react?" She stood, shaking like a leaf on a tree. The caller's eerie voice was ever present with her.

Jasion's features softened as he jumped from behind his desk, wrapping his masculine arms around her trembling body. The smell of his alluring cologne made her legs weaken. She wanted to stay enclosed in his embrace forever. *Get yourself together, Angelica*, she told herself. Common sense was kicking in; she broke from the warmth and security his arms had provided.

With a soft, penetrating stare that seemed to see straight through her soul, he asked, "what does my youth center have to do with some mysterious caller or this case? The center operates off donations, which explains the large check I received."

Unable to control her shaky hands, Jasion reached out and placed them inside his. It amazed her how he could make her feel things with just a simple touch. She rehearsed in her head what she would say once she was face to face with him. But now, she'd forgotten every single word. "Look. I'm sorry for barging into your office. I'm just a little on edge. His or her voice was disturbing. In all my years of investigating, I've never had anyone call my home or follow me. The caller made this case personal the minute he or she called my home."

"Please don't go getting yourself hurt. I don't blame you one bit for being shaken up by the caller, but this is a job for the authorities," Jasion pleaded, her hands still buried inside his.

"I'm a big girl. I can handle myself."

"I don't doubt that for one minute, but I'll feel better with the police handling this."

"I've already informed them, as well as my boss about the call."

"Great."

His brown eyes darkened under his lashes, causing Angelica's hands to sweat and shake even more. He wasn't letting go, no matter how she subtly tried to slide her hand out of his. The stiffening of his body told her that their conversation was about to take a more serious turn.

"Do you think I'm guilty?"

Her body jerked as she desperately tried to process the question he'd just thrown at her.

"You don't have to lie to me, Angelica. I'm a big boy."

"I— I don't know. I want to believe that you are," she slowly uttered. Honestly, she didn't know who or what to believe.

"Whew," he exhaled. "Your body language gave it away. You perspire on your upper lip whenever you're nervous, and you can't look me directly in my eyes."

"Jasion, for all I know, you could be using the center as a front to embezzle millions."

"Three of my closest friends and I own the center. We invested our hard-earned money into it. Those kids mean the world to us. Knowing that we're giving them an opportunity to make something out of their lives is rewarding."

His compassion for the kids and the center pricked her heart. But was it enough to erase the cloud of doubt looming over her?

"Give me a chance Angelica to prove my sincerity to you. I have absolutely nothing to hide."

He intertwined his fingers with hers, sending waves of pleasure up her spine. "Um, mm, well." Her words were caught in her throat, and her mind was clouded with mixed emotions. Should she trust him or not, were the questions she'd continued to ask herself.

"Since you didn't consider our last business dinner a date, let me take you out tonight on an official one."
"I have a deadline on a story that I have to finish," she lied, looking for any excuse to turn him down. Being close to him made her feel and think things that she didn't want to feel or think about him. After all, he was under an investigation for theft.

"You still have to eat."

"Going out with you will only complicate things," Angelica admitted.

"Not really, unless you're saying you don't trust yourself around me," he said, flashing that gorgeous smile again.

"WHAT?" she gasped. "You have a lot of nerve."

"So, where are we going?"

"I'm not afraid to go out with you." But she was. He was responsible for causing all types of feelings to run rampant throughout her body. *Were her ears deceiving her—a date, a real date with Mr. Wonderful?* She was in way over her head, too deep to turn back now. She wanted him and had developed feelings for him.

"Then where are we going and what time should I pick you up?"

She finally gave in, but it wasn't as if he had to twist her arm. "Surprise me, and seven o'clock will be fine." Angelica tried to disguise her excitement. She hoped he wasn't leading her on for his own personal gain. Her heart couldn't take another stab to it.

"I need a telephone number where I can reach you, just in case I'm running late."

"Late?" she queried, loving the way he played with her fingers without taking his eyes off her.

"You never know when the corporate office will decide to call a last minute meeting," he explained.

Angelica peeled her hands from his, as hard as it was. She picked up a pen and a sticky note from his desk and scribbled her phone number on it. She handed it to him, quickly, before she changed her mind.

Chapter Twenty

Angelica tossed and turned, entangling herself in the covers when a clap of thunder roared through the volatile night skies. The tumultuous rain thumped against the windowsill, causing her to jump with fear. The meteorologist had predicted flooding with possible electrical outages due to thunderstorms traveling at a rapid speed from New Orleans to Port City.

She'd always hated bad weather, and tonight had proven to be the worst. As a child, the kids at school joked that thunder indicated that the devil was angry with his wife. Whether or not it was true, Angelica just hoped that tonight his anger would end, and soon.

Buried under layers of covers, sleep finally rescued her from the battle of the wind and rain outside. But Angelica quickly found herself held hostage in another nightmare with her abusive mother, Gladys.

In her dream, Angelica saw herself at the age of twelve, knelt down by her bed praying. A nightly ritual she'd always shared with her father.

Young Fayth was growing tired of the abuse and being isolated from other kids her age. She wanted out. Fayth didn't know much about suicide, only that her father said it was a sin. The thought of killing herself had entered her mind, but she'd always chickened out. She was already living in Hell and thought, *why die and end up in the same place?* After praying the twenty-third number of Psalms, she continued praying in her own words. *"God, please deliver me from this torment. I want to go and be with my father."*

Angelica watched her younger self in the dream; tears raced down her cheeks. Fayth climbed into the rickety, old bed her mother moved into her room after her father's death. She recalled Gladys saying, *"Yo' ole' pappy had yhu spoiled but yhur no better than a mangy mutt and don't deserve the canopy bed he bought yhu."* So Gladys moved it out of her room and replaced it with a bed she'd found on the side of the road. Someone had placed it on the curb as trash, and that was exactly what her mother thought of her.

Pleading to go to a better place had seemed her only option. Then, Gladys stormed into her room in a drunken rage. She stood next to the bed where Fayth's trembling body lay underneath the covers. Gladys reached behind her daughter's head, snatched the pillow from under her, and covered her face with it.

"Humph, I'll show yhu torment, yhu little ingrate. I'm providin' a roof over yhur head and this the thanks I get. Yhur triflin' just like yo' ole pappy, Maurice." Gladys roared through her drunkenness. *"He mighta' left yhu all his money, but yo' behind belongs to me and I'ma gon' kick it as long as I damn well please."*

Even with the pillow pressed against her small terrified face, Fayth could smell the rotgut liquor wafting from her mother's mouth. Her kicking and sounds of struggle did little to stop Gladys from smothering her.

Death seemed better than living with an alcoholic, abusive monster, but she didn't want to die by suffocation. If Fayth had known her mother was eavesdropping outside her door, she would have prayed in silence.

"Oh, yhu gon' wish yhu were dead when I finish with yhu. I'll give yhu somethin' to make yhu wish yhu were out my house. If I had som' place else to send yo' ungrateful behind, trust… I would. But don't nobody want no mud face chile, they only want light skinned colored girls, like yo' beautiful sister, Alycee. Not som' big, pink, ashy-lips heifer like yhu. Been a thorn in my side ever since yo' old weak daddy died," Gladys growled, pushing down on her small face with all her strength.

Thank goodness, Gladys' drunkenness caused her arms to wobble like gelatin. Or, who knows what the outcome might have been that night.

She was losing consciousness or so Fayth thought. The back of her eyelids displayed an array of bright red colors with little, fuzzy dots trickling downward. Her short life flashed before her eyes. Fayth wanted God to send one of her guardian angels to scoop her into his arms and fly her to heaven to live with her father. When she'd stopped struggling and welcomed death, Gladys removed the pillow. Her mother collapsed on top of her, choking her with the fumes from that wicked brew Gladys had consumed earlier.

Fayth's father always told her Bible stories about the enemy, Satan, roaming the earth like a roaring lion, seeking whom he may devour. Gladys' unpredictable behavior and bloodshot eyes fit the description of that lion. She seemed ready to devour Fayth at any given moment. Her mother's countenance had changed that she barely recognized her. Fayth swore she was staring into the eyes of Satan that night.

Kicking and gasping for air, she screamed to the top of her lungs. She wanted this life to end, but her tortuous mother refused to even grant her that little wish.

"That lil funky tale boy yhu were bout' to kiss today at the funeral done near bout' got yhu killed," Gladys scolded. *"Nobody, and I mean nobody in this house is allowed to have a man, but me. Now get up and let me cleanse yhu from the sin of fornication."*

When Gladys walked outside and caught Fayth and JC about to share a kiss, she went on a rampage, dragging Fayth to the car like a bag of trash.

"Yhu think yhu grown, huh? Yhu wanted that boy to touch yhu. Didn't yhu?" Gladys acted out her words with her slim caramel hands, seductively, caressing up and down her body. *"Answer me, yhu lil tramp. Oh yea', I saw yhu over there with yo' fornicatin' lips bout' to kiss him. But I tell yhu what. There betta not be no babies comin' up in this hea' house or I will rip the lil sucker right outta yhu. Yhu got that, gal?"*

Fayth's lips quivered as she struggled to speak. *"Y-yesss, ma'am."* If Satan had a sister, her name would have been Gladys Hope, because evil resided in the crevasses of her black uncompassionate heart. The beatings were frequent but never to the point where she feared for her life, until now.

"Get up and go look under the bathroom cabinet and take out that cleaning powder," Gladys ordered. *"Then run som' water in the bath tub, so I can scrub the filth of sin off of yhu."*

Fayth raised her small frame from her bed, scared to resist her mother's request. She did as ordered. She was scared to death of Gladys drowning her. Who would save her? She stumbled on the tattered, stained, long dress she wore as a nightgown, thinking about what was going to happen.

Fayth had filled the bathtub halfway when Gladys staggered through the door. She ordered her to get in. Praying with all her might that her mother wouldn't drown her, she stepped in. Her naked body trembled uncontrollably as she agonized over her mother's next move.

Gladys fell to the side of the tub with a wired scouring pad in her hand and scrubbed Fayth's skin raw with the cleaning powder. She screamed to the top of her lungs as the sting intensified with each stroke up and down her shivering body.

Reliving one of many scenes from her childhood, Angelica placed her hands over her ears to tune out the screams of the young girl in her dream. She continued to watch and sobbed bitterly as the nightmare from Hell replayed her past. Drawing her legs up to her chest, she cried for mercy for the little girl.

Her horrendous torture now over, she limped back to her bedroom and crawled into bed. Gladys wobbled into the room behind her.

When wide-eyed, five-year-old Alycee stumbled into her sister's room, Gladys jumped. Alycee stood in the doorway with a rag doll in one hand and tugging on her ponytail with the other one. The color had drained from her fair skin.

Even at the age of five, Alycee knew that something wasn't right when she'd spotted Gladys standing over Fayth's bed. *"What are you doing to sista', mama? I heard her screaming."* Without waiting for an answer from her mother, Alycee ran and jumped into bed with Fayth. She straddled her legs across her sister's aching body, in an attempt to protect her from Gladys.

Tears streamed down the sides of Fayth's face as she held her baby sister close to her. They may have different fathers, but Alycee adored her, which infuriated their mother.

Gladys told Fayth that she was an abomination, a past mistake she'd wished she'd aborted. And those words followed her into adulthood.

A clap of thunder echoed throughout Angelica's small, stuffy bedroom. She awakened to find herself lying in a fatal position. She sobbed for the little girl in her dream. How she'd managed to function all these years without the restraint of a straitjacket was beyond her. She'd blamed God for her miserable life.

Maurice Hope promised her that God would answer her prayers and come to her aid when she least expected. Her father never missed a night coming into her room to kiss her goodnight or to pray with her. Fayth continued their ritual, even after his death. Now, as an adult, Angelica rejected God and all that came along with Christianity. She swore never to step a foot inside another church again. She had believed that her father was wrong about God. He was not merciful or compassionate, but tonight, she decided to make one last appeal. If there had ever been a time she needed God, it was now.

"God, if you are real. If you are everything my father said you are; why have you forsaken me? Why do you hate me so? My father taught me that we are created in your image. If so, why do you despise me? Are you chastising me for the sins of my mother? What do her transgressions have to do with me? What have I done to cause you to unleash your wrath upon me? Answer me!" she shouted in the dark room.

A wicked clap of thunder caused her to jump.

"But you won't. Will you?"

Chapter Twenty One

Angelica drove into the driveway of her best friend's white, restructured Victorian-style home to find her anxiously awaiting her arrival. Marissa's sandy blonde locks had a life of their own when gusts of wind blew them out of control. Last night's storm had been a terror. Thankfully, the only signs left of it were broken tree limbs and gusty winds, which were quickly beginning to lose their strength.

Being born into a family of great financial wealth afforded Marissa the finer things in life. Port City Industrial Oil had been in her family for over four generations and still going strong.

Sprinting towards Angelica's car, Marissa excitingly pulled open the driver's side door, practically dragging her out. Both women squealed at the top of their lungs, hugging the other with all their might. It had been weeks since the two had last spoken. The Spitzer Financial Firm case took up much of Angelica's time, which meant they had some serious catching up to do.

"I'm so glad to see you, Fay," Marissa grinned, breaking from their infectious embrace. She backed up, giving Angelica a once over. "I've missed you."

They air kissed each other's cheek.

Angelica gave her friend another hug and then drew her arm around Marissa's slender shoulders as they headed inside.

"Girl, this investigation has me buried up to my neck in paperwork," Angelica sighed. "It's getting more confusing by the day."

"If anybody can figure it out, it's you, Fay," Marissa smiled, giving her friend a gentle, reassuring nudge. "I had the chef whip us up something for lunch."

Marissa ushered Angelica down a spacious hallway, beautifully decorated in fine vintage art. She'd visited the home on numerous occasions and still found herself in awe.

100

The friends continued to catch up as they entered an inside patio made of storm glass, where a table had been set for two. They took their seats as the chef placed a plate of grilled salmon covered with cream sauce, a medley of steamed vegetables, and a bowl of fresh fruits before them. He turned, grabbed a pitcher of fresh squeezed lemonade from his cart, poured each woman a glass, and then quickly exited the patio.

Angelica was bursting at the seams. Unable to conceal her good news any longer, she blurted out, "I have a date tonight."

Stunned, Marissa nearly choked on a piece of lettuce. Straining to speak, she couldn't get her questions out fast enough. "With whom? Do I know him? What's his name? Girl, spill your guts."

"Jasion McCoy," she whispered, anticipating her friend's reaction.

"WHAT?" Marissa's petite body shook from the earth quaking news.

Angelica's lips curled into a full smile at her friend's reaction.

"Girl, you went over to Spitzer Financial Firm to investigate a story and ended up finding a man. Indeed, it has been a while since we last talked," Marissa teased, removing a strand of hair that had fallen across her flawless, tanned face. "I used to know all your business, even before it happened."

Angelica could clearly tell that her news was a pleasant surprise. "Whoa. Hold on. Don't jump to any conclusions just yet, Marissa." Waving both hands in front of her, she exclaimed, "it's just dinner, not a marriage proposal."

Although she'd prefer the latter, she knew, she had zero chance of that ever happening. Jasion probably viewed her as someone to pass the time with and nothing more. For Angelica, anything was better than being at home on a Saturday night, watching the same old romantic flick for the umpteenth time, alone. And envying the heroine as she disappears into the sunset with her tall, dark, and handsome hero, knowing there was no happy ending for her.

Angelica's heart slammed against her chest whenever she thought of the first time she'd laid eyes on Jasion. Just thinking about his rich, brown eyes, peering down into hers, and his strong, masculine arms wrapped around her waist to stop her fall caused her to blush. She'd never forget that day, even if she lived to be one hundred. Who would have thought that a month later, the two least likely set of people were going out on a date? Not a business date, but a real date. Goosebumps ran up her arms in anticipation of what the night held.

"Earth to Fay. Earth to Fay," Marissa called, snapping her fingers in front of Angelica's face to get her attention. "How long has it been since you last dated?" Touching a finger to her chin as in deep thought, she closed her eyes. "Mmm, let me see, nearing your third year." She held up three fingers.

"I know how long it's been," she added. "I'm scared."

"Scared? Scared of what… someone loving you?"

"I'm a mess. The only thing I'm good at is my job. Even that's beginning to be questionable these last days."

Looking squarely into Angelica's eyes, Marissa advised, "Fay, you only live once. To know if Jasion is sincere, you must take a chance." She paused. "Remember what my dad told you when he taught you how to swim at eighteen? To learn how to swim, you must get in the water. Well, it's time to start dating again my sister, or love will pass you by."

Angelica picked at her grilled salmon, pondered her friend's advice, and confessed, "I don't know how." Placing her fork beside her plate, her eyes began to tear up.

"Fay, what's really going on with you? Don't lie to me because I've been your friend far too long not to know when you're hiding something. She touched the corners of her mouth with her napkin and then laid it on the table.

"I had another nightmare last night about Gladys. They are becoming more frequent. What if I'm having a nervous breakdown and don't know it?"

"Have you discussed your concerns with Dr. Hawthorne?"

"No," she admitted. "I haven't been back to her since I last spoke with you."

Marissa rested her back against her chair; the disappointment was showing on her face. "Well, are you at least taking the Xanax she prescribed?" she lashed out at Angelica.

"No."

When Marissa shook her head, Angelica knew she'd let her friend down by discontinuing her therapy sessions.

"I thought I had it under control until Alycee called last month, informing me of Gladys' illness. Just the sound of her name opened up old wounds I thought had healed."

She gazed over her friend's shoulder and focused her attention and thoughts outside the glass patio window at the leaves waving in the wind. No signs of last night's storm, nothing but clear blue, serene skies as far as the eyes could see. How she wished her life were that peaceful and simple.

"I've said it a hundred times, and I'll say it again," Marissa lectured. "Go see your mother before it's too late. If you want, I'll go with you for moral support. That's the only way you're going to put the past behind you and end the nightmares."

Not liking the sound of that one bit, she tried to object, but her friend held up her hands, protesting against it, which left Angelica to pout in silence.

"You need God's help. There's no other way around it. You need Him."

Refusing to touch the subject, knowing the outcome, Angelica switched the conversation back to her date.

"What if I flip out in front of Jasion?"

"You won't, Fay. You're stronger than you realize. And don't think I didn't catch that. You're smooth, but not that

103

smooth, in trying to change the subject. I'll let it slide for now. I don't want to ruin your mood for your date tonight. Just think about what I said. Promise."

Hesitantly, she repeated, "P... promise."

"Pinky swear," Marissa crooked her baby finger.

Hooking her pinky finger together with her friend, Angelica joked, "now you're just being childish."

Since college, the women had always used this gesture for keeping the other's secrets. But today, it had grown into something much more, a friend looking out for the well-being of the other.

"Relax and enjoy your date with Jasion, then call me tomorrow and give me all the juicy details." They both burst into laughter and resumed enjoying their lunch.

Chapter Twenty Two

Jasion approached the stairwell leading up to Angelica's apartment complex cautiously. His last encounter with Mr. Nate, her rambunctious seventy-something-year-old neighbor had been an experience he didn't wish to repeat. The old man had heart but was a little on the nutty side. Tonight, he wanted to avoid all distractions.

I've made it to her door without the old man spotting me. Hurry up, Jasion. Knock on the door before he sees you, he thought anxiously.

His heart pumped at rapid speed as he looked over his shoulder for Mr. Nate's whereabouts. Why was he acting like a chump? For crying out loud, the man was over seventy-years-old. *Get a hold of yourself, J.*

Jasion took slow, methodical breaths. His nerves were getting the better of him. He'd been on plenty of dates but never had any of the other women captured his heart as Angelica had.

He fidgeted with his necktie, gave himself a once over, and then knocked on her door. Impatiently, he rocked back and forth on his heels, waiting for her to answer. The last girl that claimed his heart, causing him to feel butterflies in the pit of his stomach was Fayth. He remembered the sadness in her eyes as she sat sobbing at her father's funeral. Call it faith, but she had become his first love, and only real love, until now. They almost shared a kiss that day until Broom-Hilda, her mother flew in on her broomstick in their direction and swept her away.

His tongue rolled to the ground, eyes bulged out of their sockets when Angelica opened the door. Jasion literally slapped his cheek to see if he was dreaming. Either he'd died and gone to Heaven or God had sent one of His angels down to earth.

Say something, stupid. Don't just stand here with your mouth wide open.

Paralyzed by the beautiful creature standing before him, Jasion struggled to make his limbs and mouth respond to the signals transmitting from his brain. The only thing that he could think of was, where had she been hiding that gorgeous figure? If he had access to her closet, he'd burn every stitch of the pantsuits and oversized blazers Angelica owned. Her unflattering wardrobe hid the goddess standing before him.

Tonight, she was elegantly dressed in a lavender chiffon cocktail dress with beads and sequins adorning the neck and waist. Her sparkly, silver stilettos complimented her long, shapely, smooth legs. He didn't regard himself as an expert in women's fashion, but her transformation was evident. With shiny black curls dancing around her long kissable neck, Jasion silently thanked God for the blessing He'd bestowed upon him.

"Aren't you going to say something?" Angelica asked, snapping him out of his trance.

"You. You." Struggling to find his voice, "you look stunning. Drop dead gorgeous, Angelica." *Get yourself together, fool. You're going to scare the woman off with your babbling.*

"Thank you. I hope I'm not overdressed?"

"Noooooo." The word flew from his lips. "You're perfect."

A paper bag would have been a step up from the black outfits she normally wore. Those baggy slacks hid curves he never knew existed on her body. *Lord, help me tonight. Who would've guessed, hiding under her oversized clothing was a beautiful body screaming to get out? Please help me to remain strong and remember the covenant I made with you.*

"Come in and have a seat, while I grab my shawl from the bedroom," she said, waving him in with her hand.

Jasion's pulse quickened as he strode over the threshold, brushing passed her. When Angelica disappeared down the hallway, he tried to regain his composure. Reciting scriptures in his head for strength did little to contain his overactive hormones, so he busied himself with surveying the tiny living room. Her apartment seemed a bit bland. There were no family photos to give him a glimpse into her private life. Finally, he stopped his browsing, eased down into the plush leather loveseat and anxiously awaited her return.

When she materialized into the room, Jasion nearly hyperventilated. Still trying to process her amazing new look, he leaped from his seat. Angelica wore the sexiest smile he'd ever seen. Maybe the change in wardrobe had something to do with it.

"I'm ready—" she paused, looking oddly at Jasion. "Are you okay?"

"Never been better." Loosening his necktie to clear his airways, Jasion pulled her into his embrace and did what he'd longed to do since the moment she'd opened the door. With both hands tenderly pressed against her silky, soft face, he leaned down and kissed her mahogany painted lips. The hypnotic aroma of orchids danced off of her bare shoulders, teasing his nostrils. He loved everything about her and prayed in time she'd feel the same about him. He forced himself to pull away, planting a soft kiss on the bridge of her nose, and said, "Your chariot awaits you, my queen."

Smiling up at him, eyes fluttering with delight, he knew the kiss had taken her aback. No words transpired between them as he took her sheer lavender shawl, placed it around her slender shoulders, and led her out of the door for a romantic evening.

*****

Angelica stood by the passenger's side door, waiting while her prince charming handed over his car keys to the valet. The young man seemed anxious to get behind the wheel of Jasion's freshly waxed, black BMW. Never in her wildest dreams had she imagined dining at one of the most prestigious

107

restaurants in Port City — the Riverfront Chateau Royale. The name alone screamed money and prestige. It took months to get reservations in this place. How Jasion managed to reserve a table on short notice remained a mystery. She raised a suspicious brow at the thought, but decided to let it go tonight and enjoy herself as she glanced at the hunk standing beside her. Jasion was immaculately dressed in a tailored, black tuxedo with a skinny black necktie against his crisp white shirt. Her heart did a double flip because it showed off his lean, muscular body.

After the valet had disappeared in Jasion's vehicle, he turned, brushing a kiss across her painted lips. Her stilettos put them close to eye level. Arm in arm, they strolled inside the ritzy Chateau. For the first time in her life, other than when she'd met JC fifteen years ago, a man was making her feel alive and vibrant. Even if it was just for tonight, she was going to savor the moment.

Angelica made a mental note to thank her best friend, Marissa, for picking out her dress. She really had an eye for fashion. The dress has done exactly what she'd said it would. Angelica noticed Jasion's tail wagging when she'd opened her apartment door. He was more than just speechless. He was spell-bound by her new look.

They laughed and made small talk through the entranceway of the restaurant. An older white-haired gentleman with bushy eyebrows said, "Good evening and thank you for dining at the Riverfront Chateau Royale. Your name, Sir?"

"Jasion McCoy," he responded.

With his thin, wrinkled, pale finger, the maître d' scanned the reservation list. When he'd found the couple's name, he led them to a quiet, romantic table for two that overlooked the lit Red River. He placed the menus in front of them, and in a voice mimicking Count Dracula, said, "your server will be with you shortly." The white-haired man then turned on his heels and returned to his post.

"Wow, Jasion, this place is amaz-zz-ing," she sang. The classic sounds of jazz bellowed through the regal establishment. Angelica scanned the room, drinking in the intoxicating ambiance. *A girl could get used to this,* she mused.

"An amazing place for an amazing woman," Jasion responded. The lit centerpiece transformed his dark, mysterious eyes into a seductive blend of roasted chestnuts.

Her insides danced to the tune of his words. Yes, the Riverfront Chateau Royale had been intoxicating. The music was romantic and the window view breathtaking, but did he really think she was amazing? The handsome man sitting across from her had begun to free her heart after years of protecting it from love. She'd tried fighting against such feelings, but her emotions were winning the battle. Now she knew exactly how Cinderella felt when she found her prince. Angelica hoped the clock would never strike twelve.

"Thank you, Jasion," she whispered, trying desperately not to sound overly emotional.

"For what?" he asked, puzzled.

"For bringing me to such a lavish restaurant. Words cannot describe the beauty of this place."

"Your beauty tonight is beyond words."

She blushed.

Reaching for her hand from across the table, he caressed it with his thumb. "A woman like you deserves this and more." He raised her hand to his soft, delectable lips and kissed it.

Batting her eyelashes, she stared into his eyes. Her words caught in her throat. *Please stop taunting me with sentiments you don't mean, Jasion,* she thought. How she wished his words were true.

"Angelica, I want to get to know the beautiful woman you're trying to hide from me."

Eyes wide, lips pursed, she glanced over at him and asked, "Why? My life is boring compared to yours."

Curiosity led her to ponder where the night would take them. Their evening had started on a perfect note, and Angelica hoped Jasion wouldn't ruin it with his twenty-one questions. Instead of jumping to conclusions, she decided to hear him out.

"I think you're a fascinating woman, and I pray in time that you will begin to trust me." He leaned forward in his chair, her hand still in his. "Not just with the case, but with your heart as well."

Was she that obvious? She had reasons for not trusting him. Here, she sat across the table from one of the most gorgeous men in Port City, who may be going to prison for the rest of his life. For all she knew, tonight could be part of his plan to gain her trust, and then dump her once she'd foolishly handed over all the evidence to him. There were too many variables to sort out. Which one of her suspicions was correct, only time would tell?

"I'll try. It's just been so long—" Her words trailed off.

"So long since what?" With furrowed brows, caressing her hand, he waited for her response.

"Since I've dated," she admitted somewhat embarrassed.

"Same here."

The waiter interrupted their intense conversation, "What will the lovely lady and you, be drinking this evening, Sir?"

"I'll have cranberry juice on ice," Angelica said, prying her moist hand out of Jasion's and placing it in her lap.

Jasion never took his eyes off her, while ordering his drink. "I'll have the same as the lovely lady," he echoed, relaxing back into his chair.

Their server disappeared behind closed doors, leaving the two to finish where they'd left off. Angelica didn't know what to make out of Jasion's words. Why would a sexy, intelligent man be without a woman when there were plenty of them throwing themselves at him? She'd seen it at SFF. Women were sparring for his attention.

Later, the two finished their dinner, talked, laughed, and learned more about the other. Angelica wanted to believe every word coming from Jasion's gorgeous lips. But the investigator in her just didn't buy it.

The soothing sounds of jazz filled the air. Angelica bobbed her head and swayed her shoulders to the mesmerizing melody. She loved this place, and Jasion had been the perfect gentleman. If only he were hers and only hers. If it wasn't for the investigation, their paths might have never crossed. Was he serious about dating her after the investigation? Instead of driving herself crazy with questions she couldn't answer, she decided to enjoy the evening and let fate take its course. If they were destined to be together, it would happen. If not, she'd just pick up the pieces of her broken heart and move on as she'd done in the past. Marissa had warned Angelica to be on her best behavior tonight. So far, she had kept her promise.

"Penny for your thoughts?" Jasion inquired.

"Oh, I'm sorry," she said, smiling with her eyes. "I got a little caught up in the music."

"Well, since you're enjoying it so much, care to dance?" Pushing up from his chair, he walked over to her seat and proffered his hand.

In the past, she'd never had the nerve to do something as innate as dance in front of a room full of strangers, but here she was, for the second time, dancing with Mr. Wonderful. Without waiting for a response, Jasion grabbed her hand and led her to the dance floor. He wrapped his strong, muscular arms around her. A small gasp escaped her lips when their bodies touched, becoming one with the rhythm of the music.

This will go down in history as one of the best nights of her life. The man holding her in his arms made her feel as if she was the only woman in the room. It had been a very long time since any man had made her feel special. Leaning her head on his broad shoulders, she softly whispered, "thank you for making tonight special."

"No, thank you."

With his lips pressed against her ear, sending sweet vibrations surging through her body. Jasion seductively crooned her name, "An-gel-ic-a."

Her body tensed, sending floods of pleasure throughout her entire being.

She nervously, responded, "y-y-yes."

"Relax. You are so tense. I'm not going to hurt you. I promise."

Drawing her closer into his intoxicating embrace caused her heart to skip a beat, but sadly, he wasn't hers. She would have given anything to be that special someone he gave his mind, body, and heart to. With eyes closed, Angelica willed her mind to control her trembling. How could arms made of steel feel so warm and inviting? An uncontrollable moan escaped her lips when Jasion pulled her even closer to him. In her mind, at that moment, she had become his woman, even if it was just for tonight.

Chapter Twenty Three

The aroma of fresh baked bread filled the air, played with Angelica and Marissa's taste buds. While they stood in line, a flippant cashier, smacking and chewing her gum wildly, yelled out as hungry customers paraded through its door, "welcome to Sam's Sandwich Shop." Massive braids hung like snakes from the cashier's tiny head. How she managed to keep her neck from snapping backward from the weight was anyone's guess.

More customers poured in, taking their places in a line that seemed to be going nowhere. Craning her neck in search of the cause for the slow service, Angelica found the culprit. An elderly woman's indecisiveness was holding up the line and wearing on the young cashier's nerves. She scolded the elderly woman with one of her long multi-colored fingernails that resembled claws, popping her lips with each word she spat.

Finally, after waiting for more than twenty minutes, Angelica and Marissa paid for their orders and began to search for a vacant table.

Still on cloud nine from her date with Jasion, Angelica refused to allow anyone or anything to ruin her day. Earlier, the cashier had rung up her order incorrectly and had the nerve to cop an attitude, but Angelica just smiled, paid the difference and walked away. No one was going to ruin her day, not even the smart mouth, snake-haired cashier.

Marissa had left several messages on Angelica's answering machine last night. Curiosity was getting the better of her, and the anticipation shone in her eyes when they'd pulled into the parking lot of the sandwich shop.

Angelica purposely kept her in suspense. Before they could take their seats, like a movie director screaming *action*; on cue, Marissa jumped into her role.

"So… tell me. How was your date?" she asked. Her ears hungered for information. "I waited up last night for your call."

Nonchalantly, Angelica peeled the wrapping from around her sandwich. Using the wrapper as a makeshift plate, she poured her chips on top of it and responded, "Ahhh, it was okay." The investigator in her decided to let her noisy friend squirm a little while longer.

"Girl, you went out last night with one of the finest men in Port City. And all you can say is that it was okay? I know you're holding out on me. You better dish out the goods."

Biting into her spicy Italian sandwich with raised brows, Angelica couldn't contain the smile flirting around her lips a second longer.

"If you don't tell me what happened, Fay, I swear, I'm going to jump across this table and choke it out of you," she playfully threatened, tugging on Angelica's arm.

Since Marissa had declared to do her bodily harm, Angelica decided to give her meddlesome friend the information she craved. No need in torturing her any further. Angelica swallowed her sandwich and said, "Well, if you insist." Marissa beckoned with her hands for Angelica to hurry up.

"I had the time of my life," she squealed. "Jasion took me to the Riverfront Chateau Royale."

A couple seated nearby gawked in their direction as her excitement filled the room, but Angelica ignored them. It had been years since she'd felt that excited, especially over a man. Faith wasn't in her vocabulary, hadn't been for years, but last night the odds were definitely in her favor. Maybe the universe had finally decided to shift some good luck her way.

"Did you say, The Riverfront Chateau Royale?" she questioned, taking in a deep breath, clutching her chest. "Girl, I haven't been able to land reservations for that place."

"Words cannot describe it." Her eyes danced as she reflected on her unforgettable night. "It was breathtaking."

"Did his eyes bulge out their sockets when he saw you in that dress?" Marissa asked, giving her friend a wicked smile while sipping on her diet cola.

They high-fived each other across the table and giggled like schoolgirls, dishing out juicy gossip about her date.

"Girl, Jasion had to pick them up and place them back in his head." Their infectious laughter drew stares from the surrounding patrons.

"See, I told you to add some spice to your wardrobe." Marissa patted herself on the back. "You were going to run the man off, wearing that grim, gothic get-up."

Marissa always had something negative to say about the outfits Fayth chose, but after seeing the reaction she'd gotten from Jasion last night, maybe going shopping with her fashionista friend wasn't such a bad idea.

"I thought I was going to have to come over to Spitzer Financial Firm and talk to the man for you, myself."

"I would have called security to haul you out of the building," Angelica joked, crunching on some jalapeno kettle chips.

"Heck, if I weren't married and a tall, fine man tells me," Marissa did her best male impersonation. "I want to get to know you better after the investigation is over—"

Cutting in, Angelica asked, "what would you have said, girl?" She egged Marissa on as she took a sip of water to wash down the spicy chips.

"Why wait until later, we can start now."

"Girl, you are some kind of crazy," Angelica laughed. "I don't know what I'm going to do with you."

"It's easy to fall for a man that's easy on the eyes. That first guy you dated. What's his face?" Marissa snapped her fingers, trying to recall his name.

"Who?"

"Don't 'Who' me, you know darn well who I'm talking about. That lazy bum you dated in college."

"James."

"Yeah, him, Fay, how did you do it?" She placed her hand on her throat, pretending to throw up. "Girl, you had to take a strong drink just to look at the boy."

"See, you're wrong, Marissa. You didn't have to go there."

"Oh, yes, I did. You need to see the difference between him and Jasion. And my sister, you have made a step up in the right direction."

"I'm going to have to stop hanging around you." Angelica flicked water from her straw at her friend. Marissa was right. James had made her life a living hell. Never had she met a man who was so self-centered and disrespectful to women. His looks hadn't bothered Angelica as much as his inflated ego. James had constantly reminded her of his status as one of the top ten black quarterbacks in the south. And that she should be grateful that he'd chosen her as his girlfriend.

On the other hand, Jasion was the complete opposite. He had money, sex appeal, and a down-to-earth personality, none of which seemed to faze him. Who knows? Maybe he had been putting on an act for her benefit. If so, he'd done a great job. No matter what the future held for her and Jasion, last night would always be the most beautiful night of her life. Tomorrow, she and Jasion would be back to business as usual, but today, she planned to savor the moment.

Chapter Twenty Four

"Hope, your news segment ended just in time," Lance informed his top reporter. "The unidentified caller strikes again," he sang with enthusiasm. One thing her boss loved more than his morning cup of medium roast, unsweetened coffee was a scandalous story that could boost CBN's ratings.

CBN and CNN were running neck and neck in ratings. Once the Spitzer Financial Firm scandal broke, Lance hoped to surpass their competitor. The two stations had been rivals for as long as Angelica could remember.

"Did you record your conversation?" Angelica asked, watching Lance pace the carpeted floor in her office. He seemed to be in his thinking mode. She sensed something brewing in that brilliant mind of his. Whenever a major story broke in Port City, his behavior changed from the laid-back general manager to the sharp nose reporter he once was. Sitting behind a desk and pushing papers hadn't dulled his skills to sniff out a great story.

"Yes, and I want you to set up another meeting with Mr. McCoy and play it for him. Maybe he knows more than he's leading us to believe."

Back to reality, her fairytale weekend was now officially over. She had a job to do. A job she now regretted. With her feelings now growing stronger for a man with possible legal troubles, she believed she was in way too deep. If Lance had any idea what was going on between her and Jasion, he'd snatch her off the case. No one, not even she— his top investigative reporter, jeopardized an award-winning story. "Sure, Lance. I'll call Mr. McCoy and ask that all of Spitzer's employees of interest to the case meet in one of the company's conference rooms," she said, trying to hide her disappointment.

"I know that I don't have to tell you this, but pay close attention to their body language as the tape plays, especially Mr. McCoy's."

She flinched at the mention of Jasion's name. "How long have I been doing this?" Angelica asked through clenched teeth, propping her hand on her hip and cocking her head to the side as if waiting for his answer. Lance's stiff face broke into an infectious smile. "I don't miss a thing. Trust me. I'll get my story one way or another."

"I know you will. Just don't get hurt in the process," Lance advised his colleague and friend. "By the way, Nicole Swaggart, a mental patient reported as armed and dangerous, escaped from Forest Oaks last month and is still on the loose. She took down two men twice her size at the facility. I assigned that new reporter, Keith Locket, to the story. He's been complaining about the cookie cutter stories he's been covering, so I've given him the opportunity to get his feet wet. I breathe a sigh of relief each day he returns unharmed. From what I gather from the police report, Ms. Swaggart will take down anyone who gets in her way. I have enough on my mind without worrying myself sick over you.
Watch your back, Hope. Keep your eyes and ears open."

"I'll be careful."

With a string of anonymous calls pouring in and Angelica and Jasion's cars being sabotaged, Lance had reasons for concern. She had to be on the right track. Her instincts never led her wrong. Angelica pushed the play button on the recorder, and the eerie voice emerged.

"The house that Jack built will soon tumble down, along with anyone who gets in my way. Those bigwigs at Spitzer Financial Firm will pay. They've crossed the wrong person. I'm going to sit back and watch it all unfold on television. Port City's PD will haul those Judases off in handcuffs. No one crosses me and gets away with it. NO ONE!" the caller shouted, causing Angelica's body to jerk.

She clicked the off button. Appalled, she commented, "The caller sounds more threatening with each call." Anger grew from the pit of her stomach as she flopped into the chair behind her desk.

"I'm just glad the authorities are working hard to catch this nut before someone gets hurt." Brushing his salt and pepper hair away from his pasty forehead had exposed Lance's worry lines. "And I don't want it to be you. I'm warning you, Hope. Don't take this creep's threats lightly."

"I promise not to take any unnecessary chances," she shrugged, crossing her fingers underneath her desk. Angelica loved a challenge, just as much as her overprotective boss had. "What if the caller has a score to settle with Spitzer Financial Firm? And has the run of the building without anyone questioning his or her comings and goings? Someone Mr. Lexington trusts? The perpetrator would have easy access to valuable information. With a click of a button, he or she could transfer money into outside accounts, while placing bogus profits into investors' portfolios without anyone catching it until it was too late."

"Hot darn, Hope," Lance shouted with zest in his voice. "I think you are on to something."

An uneasy feeling came over her. Solving the case might prove Jasion's guilt or innocence. She hoped for the latter. Angelica desperately wanted his name cleared of all wrongdoing. Although he hadn't been officially charged with a crime, as of yet, she vowed to dig deeper for any clues that might eliminate him as a suspect. Her heart ached at the thought of him going to jail. The man who'd held her in his arms and showed her the time of her life couldn't possibly be a thief.

Why had she suddenly begun to worry over Jasion's dilemma? Could it be? Was she falling in love with this man? The youth center had been the one thing that concerned Angelica. It had left a big question mark over his head. He'd admitted to receiving large donations from many of Port City's businesses and churches. When she'd visited the center, along

119

with the detectives, there was state of the art computer systems worth thousands of dollars, with computer programs that a person could use for illegal activities, if he so desired. Her heart sank in her chest at the thought.

*****

"Thanks for the coffee, Caleb," Angelica said, stopping in front of Ms. Kennedy's desk, where Jasion and her seemed to be having a serious conversation.

After Angelica and Lance's discussion this morning, she thought it best to get the ball rolling as soon as possible. By mid-morning, she'd have Mr. Lexington round up the employees of interest in the conference room and play the recording of the anonymous caller.

With a flirtatious smile, Caleb responded, "anytime, Angelica."

Caleb strolled off, giving the impression that there was more between them than a mere cup of coffee. Like lasers, Ms. Kennedy's eyes seared through Angelica while Jasion directed his displeasure in Caleb's direction. He looked as if he wanted to rip the young man's head off. Was there something more between Jasion's secretary and Caleb? Call her paranoid, but the 'stay away from my man' stare was written all over her narrow, brown face.

"Good morning," Angelica greeted, ignoring the cold look she received from them both.

Ms. Kennedy spoke dryly, while Jasion tried to mask his annoyance, and greeted her cordially. Feeling as if she'd walked into the Twilight Zone, Angelica brushed past Ms. Kennedy's desk and headed into Jasion's office. He trailed on her heels, closing the door behind him.

"What was that all about?" he questioned, tossing the files in his hands onto his desk.

"Excuse me." she paused. "What are you talking about?"

"You, having coffee with Caleb," he scowled, speaking disapprovingly. "I didn't know the two of you were seeing each other."

"Oh, so you're jealous."

How could a gorgeous man that has everything to offer a woman be jealous of that cocky young man? Besides her ex-boyfriend, James, she had never met a man that talked incessantly about himself as Caleb. He wasn't even in Jasion's league. Having coffee with him was a coincidence. Angelica decided to stop by the company's cafeteria when she ran into Caleb, and he'd offered to buy her a cup of coffee. She didn't have the heart to refuse him.

"Jealous?" he snorted, cocking his eyes in her direction.

"Then why are you giving me the third degree about having coffee with Caleb?"

"Just drop it." He threw up both hands in defeat.

The tension of seeing her and Caleb together showed in his demeanor. It wasn't as if she and Jasion was a couple. True, they had a great time over the weekend, but he hadn't informed her that they were an item. She could drink coffee with whomever she darn well pleased.

To Angelica's knowledge, Ms. Kennedy and Caleb didn't see each other. What reason had she for giving her that nasty look when she'd passed her desk? Was there more going on between the secretary and the computer technician than she knew about? If so, she had no plans of taking part in any workplace drama. She had enough problems of her own.

"Drop what, Jasion? You attacked me."

He charged in her direction and shouted, "attacked you?"

Jasion's quick movement in her direction triggered flashbacks of her abusive past. Images of Gladys invading her personal space caused her to go into defense mode. Both her hands flew up to protect her face from the blow she thought was coming. It wasn't as if Jasion would have been the first man to strike her. The violence of her childhood had flowed over into her romantic relationships.

"Angelica, what's wrong?" her reaction disturbed him. "Please tell me you didn't think I was going to hit you?" He grabbed her in his arms.

"I'm fine," she retorted, trying to pull away, embarrassed by her reaction.

"No. There's more going on with you than you're willing to admit." He kept a firm grip on both of her arms, pinning her still. "Were you physically abused?"

"No," she lied, looking up at him with a straight face.

"Then why did you cross your hands to shield your face? That was the reflex of an abused woman." He paused. "My center teaches a class on how to detect the warning signs of a battered teen or adult, and your reaction mimics one of those signs we teach."

"I told you. I wasn't abused." Angelica became agitated as she tried pushing him away, but Jasion's strapping arms wouldn't budge.

In a calmer tone than earlier, he added, "I would never hurt you. I—" He stopped, lifting her chin with his forefinger. Jasion brought her lips to meet his and kissed her softly, lovingly, and passionately.

Her legs became weak as he stroked the delicate hairs on the nape of her neck with the tips of his pulsating fingers. Like an expert, his lips continued working their magic on hers. For a split second, she'd thought he was going to engulf her entire face. He had kissed her before but not with such hunger and wanting. She surrendered, allowing him to ravish her mouth. The more she tried pulling away, the tighter he held on to her. How long would she be able to hide her secret from him? Jasion was nobody's fool by any means. He had her pegged right with his suspicions of abuse.

The room spun as she clutched Jasion's powerful shoulders to maintain her balance, but the hold he had on her made falling impossible. Only a man in love kissed a woman with such fire and vigor. Surely, Jasion wasn't in love with her? Or was he?

Finally, coming up for air, Jasion asked with bated breath, "Angelica, I would love for you to go to church with me tonight."

She tried steadying herself after that amazing kiss he'd just laid on her. Stunned by what he'd just posed, she replied, "I can't. Not now, I'm not ready."

"I won't press the issue. But think about it. Only God can heal whatever it is you're trying to deal with on your own." His tall frame bent down, peppering kisses across her forehead.

Angelica didn't want to discuss church, so, she switched back to the reason why she was there. "We're going to have to stop this, Jasion. It violates the employee Code of Ethics Policy." She backed away from him.

"I know, but I don't care."

He moved in closer, trapping her like an animal corners its prey. Her back was against his file cabinet.

She changed the subject again. "The station received another message from the anonymous caller. That's what the meeting is about today.

I need to focus on doing my job. I can't do that when you're toying with my emotions."

Trapped with nowhere to run, Jasion smile down at her and said, "I'm not toying with your emotions, sweetheart. I'm trying to claim your heart."

"I had a great time on our date, but we have to be realistic. We come from two different worlds. We can't be together." She was fooling herself. Angelica wanted Jasion more than any man she'd ever known, except for JC. She had wanted him as well, but fate had torn them apart.

"What are you afraid of, Angelica?" he asked with furrowed brows, both hands now tenderly pressed against her cheeks.

"You." Her personal space was now invaded by his presence. Why was he making this so darn difficult? Once he'd learned of her past, he probably would head for the nearest exit. She must protect her secret. Sure, she had issues, but Jasion might see her as damaged goods.

"Why are you afraid of me? I—I," he stuttered, looked away, and then quickly returned his gaze to her. "I care about you, Angelica."

Unable to look at him or process his admission, she stared down at the freshly vacuumed floor.

"Did you hear what I just said? I have feelings for you. Code of Ethics or not, it doesn't change the fact of how I feel."

Sweeping a loose curl from her face, Jasion brought her lips to his and showed her how much he cared.

She mumbled through the kiss, "I care for you, too." But Jasion showed no sign of comprehending what she had admitted. He was on a mission with her lips. A mission, she believed to claim her heart.

*****

By mid-afternoon, Angelica had met with the key employees at Spitzer Financial Firm. She played the recording of the anonymous caller and watched their body language, just as Lance had ordered. Caleb seemed a tad uptight, which set off the alarm in her head. The other employees' eyes were fixated on the tape recorder while Jasion eyed her. His intense stare caused her to perspire under her clothing. This man had her, for the first time in a long time, thinking about giving him the key to her heart. But going to church was out of the question.

Chapter Twenty Five

The sappy music blared throughout the movie theater as Jasion and Angelica watched the onscreen lovers declare their undying love for one another. As staged as it was, Jasion coveted the actor's happy ending. With arms wrapped around the woman he wanted to express his perpetual love to, he questioned their future. Would their love be everlasting or just two lonely people thrown together temporarily? Whatever the reason, Jasion thought life couldn't get any better than him sitting in a dark cinema next to the woman who could possibly become his future. Instead of focusing on the movie, he spent most of his time stealing glances at Angelica. Her beautiful, radiant silhouette shone through the dim lighting in the theater. His heart beat with excitement at how blessed he was to have her in his life, even if it was just for a short time. Beside Angelica, Fayth had been the only girl who'd evoked such emotions within him.

Ever since the day Angelica freaked out in his office, projecting what many psychiatrists called, "the battered woman syndrome," they'd been inseparable. That day still haunted him. What monster could have hurt one of God's delicate creatures? Jasion's nostrils flared with anger at the thought. He wasn't a violent man but would put a serious hurting on the person who'd abused her. Whether she'd own up to it or not, he recognized the signs from the classes that he offered at his center.

Keeping his hands to himself remained a challenge. So he believed it would cause less temptation on his part if he and Angelica didn't hang out at each other's homes. He'd had countless of unfulfilling liaisons with women and had vowed to give himself solely to his future wife. Angelica could possibly be the one, but first, she had to tear down the brick wall standing between them. Jasion promised God that the next woman who shared his bed would indeed be Mrs. McCoy and not a one-night stand.

Her resistance to church posed a problem against any future they might have together. Jasion prayed that her faith and trust in God would change, or there wouldn't be a happily ever after for them. His heart grieved over her unbelief. He was a minister, for crying out loud. How would it look; the wife of a minister, who'd never attended church? How could he compel others to come when his own spouse didn't?

Angelica stirred against his arms, breaking Jasion out of his conflicting thoughts. "Are you enjoying the movie?" he whispered close to her ear to keep from disturbing the other moviegoers.

"Yes," she whispered back, repositioning her body in her chair.

Brushing his hand through her wealth of black hair, he refocused his attention on the romantic flick. God had indeed given him favor by sending her into his life. Yes, she was opinionated and headstrong, but he understood her position. A woman in her profession had to be resilient, or the male chauvinist bullies in the business world would not take her serious. If only she'd possessed more aggressiveness when it came to her personal life, each time he'd tried breaking through the tough barrier around her heart, she would close him out. Jasion could see the pain in her eyes. He'd seen it months earlier at their luncheon when she had begun to cry. He figured she was secretly dealing with some heavy issues; issues he wanted to help her through if only she'd let him

Hours later, Jasion and Angelica strolled along Port City's river walk hand in hand. Music filled the streets as shoppers rushed in and out of stores. Jasion closed his eyes, inhaling the scents of foods that filled the air. Slowly, he opened them to the warm and inviting smile of an angel. How he wished everyday could be this heavenly. The twinkling stars beamed with excitement throughout the night skies. The rain that forecasters had predicted never made an appearance. He watched as children chased one another up and down the strip as the beautiful woman who'd stolen his heart walked alongside him.

The investigation was never far from his mind. If the detectives would stop dragging their feet on the case, he could move on to the next phase of his life. No matter how Jasion tried letting loose to enjoy himself, his impending fate always came crashing back into his thoughts.

"What are you thinking about, sweetheart?" he asked, squeezing her hand. "You've been quiet ever since we arrived here."

"I wish we could have met under normal circumstances," she responded. Angelica let go of his hand. Reaching into her jacket pocket, she pulled out a coin and tossed it into the fountain.

"What did you wish for?" he asked, pressing his arms around her petite midriff. It amazed Jasion how something good could come from a bad situation. His mother and sister had always been his rocks after his father's passing, but God had sent him something more— a friend, and hopefully in time, a wife, and lover.

"If I tell you, my wish won't come true." She smiled with his face nestled in the hollow of her neck.

"Whatever it is." He gently spun her around to face him. "Trust God to bring it to pass. We were brought together because we have something each other need and want." Pulling her into his arms, he smiled down into her sultry, brown eyes.

"And what is that?"

"To be loved... the right way." He tapped the tip of her nose with his finger, causing a giggle to escape her luscious lips.

"How do you know when you've found it?"

"God will speak to your heart."

"What if God doesn't speak?" she asked innocently, with raised brows.

"He will." He paused, brushing a kiss across her lips. "He always does."

When she rested her head against his chest, he wondered about the severity of her pain. What monster destroyed this beautiful woman's faith? The coward had better prayed they never meet. No woman on God's green earth deserved such treatment at the hands of the man who was supposed to love and protect her.

God, give me the wisdom and knowledge to usher Angelica into your presence. I don't know the extent of her issues. But you do. Restore her faith, bring her back into Your kingdom, and show me how to love her the right way.

Chapter Twenty Six

Marissa whipped her red Ferrari into a vacant parking space at a family friendly, Tex-Mex restaurant. She and Angelica hopped out of the vehicle and headed inside. The greeter gave them a hearty welcome and then proceeded to escort them to their table.

Marissa's seat faced the restaurant's exit. She'd noticed an anxious, little boy, his face pressed against the crane machine filled with stuff animals. As the mechanical claws snatched the toy, anticipation filled his eyes. An older man successfully maneuvered the toy animal toward the drop box where the youngster's tiny hands reached inside to retrieve his prize.

"Fay, I'm going to let you in on a secret. I love my husband but two weeks together on a cruise had me wanting to throw myself overboard. Girl, Kyle snored so loud in our cabin that I wanted to smother him. A couple in the neighboring bunk called security. I woke him up to tell him there were complaints about noises coming from our sleeping quarters. And he had the nerve to say," Marissa deepened her voice to sound masculine. "Well, you need to quiet it down, so other people can sleep." She burst into a gut busting laugh. "Can you believe that? When we arrived home, I was so tired that I slept two days straight."

"Now that's hilarious. I can't believe you didn't tell him that he was the problem," Angelica said, using her forefinger to wipe away a tear that had escaped the corner of her eye from laughing so hard.

"You know I wanted to, but I was so sleepy that I just didn't have the energy to do so. It would have only led to a debate about, which one of us snore the loudest."

Marissa continued to fill Angelica in on her romantic getaway from hell when a couple with a small child preparing to leave the restaurant caught her attention. Without alerting her friend to her discovery, Marissa tried to entertain Angelica with story after story about her vacation.

Keeping her friend distracted while she spied on the man who tried to win the little girl a stuffed animal, had become her mission. She prayed that Angelica wouldn't notice her discomfort until she could be certain her eyes weren't playing tricks on her. Her vision was accurate. Marissa's anger had gone from simmering to boiling point in a matter of seconds. *How could he do this to her? Something of this magnitude will set her back after she'd taken great strides to love again. This will destroy her for sure.*

Marissa felt her eyes turning into razor-sharp daggers, ready to take out the enemy. She wrestled with her dilemma. Should she tell Angelica or leave her in the dark? She couldn't allow this man to play her friend for a fool. If there were any other way to handle the situation, she would. So, Marissa decided to do what any good friend would. She didn't want to play the devil's advocate, but she had to do what she had to do.

"Girl, you act as if you've seen your worst enemy. What's so interesting over there?" Angelica asked, turning to see what had Marissa about to erupt. And there it was, hitting her smack dab in the face. "Oh, my word… this can't be happening," It felt as if someone had socked her in the stomach. Tears filled her eyes as she stared from her seat at Jasion and an unfamiliar woman and child laughing and hugging over the fact that he'd won her a stuffed teddy bear. Angelica was devastated. He had lied to her.

There he stood, brazen as ever, with a wife and kid. She felt stupid for falling for another man's lies. Now she understood why he'd never wanted to go to his place, lying, that the temptation of being alone with her was too strong. She should have known better than to fall for his celibate song and dance. What a load of bull he'd fed her. She could kick herself. When was she going to learn never to trust the words coming from a slick-talking pair of britches? Her gut instinct had warned her that he was just too handsome and intelligent not to have a woman waiting for him at home. There he stood, no better than the next man who'd lie through his teeth to her. With steam shooting from her ears, she wanted to waltz over to where they were and inform his unsuspecting wife about her lying, cheating, cold-hearted husband, but her feet weren't getting the signal from her brain. It felt as though someone had poured cement in her shoes.

Angelica looked on in disgust as Jasion and his family left the restaurant and drove off, laughing and enjoying their perfect life. A life she'd hoped for them to share together one day. He'd lead her to believe that it was possible for them to be together once the investigation ended. This was the lowest Angelica has felt in months. God had failed her again. If it were possible, she'd strangle herself for falling prey to Jasion's deception. She'd believed him when he'd said that the two of them had what the other one needed. Yes, she desired true love, but what did he want from her?

Well, Gladys, you were right. I'll always be alone, she thought.

A bubbly, blonde, petite young server interrupted Angelica's pity party.

"Hi, my name is Leeann, and I will be your server today. What can I get you two ladies to drink?"

"We'll be leaving," Marissa said sharply, grabbing their belongings.

"Did I say something wrong?" the server whined through her nostrils.

"Sorry, I didn't mean to yelp at you," Marissa shrugged apologetically. "My friend has suddenly become ill."

"I'm sorry, ma'am. I hope your friend feels better," the server said, concerned.

Angelica had passed ill. She was downright devastated, to say the least. She couldn't eat anything even if she'd tried.

Marissa reached for her arm, handling her with kid gloves. Her friend was always there to pick up the pieces of her broken life.

When the two exited the restaurant, Angelica burst into tears. "Why did he lie to me? How could he have hurt me like this? I would have eventually found out."

"I don't know why some men do the things they do, but, looks can be deceiving. I just don't believe Jasion is that stupid. True, the sight of him with another woman, at first glance made me wanted to walk over there and choke him myself. We don't want to jump to any conclusions just yet, Fay."

Angelica wasn't in the mood for Marissa's positive outlook on the matter. For crying out loud; she was upset. "What are you saying, Marissa Michele Cartwright?" Only in anger did Angelica referred to her friend by her full name.

"Are you taking his side? We both saw him with our own eyes," she snapped, shooting her friend a sidelong glance.

"All I am saying, Fay, is don't get yourself all worked up over something that hasn't been proven yet. You are an investigative reporter, aren't you?"

"Yes," she said, pitifully.

"Then investigate."

"What's the point? If he's not married, then he has a child. And I don't have time for any baby mama drama." Angelica slid into the passenger's seat of the car, buckled her seatbelt, laid her head back against the headrest, and sulked. "These young girls today are crazy. I'm not trying to cross into some possessive chick territory. I've done enough 'Jealous Lovers' stories to last a lifetime, and I have no plans of ending up in one of them." She forced out a sarcastic laugh.

Angelica hated that Marissa continued to be the voice of reason on the drive back to her apartment. As usual, she tried tuning her out, but it didn't work. How could her friend give Jasion the benefit of the doubt? Marissa saw him at the restaurant with another woman just as she had.

They arrived at Angelica's apartment. "Look. I am going to stay here with you tonight," Marissa insisted, placing her purse and car keys on the coffee table.

"You have a husband. I can't expect you to babysit me every time I have a crisis. I feel as though I'm becoming a charity case." Angelica plopped down onto the sofa, pulling one of the throw pillows close to her chest.

"Kyle will understand. Besides, he had to fly to New York this morning on business, so I am all yours. Plus, I don't want to stay in that huge house alone."

"I don't want to be alone either. Jasion and I were supposed to have dinner later tonight, but I'd rather eat with a pack of wolves than with him," she barked, rolling her eyes heavenwards.

"I need to make a quick run home to pack an overnight bag, and then I'll be right back. We're family, Fay, and families help one another to get through those rough spots. I will always have your back, your front, and your sides," she joked.

Angelica knew her friend meant well when she tried cheering her up, but she wasn't in the mood for any of Marissa's witty remarks.

"I'll whip something up for us to eat while you're gone since I ruined our lunch," Angelica offered.

"You didn't ruin my lunch, sweetie," Marissa replied, patting her friend on the shoulder. "I'll pick up something to eat on the way back. Go take a hot, relaxing bubble bath, so that when I return, we can have some much-needed girl talk."

As soon as Marissa disappeared out of the door, Angelica followed her orders and ran herself a hot bath. She added a couple of drops of her favorite lavender bath oil. The fragrance seemed to help her unwind after a stressful day at work. Angelica hoped that it worked its magic tonight because she had passed stressed. She was peeved off. With nothing but idle time on her hands while awaiting Marissa's return, Jasion's deception reclaimed her thoughts. The pain made her want to submerge her entire body under water and never come up for air. This was truly one of the most humiliating days of her life.

The sound of the telephone resonated through the partially opened door, but the soothing hot water held her hostage. She decided to let it go to voice mail, knowing it could only be one person, Jasion. His deep voice chimed in, sending sharp pains through her broken heart. She listened to the two-timing liar invading her safe haven.

"Sweetheart, this is Jasion. When you get this message, please call me back," He hesitated. "I've left several messages on your cellphone and even your work number. I'm getting worried, Angelica. Please call me."

"Huh. Worried, you adulterous piece of crap," she mumbled, rolling her eyes into space.

"Don't worry about the time. I'll be up late waiting for your call."

"Hold your breath."

Determined not to cry or play the victim anymore, Angelica licked her wounds and decided to move forward. No account men had claimed enough of her energy. She'd accepted the fact a long time ago that she might be spending the rest of her life alone. Every man she'd dated had done nothing but make a fool out of her. Angelica had been used, abused, and taken for granted, and it was about to end. Jasion didn't care about her. She realized that now. His only concern was to keep his cheating behind from going to prison.

Thankfully, she'd found out the truth before her heart had been completely stomped on. But it was a little too late; she had fallen madly in love with a married man, a man who would never be hers.

Chapter Twenty Seven

Jasion decided to channel his energy elsewhere, instead of impatiently waiting for Angelica to call. Grabbing his briefcase, he began fishing through the sea of papers for files on the investigation, only to discover they weren't there. Against his better judgment, he left home.

Arriving at Spitzer Financial Firm unannounced to retrieve files he'd left on his desk Friday afternoon, he began to have second thoughts. Since the investigation, no employees were to enter the firm on weekends without prior authorization from security.

Security buzzed Jasion into the building but not without him stating his reason for being there. After the interrogation, which made him feel like a common criminal, he headed towards the elevator. On the ride up, his mind strayed to Angelica and her whereabouts. With the anonymous caller on the loose, he worried about her safety.

It wasn't like Angelica not to call, especially knowing they had a date tonight, so Jasion figured she had a good reason. *Maybe her boss had her covering a story at the last minute*, he told himself.

Whatever the reason, his plans were ruined. He'd wanted to ask Angelica to date him exclusively. For nearly a week, they had been inseparable. Surely, if things were moving too fast, she would have told him, instead of standing him up. He prayed that she hadn't found out about his little secret before he had the chance to explain.

The elevator door opened. Stepping out, he headed to his office and then spotted a man's shadow moving in the opposite direction. It startled him. Jasion assumed that security had allowed another employee into the building. He unlocked his office door, stepped inside the dark room, and switched on the lights to grab the files from his desk. They were nowhere in sight. He tore his office apart in search of them.

Snatching open his office door, he looked up and down the hallway. He had an uneasy feeling. There was movement near the emergency exit. He ducked back inside his office, picked up the phone, and called security. He told what he'd witnessed, but kept quiet about the missing files. Jasion was anal when it came to the way he left his desk. He should have known from the moment he entered the room that something wasn't right.

Security looked around the hallways and stairwell but stated that no one had been in the building since the close of business yesterday. His anticipation about his date with Angelica had affected his better judgment. Now important documents were in the hands of god knows who.

"Damn," Jasion muttered under his breath. It wasn't like him to swear. Thinking of Angelica twenty-four-seven had caused him to slip. Those files contained information for his eyes only. He'd practically handed his head over on a silver platter, and to make matters worse, he had no clue where Angelica was and hoped she wasn't on to him.

"Son, you're seeing things. This place is airtight. The only way anyone can get into this building is through me. Hidden surveillance cameras are planted throughout the firm," he informed Jasion, twirling his flashlight in his hand.

"Yeah, perhaps you're right." Jasion knew better. Someone had been in the building. Not wanting to argue with security about what he'd seen, Jasion locked his office door, and the guard escorted him downstairs and out of SFF. There was no point in disputing the security guard's claims. If anyone had broken into the building, all he had for protection was a flashlight and a chain full of keys.

Jasion decided to drive over to Angelica's place after leaving the firm. He would not rest until he'd heard her voice and seen her beautiful face. This woman had begun to control his entire being. Even her happiness had become his concern, and if she wasn't, he wanted to know what he could do to make her happy.

Time after time, he questioned what man had broken her heart and what he could do to repair it? After the disappearance of his first love, Fayth, true love had finally found him again. Thanks to Angelica.

His proposal to Nicole Swaggart was done out of loneliness and lust. Love had nothing to do with it. On the other hand, Angelica was everything a man could ever want in a woman. Besides her beauty, she was intelligent and compassionate about the things around her. Nicole was self-centered and mean-spirited toward others. Jasion was thankful that he'd seen straight through her before he'd made the worst mistake of his life. He wondered whatever happened to Nicole. It seemed as if she'd vanished into thin air, which was fine with him, but she hadn't gone peacefully. Nicole had promised Jasion after he'd broken off their engagement that she'd make him pay for humiliating her.

Pulling into Angelica's apartment complex, he noticed her car parked in its usual spot. Confused as to why she hadn't returned his calls, Jasion immediately jumped out of his vehicle, making his way upstairs, but not before a run-in with Mr. Nate, which he wasn't in the mood for.

"Whut yhu prowlin' roun' hea' fo' at this time of night youngblood?" Mr. Nate questioned with his hands tucked inside his soiled bathrobe.

"Good evening, Mr. Nathaniel," Jasion greeted, praying the old man would take it easy on him tonight. "Just coming to check on Angelica and make sure she made it home alright. That's all."

"Yhu see hur car parked downstairs, don't yhu? Well, she's okay." Mr. Nate cocked his head to the side as the nightlight revealed his overgrown, bushy gray hair. It resembled a cotton patch.

"I'll feel better if I see for myself." Jasion couldn't understand why the old man made him nervous. Mr. Nate could stare down a bear without batting an eye, and his wrinkled hands always seemed to be searching around for something inside the pockets of his robe; hopefully, not a weapon.

"No… yhu're after somethin' else. I wasn' born yes-ta-dee, boy."

"Honestly, Mr. Nathaniel, I'm just checking in on her and nothing more. I promise." Then, Jasion quickly made his exit.

"Well, in that case, gwon'on, and yhu betta be tellin' the truth or I'll put a serious hurtin' on yhu."

"Yes, Sir. Take care," Jasion said, rushing off. He refused to look back, for fear of getting Mr. Nate started up again with his shenanigans.

Jasion knocked on Angelica's door several times without an answer. If he didn't know any better, he would have thought she was purposely avoiding him. The door opened, but it wasn't Angelica. "Hi, Marissa. Is Angelica home?" he asked, perplexed.

"Shh. Lower your voice. She's asleep," Marissa snapped, furrowing her brows.

"What's going on? I've been trying to reach her all day." The alarm in his head sounded off. Something wasn't right; he could tell by Marissa's voice, and by the way she was giving him the cold shoulder.

Jasion had met Marissa last month when she and Angelica were dining at the same restaurant where Spitzer Financial Firm held their usual Thursday business luncheon.

"Don't stand there acting all innocent." She stood blocking the entranceway of the door.

"Excuse me?" Jasion had no idea what Marissa was getting at.

"Look, I have to go. My friend has been hurt by no-good, lying men before, and I will not stand by and allow it to happen again," she scowled.

Jasion saw and felt the woman's annoyance, but why was she directing it at him? He turned and looked behind him to make sure she had been indeed referring to him. Or was he reading too much into her words? He hadn't seen Angelica since their movie date and had no idea what was going on.

"What are you talking about? I would never purposely hurt Angelica," he replied, rubbing his head, trying to make sense out of her words.

"I've talked too much already," Marissa said, pushing the door closed.

Jasion blocked her from doing so by placing his foot in its path. "Would you care to enlighten me about what's going on?" By now, he was growing tired of her talking in circles. If she knew something, she needed to just spit it out.

"Angelica will talk to you when she's good and ready. It's not my place to tell you anything. Now run on back home to your wife and child," she said, slamming the door in his face.

Chapter Twenty Eight

"Rise and shine, sleepy head. We got some churchin' to do," Marissa ordered, pulling the covers off of Angelica.

"Noooooooooo. It can't be morning already. I thought you were going back to your place to pick up a change of clothes," Angelica groaned, trying to pull the covers from Marissa's hands. "Just what do you know about churchin'? Girl, you're Catholic."

Marissa continued her tug-of-war with Angelica over the covers but quickly gave up, when the tiny bedroom seemed to close in on her. How anyone managed to function in such a small sleeping space was a mystery to her. The bedroom lacked spunk, like her wardrobe. Angelica's décor screamed for a makeover. She strolled over to the window and drew up the Venetian blinds, allowing the sunlight to cheer up the gloomy place.

"Kyle and I joined a Non-Denominational Church years ago."

"Well... excuse me, Mrs. Non-Denominational."

Returning to where her sleepy friend lay buried underneath layers of covers, Marissa asked, "how would you know what churches do nowadays? You haven't attended one since you moved out of your Aunt Beatrice's house."

Angelica yelped from underneath the covers like a brooding child. "I wouldn't have gone then if she hadn't forced me to." Finally, pulling the covers from over her head to the welcoming light of the day, she asked, "when did I agree to go to church with you?"

"Right after you took a sedative. You had a hard time falling asleep." Marissa didn't have the heart to tell Angelica that Jasion had stopped by. "Now don't go chickening your way out of it. I told you last night about my employee, Sheryl Blake. You remember her, don't you?"

140

"Yeah, sweet lady," she said, yawning and stretching.

"Well, she and her husband want us to come out and hear their daughter, Brianna, sing her first solo with the youth choir at Bountiful Blessing Ministry."

"I don't know about that, Marissa." Shaking her head in disagreement about church, she sat up.

"Please, Fay, just come and support little Brianna," she pleaded. "No strings attached and no trying to force religion on you." Crossing her fingers behind her back, she prayed that her friend would say yes.

Wrinkling up her nose, Angelica said with reservation, "This is against my better judgment... but okay. For little Brianna, you'd better be glad it's for her or else." She pulled herself out of bed and dragged in the direction of the bathroom.

Words could not explain Marissa's surprise and happiness. She'd been begging Angelica for years to attend church with her and now that day had finally come. Although she had never attended Bountiful Blessing Ministry, she'd heard that fourth Sundays were standing room only. The church had some of the most talented youth in the city, and she couldn't wait to see what God had in store for her and Angelica this morning. It wasn't an accident that Angelica had agreed, but by His divine power. Marissa believed that a miracle was going to take place in her misguided friend's life today.

Church wouldn't be an easy feat for her friend, but it was a start. In order to help Angelica renew her relationship with Christ, Marissa had to allow God to work on Angelica's heart. She'd already done her part in planting the seed. Coming off too strong might push Angelica away from the church for good, so she decided to allow things to happen in God's perfect timing and not hers.

Yes, Lord, this is going to be a great day. Touch my sister's heart, Father. Show Yourself mightily in her life. Let her know that You, and You alone are God. I want her to know and experience what it's like to have total and complete trust in You and not her job or her own carnal wisdom. I stand in your

141

presence now, Lord Jesus, interceding for my lost friend. Help her to know the joy and peace in serving You. You said, Father, that You are shelter from the storm. Fay, has had many storms in her life. Cover, shield, and heal her from past and present storms. In the name of Jesus, I pray. Amen. Marissa prayed, knowing that her friend's spiritual survival depended on it.

"Girl, what are you doing on the floor?" Angelica asked, returning from the bathroom, puzzled. "Why are you crying? When I left the room, you were singing and dancing."

"Oh, I'm happy. I'm very happy," Marissa said, rising from her knees. "Let me go and wash up, and then we can leave."

"Whatever's gotten into you, I hope it doesn't rub off on me," she mumbled.

Marissa turned and asked, "you say something, Fay?"

"Um… no. I didn't say anything."

Marissa had heard exactly what Angelica had muttered under her breath.

Later, she emerged from the bathroom fully dressed in her church attire. "Are you ready, Fay?"

"As ready as I'll ever be," she said, unenthusiastically.

"Well, you look great, and if I didn't know any better, I'd think you were going to snag a man."

"Don't you start, or I'll change my mind," Angelica countered, adjusting her skirt in the full-length mirror. "I already think this church thing is not a good idea."

"Sorry," she apologized, shooting her beautiful, insecure friend a sly grin. "Brianna's mom told me that the new youth minister had worked miracles with the kids at the church. He spends most of his free time making sure the church and youth center create activities to keep them involved and off the streets. Who knows, Fay, maybe he's single. I just might ask her to introduce him to you." She couldn't resist taking one last pot-shot at Angelica.

"Hold on one minute, don't go trying to play cupid. I need to get myself together first. Hell... Oops." Angelica quickly covered her mouth after the foul language slipped out.

Fayth's slip of the tongue didn't seem to faze Marissa.

"I'm like a stick of dynamite, ready to go off at any moment. Please, don't go doing me any favors," Angelica said, emphatically.

"Okay. Okay. Okay, I won't. Let's go before we're late."

Chapter Twenty Nine

When Marissa and Angelica arrived at Bountiful Blessing Ministry, they circled the enormous parking lot several times without finding a place to park. The church seemed miles away when they finally parked, so they decided to wait on the church shuttle bus to chauffeur them to the sanctuary. BBM held at least two thousand people, and today, by the number of cars in the parking lot, it was standing room only.

People had come from near and far to help celebrate the church's Annual Youth Explosion. As they rode through the spacious lot, the feeling Marissa had earlier at Angelica's apartment began to speak to her spirit again. She knew they were in the right place, at the right time.

Yes, God was up to something wonderful today, she thought, shivering with anticipation.

"I know you're not cold?" Angelica asked, breaking the silence. "It's eighty degrees out here."

"No. I was just thinking about something." She looked and smiled at her unsuspecting friend. Marissa knew that Angelica's life would never be the same after leaving the house of the Lord.

"Finally. We're here. I hope this isn't one of those churches where they bully visitors into joining. They overextend the invitation to discipleship until someone gets tired of their begging and pleading, and then joins."

"Well, I hope not either, but I'm all for a soul being saved. I just don't agree with ministries that coerce visitors to join for their own financial gain."

They stepped off the shuttle bus and walked into the foyer of the church, where sounds of celebration rang throughout the building. Marissa hurried through the sanctuary doors to join in on the festivities while Angelica lagged behind.

The usher directed the women down to the fourth row, where two seats were miraculously vacant. Marissa couldn't believe it. With all the people packed inside the church, she thought for sure that they would have to sit in the back and watch the service on the Teleprompters.

Through her peripheral vision, Marissa could see that Angelica was uncomfortable sitting so close to the front. Once they'd taken their seats, Marissa rested her hand on top of her friend's hands, giving them a reassuring squeeze.

Everyone stood as the worship leaders came onstage, leading the congregation into a song of praise and worship. The large platform accommodated the praise dancers and the biggest choir Marissa had ever seen in one church.

Angelica looked like a deer caught in headlights when Marissa glanced over at her. Praise and worship seemed foreign to her friend although Angelica grew up in a black Baptist church. The way people worshiped today had changed drastically since she'd last attended and Marissa could see the amazement in her eyes.

Once the worship segment ended, a handsome young man graced the stage. "Church, let's put our hands together for this next little angel. This is her solo debut," he announced, "Miss Brianna Blake."

The congregation rose from their seats and clapped as the young girl took her place center stage. Marissa spotted the proud parents videotaping their daughter. The joy on their faces was evident as their child sang with such conviction about the goodness of the Lord. Marissa glanced over to discover a teary Angelica.

When Brianna finished her solo, the congregation applauded, giving her a standing ovation. The young child truly allowed the Holy Spirit to use her as she belted out, *His Eyes Is On The Sparrow.*

The same young man, who'd introduced Brianna, now led the congregation in a devotional hymn. As the church remained standing, Marissa noticed two familiar faces across the church, seated in the front row. She'd seen them before. Suddenly, like a ton of bricks, it hit her, and she unintentionally blurted out, "The Tex-Mex restaurant."

"Shhhhhh. You're too loud," Angelica scolded. "Even I know better than to talk in church."

Lord, You told me this was going to be a good day. I felt it in my spirit. Please don't let Fay spot them, because this may turn her away from the church for good, she prayed while trying to keep a smile plastered on her face.

It was the same young woman and girl that she and Angelica had seen yesterday. Marissa's heart raced a mile a minute. She tried to come up with a plan for getting Angelica out of there without her spotting them.

"As Bountiful Blessing Ministry's Sons' of the House come out to take their seats, I would like to introduce to you our new youth leader. You already know him as a promising young minister here at the church, but this young man has turned our youth department around. Kids are getting involved, not only here at church, but in the community as well. Church, put your hands together to show this young minister some love... Minister Jasion McCoy."

*****

"Fay. Fay!" Marissa yelled, trying to shake her friend out of her trance. The color had drained from Angelica's traumatized face. "Are you all right, Fay? Say something."

A heavyset woman wearing a hat that resembled a bouquet of flowers shot them a nasty look, but Marissa could not have cared less. Her only concern at that moment was for her dear friend, who'd been like a sister to her over the years.

"I need to sit down. I feel sick to my stomach. He's pretending to be a man of the cloth. Jasion has a wife and child, all the while saying that he wants to be with me. That hypocrite," she said, looking in his direction with disgust.

"I'm so sorry, Fay. I didn't know he was a member of this church, let alone a minister. I only wanted to come and support Brianna. Please believe me." Marissa pleaded for forgiveness.

"I know you didn't do this deliberately, Marissa, so stop beating yourself up over it. I'm good. We're going to stay, so that later on, we can congratulate Brianna on her beautiful solo afterward. You have given up so much for me over the years. Now it's my turn to deny myself for you," Angelica declared, raising her head with dignity.

Before Angelica and Marissa could utter another word, Jasion began to speak to the congregation. "Church, it is truly an honor to stand and proclaim God's Word," he said, smiling at the crowd.

Angelica and Marissa sat in their seats, appalled as the woman in the hat kept giving them a disapproving look.

Marissa turned to her friend and mouthed, "if that lady rolls her eyes in this direction one more time, she'll be picking them up off the floor." She wasn't a violent person, but today, her temper had soared into overload.

"My family is here today to show their support. I would like for my mom to stand, and I know my father is looking down on us from heaven," Jasion continued, as the congregation clapped in recognition of his mother. "Last but not least I'd like to thank a very special lady whom I love dearly. You can say she's my biggest supporter."

As Jasion spoke, Marissa looked over at Angelica, pointing toward the exit. She couldn't put her friend through any more humiliation. Listening to that Judas standing there, gloating about his wife in her friend's face was a hard pill to swallow. If a bolt of lightning came surging through the church and struck him down, it still wouldn't be justice for the pain he'd caused Angelica.

If Jasion lied so easily about being single, what else was he hiding? With Port City's declining economy, a youth center like his needed money, and lots of it. Where was Jasion getting the financial backing to support such a large facility?

As Angelica and Marissa tried sneaking out, Jasion continued his introduction. "I would like for my sister and beautiful niece to stand. Church, this is my best friend. When I need a shoulder to lean on, she's always there. Now don't get me wrong, my parents were very supportive, but my sister and I have a very special bond."

"SISTER!" The friends shouted in unison as they stood in the middle of the aisle with their mouths hanging to the floor.

"Hurry up. Let's sit back down to keep from drawing attention to ourselves. I'm glad everyone is into what Jasion is saying and not paying us any attention," Marissa said, heading back to her seat.

"You mean to tell me that I've made myself miserable for nothing? Oh, my goodness. I feel like such a fool," Angelica sighed, slapping her forehead. "I've alienated this man for nothing. Now I really do feel sick."

"Shush." The woman in the hat hissed, shooting them another fiery glance.

"You know what? I'm so happy and relieved about what just transpired that I refuse to let her get under my skin," Marissa stated.

"So am I," Angelica agreed.

They both turned and smiled at the woman.

The woman returned the gesture.

Then, Jasion began to pray.

When he finished, he opened his Bible and asked, "God's people, turn your Bibles with me to Job, chapter twenty-three, and we'll commence reading verses two through five. I will be reading from, The Living Bible, for those of you who are using other translations. When you've found it, say amen," he paused, looking out into the crowd. "I still hear some pages turning."

Amen rang throughout the sanctuary.

And he read.

"My complaint today is still a bitter one, and my punishment far more severe than my fault deserves. Oh, that I knew where to find God—that I could go to his throne and talk with him there. I would tell him all about my side of this argument, and listen to his reply, and understand what he wants," Jasion finished.

After the reading of the Scriptures, Angelica glanced around the building in amazement at how people were testifying and praising God. So much so, that Jasion had to wait until the church quieted down to proceed.

"I gather I'm not the only one this morning that need to be reminded that our trials are temporary. God not only knows what we're going through, but is there even when we at times can't feel His presence," Jasion testified, rocking and waving his hands in the air with joy.

"Amen, young man. You sho' 'nuff preachin'," a voiced cried out from among the pews.

Unable to fully process the praising and the shouting around her, Angelica couldn't deny that something supernatural was taking place.

"My text this morning is, Where Was God? You may be seated all over this great church," Jasion added.

Angelica had asked herself that same question time and time, especially after the death of her father. She believed that God had forsaken her and placed her in harm's way to fend for herself. And often, wondered if He even cared that she was being kicked, slapped, and demeaned by the hands of her mother. Was there a God? If so, He'd abandoned her a long time ago? Angelica could relate to Job's frustration, and she had the emotional scars to prove it.

"How do I handle situations in my life when God's presence can't be found? How can I stay focused and committed to doing God's Will when He doesn't answer me? Well, saints, many of you have asked these same questions. What do you do when your back is against the wall?" Jasion asked, revving enthusiastically.

"Amen, minister. What do you do? " A female parishioner hollered from her seat.

"I see there's someone in the congregation who can identify with the message I'm preaching this morning." Jasion began to pace back and forth on the platform. "Church, can you imagine living a blessed life one day and then having it all snatched away in a matter of seconds? To have a clean bill of health, a wife and kids who are doing fine, plenty of money in your bank account, and a nice home. Only to lose everything in one day and to top it off, the very God who said that He'll never leave you nor forsake you, can't be found. What do you do? Will you complain, get mad, leave the church, or turn your back on Him? No, saints, you don't give up. What helped Job through those rough times is that his relationship with God was intact before trouble found him."

"Hallelujah. Speak, Lawd.

We need a word up in here today." An elderly man from the deacons' corner cried out.

"Preach, Son. That need to be said," the senior pastor shouted.

"Ain't no harm in praising Him. Ain't no harm at all, because He is worthy," Jasion shouted into the microphone. "Job praised God for what He'd already done for him, even if God didn't heal him or give him any relief. He is still worthy to be praised."

Before Jasion concluded his sermon, he read, Job chapter twenty-three, verses eight through ten from the King James Version. "Behold, I go forward, but he is not there; and backward, but I cannot perceive him: On the left hand, that I cannot see him: But he knoweth the way that I take: when he hath tried me, I shall come forth as pure gold."

Angelica watched in awe at what was transpiring around the congregation. People were out of their seats, raising their hands in total submission to the word Jasion was preaching. Men and women, young and old, were crying their hearts out to God.

Jasion carried on, "God asked Job a very simple question out of a whirlwind: where were you when I laid the foundations of the earth? Tell me, if you know so much." Jasion quickly ended his sermon. The cries of the people were so loud that it drowned him out.

Thirty minutes had passed since Jasion had begun his sermon.

"Bountiful Blessing Ministry, we're all guilty of blaming God for our misfortunes. He is a forgiving God, even His only begotten Son, Jesus, felt abandoned on the cross, when He cried, "My God, my God, why hast thou forsaken me? But Jesus saw the bigger picture. He knew we needed an example to follow when the time came for us to carry our crosses,'" Jasion stated.

Angelica collapsed in her seat, sobbing uncontrollably. Marissa tried consoling her as the woman in the hat used her church program to fan her. She'd never experienced the Spirit of God moving in her in such a mighty way. Never in her wildest dreams had she expected an outpouring such as this.

Jasion continued. "As the praise team sings, 'Great Is Thy Mercy,' if anyone in this house can identify with this message and want prayer and deliverance, please come down to the altar." He stretched forth his hands toward the congregation. "Don't leave here today carrying the same old issues back home. God wants you to leave it here today. There's nothing too hard for Him. We serve a loving and merciful God, who's waiting on you to surrender."

Crowds of people pressed their way to the altar, kneeling and pouring their hearts out to God.

"Fay. It's time to let go of the past and turn it over to God," Marissa pleaded, tugging Angelica's arm. "I'll be with you. I will not leave you. Let's go."

"I'm scared. I've strayed for so long," Angelica cried while the woman in the hat continued to fan her.

"Suga', you don't have to be afraid of God. Listen to your friend. I don't know what's going on in your life, but there's nothing too hard for Him," the woman advised.

"God doesn't care about me," Angelica lamented, choking on her tears.

"God loves you, baby. He will give you the strength to persevere when Satan puts his stumbling blocks in your path. The three of us can go together," the woman in the hat encouraged her.

"You don't know me. Why do you care?" Angelica snapped, glancing up at the stranger through her tears.

"Because of God's love, that's why I care."

As the woman in the hat had promised, the three of them walked together down the aisle of the church. Both Marissa and their new elderly friend held on to Angelica's arms to keep her steady.

Chapter Thirty

Jasion spotted Angelica from the pulpit. Stunned, he rushed down the side stairs that lead to the altar and pressed his way through the crowd to her. He couldn't believe that he hadn't noticed her until now. His heart leaped with joy. His mind raced as to what could have possibly compelled her to come to church.

"Angelica! Angelica!" he cried out as he reached out for her through the crowd of people. She appeared fragile and weak when he finally approached her. "I'm so happy to see you. Come with me. I knew something was wrong. I sensed it the day you first entered my office. You put up this wall to protect your heart. Allow God to free you, Angelica. He can do it. He can make you whole again."

Jasion signaled the church intercessors to come and assist him. Marissa and the woman in the hat followed closely behind. They positioned themselves around Angelica and Jasion in a prayer circle. He prayed that God would remove the demonic forces that held Angelica in bondage.

She cried in Jasion's arms as the prayer warriors surrounded them, calling out the demonic spirits. "Where was God, when my mother abused me as a child? If God loves me, why did He turn His back on me when I needed Him the most? I was a little girl, left all alone with no one to love or protect me."

Jasion continued to pray as Angelica voiced her complaints.

"Why did God leave me to suffer all alone? I was a good girl. I didn't hurt anybody. Why?" Angelica screamed out in anguish. Exhausted from emptying herself, she collapsed into Jasion's arms.

"God never left you, Angelica. He was there all the time, protecting you through your abuse. Sometimes we don't understand why God allows things to happen to us, but there is a reason. God has placed in you a gift that will help others through their tragedies. There's some child, woman, or man who need to hear your testimony." Jasion said, lifting her chin. "Release the hatred and pain, Angelica. Leave it here at the altar. Stop giving the devil victory over your life." Jasion placed his hand on her forehead and prayed. "This day, I command you, Satan to loosen your hold on God's daughter. She doesn't belong to you. And Father, breathe Your healing power into her right now. Show Yourself mightily into Your child's life. Manifest Yourself, Lord, that Angelica may know that You are real and You alone are God."

Jasion prayed with power and authority from on High. He proceeded to anoint Angelica's head with oil. After praying for her deliverance, he held her close in his arms as she surrendered to the power of the Holy Spirit.

Chapter Thirty One

Three Months Later

Angelica had been attending Bountiful Blessing Ministry regularly since her spiritual awakening. Jasion, along with his pastor, had been instrumental in teaching her how to forgive her mother as well as forgiving herself. After renewing her faith, she decided to make the dreaded, overdue trip back to her childhood hometown, Augusta, Louisiana. For months, Angelica's younger sister, Alycee, had begged her to visit their dying mother before it was too late. Now, with the support of Jasion and Marissa, she had the courage to face those demons she'd left behind more than fifteen years ago.

Due to an explosion at one of Marissa's family oil refineries, she was unable to make the trip. Regarding herself as the queen of matchmakers, she thought Jasion would be the perfect traveling companion in her absence, and Angelica couldn't have agreed more. She'd fallen head over heels in love with him.

Angelica didn't know what to expect once she arrived in Augusta. The memories of a twelve-year-old girl, dodging her mother's power-packed blows, raced through her mind.

She shrugged at the thought. Gladys had been everything but kind to her. Thanks to Marissa, Jasion, and her new church family at BBM, she'd learned what loving someone unconditionally meant. Angelica knew it wasn't going to be easy, but she had to love her mother in order to move forward in her life.

"Thank you for accompanying me, Jasion," Angelica said, hopping into the passenger's seat of the Jeep Grand Cherokee he'd rented for the trip. His BMW didn't stand a chance against the badly, damaged roads in Augusta. Even as a young girl, she remembered the smaller towns were the last to receive funding for repairs on their country roads.

"My pleasure," he smiled, rushing around the SUV to close her door. "Besides, I get the chance to visit my family who lives in the neighboring town.

"I don't think I could have done this alone."

With the investigation going nowhere, Jasion surprised Angelica, showing up on her doorstep to deliver the good news about his taking a two-week vacation from Spitzer Financial Firm. Acting on impulse, she leaped into his arms with joy. Mr. Nate's threats didn't seem to faze Jasion when he held her in his arms, sprinkling kisses all over her face.

Now heading four hundred miles south to the place Angelica had once called a child's worst nightmare, she began to fear the unknown. Gazing out of the window at nothing in particular, her stomach twisted into knots. She tried putting on a brave front for Jasion, but inside, her nerves were getting the best of her. The more Angelica kept telling herself that she could do it, the more she kept hearing Gladys' scolding voice, shouting, *"You're weak. You're nothing. God doesn't listen to reprobates."*

"You're awfully quiet," Jasion said, taking one of his hands off the steering wheel and laid it across hers.

"What did you say?" she asked, turning from the window to meet his warm and engaging smile.

"What are you thinking about?"

"Nothing important, I'm just admiring the bed of flowers growing alongside the interstate." Angelica didn't want to ruin things, so she withheld the truth. How could she tell him that she was afraid to face her demons? Maybe the trip had been a bad idea. What would she say to Gladys? How would she approach her abusive mother after years of estrangement? Years she didn't regret. All those questions seemed to filter through Angelica's cluttered mind. Walking up to Gladys, giving her a big hug and kiss would feel awkward. They had never had that type of mother-daughter relationship. Angelica knew

Gladys preferred to roll over and die before showing any type of affection toward her.

"You've been fidgeting with your hands for the longest."

"You need to watch the road, Mister," she playfully scolded. "And not me."

"If you weren't so beautiful, I could," he replied, easing over into the right-hand lane of the highway. "You're a distraction. Now, what do you have to say about that?" He caressed her cheeks.

"You're nuts, Mr. McCoy," she laughed. His affectionate gestures helped to ease her fears. "That's what I have to say about that. In the meantime, please keep both eyes on the road. I do want to make it to our destination in one piece."

After driving for what seemed like an eternity, they pulled into the first eatery they spotted along the highway — Big Mama's Burger Pub. The two climbed out of the SUV, stretched their arms and legs, and then went inside. They claimed a booth near a jukebox located in the back and then placed their orders. Pictures of past and present country singers lined the freshly painted walls. Checkered tablecloths draped the tables, giving it that down-home, southern appeal.

"This is a cozy little place," Jasion said, observing the place from his seat.

"Looks can be deceiving. I wasn't expecting it to be so sanitary inside."

"I know," he whispered after one of the busboys passed their table. "I'm not trying to change the subject, but we have officially dated for three months, and there are still some things I don't know about you." His playful mood had taken on a more serious tone.

"Like what?" she asked, carefully, knowing full well what he was referring to. Angelica didn't want to discuss every detail of her childhood with Jasion, at least not yet. Each time he'd pressed for information, she'd clammed up. Talking about it just opened up old wounds.

"I want to know the unedited version of what happened to you." Grabbing her hand from the table, he kissed the inside of her palm.

I knew it. Why can't he just drop it? He has to keep pressing and pressing. I'm not ready to share. And when I am, I'll be careful not to mention my real name; a name that has brought me so much pain and unhappiness. "I really don't want to talk about it, Jasion. The memories are just too painful."

"I want to know," he demanded, furrowing his brows. Still holding her hand, he sought her gaze with his pleading, brown eyes. "I'm in love with you, and I plan to learn all there is to know about you."

"Wow." She dropped her head, stunned at how easily Jasion poured out his heart, rendering her speechless. Afraid to admit her feelings, she avoided eye contact, but Jasion, being the man he was, lifted her face and stroked her cheeks with the back of his hand. His touch made her drunk with desire. She needed time to process their relationship to be sure that she wasn't confusing her physical yearnings for love.

"So all you have to say is wow?" He held her hand to his clean-shaven cheeks. "Do you have any feelings for me, Angelica?"

How was she going to squirm her way out of this one? Angelica did love him. Jasion had been the first man in years, who had made her feel alive, but was it enough? So, she answered his question with a question. "Jasion, why do you love me?"

"The first day you walked into my office, you took my breath away," he confessed. "God revealed to me in a dream that night not to let you get away. At first, I thought surely He couldn't be referring to you."

She gasped.

"You were rude," he smiled, toying with her fingers. "You had this wall built up around you that seemed impossible to break through. I thought that maybe I'd heard God wrong. As each day passed, I began to see the real you. Underneath your tough layers, is a warm, caring, gentle soul that needs to be loved."

Angelica's eyes welled with tears. How could she not love this man? She didn't want to withhold her feelings from this passionate soul any longer. But when she tried expressing her feelings, the words were caught in her throat.

"I don't want to rush into anything too soon, Jasion."

His chest deflated, disappointed by her admission.

Angelica just couldn't express herself the way he had. She wasn't as open with her feelings as he.

"I understand," he said, deadpan. "It's no fun being in love alone. I've been down that road before, and I don't want to end up there again."

"So have I." Her words had hurt him; she could see it in his eyes. "I'm sorry, Jasion."

He cleared his throat, released her hands from his, sat back in his chair, and said, "I still would like to know what happened to you as a child, Angelica."

Dredging up the past took every ounce of her strength. The incidents surrounding her abusive childhood left scars to last a lifetime. As Angelica tried to figure out how to start her story, Jasion sat with his arms folded, anxiously waiting. She cleared her throat, regained her composure, and shared the vivid details of her abuse. Jasion flinched each time she spoke of the different beatings. Taking a deep breath, she rehashed how Gladys had fingered her private parts for proof that she wasn't having sex. Angelica dropped her face into the palms of her hands, ashamed to look at the man in front of her. *What will Jasion think of me after he hears every sordid detail of my dysfunctional life?*

Before she realized it, Jasion had left his seat and sat next to her. His touched seemed to calm the raging inferno inside her. Her mother had really done a number on her. How could she love anyone, especially the man next to her, when she hated herself? Gladys' disapproving words about her physical appearance continued to replay in her head. What mother would call their child a worthless, black whore?

Stroking his strong masculine hand against her wet cheeks, he leaned in to kiss her forehead.

She felt undeserving of such a man as he. No matter how gruesome the details were, he continued to listen. The men in her past ignored her pain, telling her that she needed to get over it. Her abuse and what she'd gone through meant nothing to them, but the man seated next to her wasn't ashamed to cry, to laugh, or to bare his soul. She wanted to love him and give him her heart, but fear stood in the way. Fear that he would leave her as the others had after learning about her deep emotional issues.

Chapter Thirty Two

Animals treat their young better than Angelica's mother treated her, Jasion thought, pulling onto the dirt road that led to his aunt and uncle's farm.

She'd laid a doozy on him back at the Burger Pub with her tales of abuse. Thinking about it sent chills through his body. Why no one had ever bothered to report the crime to Child Protective Services baffled him. The way he saw it, the neighbors who'd kept quiet about the abuse were just as guilty as Angelica's mother.

The similarities between Angelica and Fayth's childhoods were unbelievable. Jasion recalled how he had watched powerless, as Fayth's mother had struck her in the face and then dragged her away. The kiss he and Fayth had almost shared had caused her mother to go berserk. Jasion wondered *had she also suffered the same abuse as Angelica?*

He made a left turn onto a gravel road, passing a sign that bore his family's name. "I can't wait to see my aunt and uncle," Jasion rejoiced, smiling from ear to ear. "Finally, I get a chance to eat some real down home cooking. Uncle Bill tried teaching my sister and me how to ring a chicken's neck and prepare it for dinner."

"HE WHAT?" Angelica shouted with a horrified look. "Oh, my goodness, I would die if I had to kill what I ate."

"Shoots, girl, that's som' good eatin'," he teased, in a southern drawl while sucking his teeth.

"I don't think so." She cut her eyes at him from the passenger seat. "Please tell me that we're not killing our own dinner tonight?"

He loved the way she squinted her big, brown eyes at him at the thought of having to kill her dinner. "I won't let you get those pretty little hands bloody."

"Yuck." She shook her head, frowning. "Thanks, I appreciate that."

Jasion continued up the bumpy makeshift road leading to their destination. Thankful he'd driven the SUV, instead of his car.

The woman accompanying him was the best part of the trip. Although she had many issues to work through, her story made him love her even more. God had warned him that his future wife would come to him broken. Now he had to be patient and help her through the healing process. He had to place his macho ego on the back burner for now. Pressing her with more questions that she wasn't ready to answer might push her away. He knew Angelica cared for him, but he had to wait until she was willing to admit it. He regretted having been short-tempered with her back at the Burger Pub. His bruised ego had gotten in the way when she didn't tell him that she loved him back.

As the bumpy road bounced them up and down in their seats, Jasion said, "Angelica, you're going to love my aunt and uncle. They are two of the most loving people you'll ever meet. Now don't get me wrong. They've had their share of problems in their younger days, but thankfully, they worked through them. Couples today just don't do that anymore. Many feel that it's easier to walk away from a troubled marriage than try and iron out the rough spots." He shot a quick glance in her direction.

"They sound like a cute couple," Angelica added. "I don't mean to be nosey, but what happened that almost broke them up?"

"Uh," he hesitated. Jasion wasn't quite sure if he should discuss his aunt and uncle's personal business. After some serious thought, he decided to answer her question since he and Angelica appeared to be slowly moving past the friendship stage. "Some woman at a nightclub over in Augusta came on to him. One night, my aunt and uncle got into a big argument. About what, I don't know. My uncle stormed out of the house, speeding off into the wee hours of the night, to who knows where. Uncle Bill never came home, which made my aunt to be worried. She thought that something terrible had happened to him. The next day, one of her gossiping friends called to inform her that my uncle was seen leaving a bar with some strange woman. Sure enough, Aunt Claire learned he'd spent the night in a motel with her."

"That's so sad. I know it broke your aunt's heart. It would have mine," Angelica responded.

"Yeah, it was sad," he agreed, shaking his head. "Enough of that gloom and doom. They're together and have been happily married for over forty-five years. That's all that matters now."

"You're right."

Pulling into his family's farm, Jasion could see his aunt and uncle wobbling off the front porch. He'd informed them that he and Angelica would arrive before dark. Excitement wasn't the word he'd use to describe how he felt. It had been a while since his last visit. He'd missed several family reunions because of work, but he'd promised himself that when the dust settled after the investigation, he was going to make time for his loved ones — especially for the woman who'd stolen his heart. Most definitely, something had to change.

He wasn't going to miss out on love, twice. Every summer he visited his aunt and uncle, Jasion would beg them to drive him over to Augusta. He searched high and low for the girl he'd met at the funeral. He had continued to do so each summer until he'd turned eighteen and left for college.

Jasion couldn't get out of the vehicle fast enough. Rushing around the car, he opened Angelica's door like an excited, little boy going to the county fair for the very first time.

"Hey, boy, come give yo' old uncle a hug," Bill said, chuckling with his pipe clutched in his trembling hand.

Some things never changed. Jasion's uncle still wore the same denim overalls with a red flannel shirt. His hair had grayed since Jason's last visit. Surrounding his once slim waistline was a potbelly.

"Oh, son, yhur so tall and handsome. Turn around, let me get a good look at yhu," Claire said, spinning Jasion around. "We-ee-ave missed yhu somethin' awful aroun' hea'. I can't believe that yhu're hea'."

Crow's feet were etched outside her twinkling eyes as they began to well up with tears.

"I missed y'all, too." Jasion reached behind him, pulling Angelica to his side. "I have someone special that I want you two to meet."

The elderly couple looked Angelica from head to toe, and then gave her a big bear hug and hearty welcome.

"Nice to meet you, Mr. and Mrs. McCoy," Angelica greeted, shyly. "Jasion has told me so much about you both."

"Youn' lady, call me Aunt Claire. No need for the for-ma-la-tees roun' hea'," Claire sang, opening her arms to embrace Angelica again. "Chile, yhu looks familiar. Is yo' folks from aroun' these parts?"

"Now Claire, don't go thinkin' yhu know everybody." Bill chimed in before Angelica could answer. "Come on, yhu youn' whippersnappers, let's grab ya'lls bags and go inside befo' these mo-squi-toes eat us alive."

"I hear you, Unck. It's been a while since I last visited, and I can't wait to dig into some of Aunt Claire's mustard greens and homemade cornbread. My mouth has been watering for her vittles since we started out on this trip," Jasion said, rubbing his growling stomach.

"This chile looks like she can use som' meat on her bones. If yhu stay aroun' hea' a spell, I'll have yhu fattened up in no time," Claire teased, slapping her thigh as she broke into laughter.

Later that evening, Jasion and Angelica headed outside for some alone time. He loved reminiscing about the past with his aunt and uncle, but he hadn't spent much time with Angelica since they'd arrived. The two sat on the front porch before hopping in Jasion's SUV. Like a young schoolboy, he wanted to show Angelica all his favorite hangouts and where he'd spent most of his days in Claysville. The town was small, but he loved the down home feel. Country life seemed more simple and serene. Quite the opposite when it comes to city life, where people were always in a rush to go nowhere fast.

Dusk began to settle as they made their way back to the farm. "So, how do you feel being so close to home?" He held her hand in his.

"Strange," Angelica admitted, taking in deep breaths of the country air. "I swore never to return to Augusta.

Jasion helped her out of the vehicle and led her to the backyard of his aunt and uncle's home. With his arm around her narrow shoulders, he couldn't wait to show her his favorite tree, where he had spent most of his lazy days during the summer dreaming about Fayth. But common sense told him to keep that bit of information to himself. Although he and Fayth spent only two weeks together, they were the most memorable weeks of his life.

"I'm proud of you, Angelica. You've made great steps in the past three months," Jasion complimented, kissing the top of her head. He then pulled her down onto the blanket underneath the tree where he secretly had his aunt to prepare some snacks they will eat when they returned from sightseeing. The surprise on Angelica's face was worth it.

With her hands covering her mouth, she was speechless at his romantic deed.

"Sweets for my sweet."

His aunt had prepared strawberries dipped in chocolate, cheese and crackers, freshly squeezed lemonade, and handpicked blueberries. Jasion grabbed up one of the strawberries, guiding it to Angelica's kissable, glossed lips, before taking a bite out of it himself.

"Mmm mmm, they're delicious," she moaned, her eyes rolling back in her head.

"Yes, it is. I've been living in the city far too long. I'd forgotten how good fresh grown fruits taste," he stated, wiping both their mouths with a napkin.

"A girl could really get used to this," she smiled.

"Angelica, I pray in time, you'll learn to trust me. I'm not the enemy," he said, tapping the bridge of her nose with his finger. "I will never do anything intentionally to hurt you."

"I know you're not the enemy, Jasion." She diverted her attention elsewhere to keep from looking at him.

With the tip of his finger, Jasion guided her face back to him, commanding her full attention. He knew he'd made her uncomfortable, but he wasn't her enemy.

His only desire was to love her. Jasion wasn't like the other men in her past, and he was determined to prove it. He'd never felt so complete until the woman in front him stumbled into his life. He had never wanted a woman as much as he did her. True, he loved Fayth and still did, but she had become a fading memory. Thoughts of Fayth had caused him so much heartache, and he was ready to set her free. Angelica had now become the woman he wanted in his life, permanently, and he would stop at nothing until he claimed her heart, no matter how long it took.

"You know what I called this tree as a boy?"

"No, what?" she inquired.

"My thinking tree." Lying on his side, Jasion rested his head on the palm of his hand. "When something was bothering me, I would come here and sort out my problems."

"Did it work? I mean, were you able to get the answer to your problems?"

"Sometimes, yes. Sometimes, no," he replied, reaching for her hand to lower her down beside him.

His aunt and uncle's backyard brought back many forgotten memories. The tree house his uncle had built for him and his cousins was still standing. The swing, made out of Cypress wood, still hung in the same spot. The backyard seemed untouched by time.

He and Angelica decided to lie on their backs. Like little kids, they tried guessing what each cloud resembled. Jasion was grateful for their time together. Back in Port City, things were so hectic that the two hardly had time to breath.

"Of all the places for a young boy to hang out, why under a tree?" she asked, gazing at the sky.

"Life," he answered. He didn't want to go into the details of his first love. One lesson his father had taught him as a young man was, never discuss a past girlfriend with the present one.

"Life," she paused, untangling the necklace caught in the nape of her neck. "You were a kid. What did you know about life?"

"Enough about my issues," Jasion laughed. "Why do you keep that chain buried under your shirt? It must be very special?" He prayed it wasn't from a past lover. A love she couldn't get out of her system. The last thing he wanted to do was compete with the memory of an old boyfriend.

"It's nothing." She sat up.

"It must have some type of sentimental value because you wear it all the time."

"This necklace is the only good thing that came from my childhood," she said with her hand clutched to her neck.

Jasion rose up beside her. Without permission, he reached around her neck, in an attempt to take a peek. Before he could do so, Angelica slapped his hand away, shot off the blanket and stormed into the house.

Chapter Thirty Three

Strong arms wrapped themselves around Angelica's waist. Yesterday, she'd lost her cool in the backyard with Jasion when he tried peeking at her necklace. It was the only tangible reminder of JC. How could she explain the reason for wearing an old boyfriend's necklace? Her reaction now seemed a little hasty by slapping his hand away, but he'd caught her off guard.

The smell of his masculine scent tickled her nostrils as he moved in closer behind her. Having him so near caused her hair to stand on end. She wanted him, but being the gentleman he was; she knew he wouldn't act on any physical impulses. Jasion thought with his head. When things seemed to get hot and heated between them, he'd be the first to step on the brakes. In the meantime, she just hoped their relationship would continue to flourish because the physical torture was proving harder to resist.

"Are you still mad at me, beautiful?" Jasion asked, peppering her with kisses.

Pursing her lips, she responded, "I can't stay mad at you. I'm sorry I overreacted."

Jasion spun Angelica around, lavishing her with more kisses of endearment. "I'm glad because my aunt and uncle are preparing a good ole' fashioned barbecue today. They have invited a few close relatives, and I can't enjoy myself, knowing that you're still angry."

"Rest your nerves, silly boy. All is well." Surprising even herself, Angelica did something she'd never done since dating him. She made the first move. Pulling his broad shoulders down to her, she wrapped her arms around his neck and devoured Jasion's lips. When they finally came up for air, he gave her a surprised look. Speaking just above a whisper, she confessed, "You don't have to wonder about my feelings for you any longer. I love you too, Mr. McCoy."

*****

Jasion was on cloud nine. With Angelica planting the kiss of a lifetime on him this morning, he thought his day couldn't get any better. Confessing her love for him nearly made his heart leaped from his chest with joy. If she'd told him her feelings back at the Burger Pub, he would have proposed marriage to her on the spot. After the family barbecue, he'd planned to do just that.

"Hey, boy, watch them steaks befo' yhu burn'em up," Uncle Bill yelled, shaking his finger in Jasion's direction. "Yhu betta' get yhur head out of them clouds befo' yhu mess up som' good eatin'."

The menfolks in the backyard laughed. It was a known fact among Jasion's family that Uncle Bill didn't play when it came to the meat he butchered.

"Oh, shoots," Jasion blurted, jumping back as the flames roared from the grease dripping off the steaks. The thought of him proposing to Angelica caused him to lose focus on the present task. He quickly took the cooking tongs, flipping the steaks over. "Sorry, Unck, my mind was someplace else."

"Well, yhu betta get it back on tendin' this hea' meat befo' I make yhu go out thera' and slaughter another one of them cows."

By now, the malefolks were laughing hysterically. If Jasion couldn't stomach wringing a chicken's neck, he sure couldn't handle slaughtering a cow.

Aunt Claire stuck her head out of the screen door. "Whut's all that key-mo-tion out hea'?" Do y'all need us women to come out thera' and keep an eye out on ya'll?" she asked, yelling with her hand propped on her round hip. "Lawd, Bill, why yhu got that chile on that grill, yhu know the boy's mind cans't never stay focus on more than one thang at a time

Jasion lifted his head from tending the meat, glancing at his aunt. "Thanks, Aunt Claire, for the vote of confidence," he replied. He then turned and rolled his eyes at the menfolks who were laughing at the tongue-lashing he was receiving from his aunt and uncle about his cooking.

"Oh, baby, yhurs welcume, jest don't burn the meat, yhu hea'."

"I'ma stand by him, babe, so's if he starts to daydreamin' ugin', I'ma be close enough to slap him back into reality," Uncle Bill winked at his wife, and then she quickly disappeared inside. "Unck, now tell me you don't mean that," Jasion groaned, turning his attention back to the grill. "I see I'm still the butt of everybody's jokes around here. Some things never change. You would think as long as I've been gone, seems like the two of you would have found someone else to pick on. Little do you know; I've become a great cook since living on my own."

"Boy, stop yo' fibbin', yhur mama says yhu over at her house lookin' for somthin' to eat at least three days out of the week," Uncle Bill stated.

"Humph. We'll be the judge of that when dinner is served," a male relative yelled from the card table.

"Oh, your steak will be fed to Unck's old bloodhound, Duke, "Jasion hollered back.

"Man, that old bloodhound won't sniff your steaks, let alone eat it," the relative joked.

"Keep talking, cuz," Jasion playfully warned, shaking his cooking tongs at the loudmouthed man.

He'd taken wisecrack after wisecrack about his grilling skills, but he enjoyed every minute of it. Jasion didn't realize how much he'd missed his family until now. The trash talking, cookouts, and outdoor activities were a part of their summer traditions. The only people missing from the festivities were his two cousins, Philip and Terry Johnson. They were like the brothers he'd never had. The three became inseparable as kids. They referred to themselves by their first and last initials. JM for Jasion McCoy didn't click the way PJ and TJ had. So, Jasion took the letter from his middle name — Christopher. To this day, his cousins refer to him as JC.

Chapter Thirty Four

The women resembled worker bees, buzzing around the kitchen, preparing side dishes for the steaks the men had grilled. Aunt Claire —The Queen Bee — gave the orders, and the women carried them out. Angelica wasn't accustomed to a kitchen full of women scurrying in all directions. It was a bit daunting. Aunt Claire probably sensed her uneasiness and wobbled over to where she stood.

"Angelica, do yhu know yhur way aroun' the kitchen, suga'? Cus yhu look a bit lost."

"Confused is more like it," she answered, peeling the potatoes. "I'm not used to being around so many people. I mean, seeing a family come together without anyone getting offended when you tell them what to do. I envy that."

"Aw, Suga', wee-ee-ave do this all the time. Sit for a spell," Aunt Claire suggested, patting the stool next to her. "Do yhu have any kinfolks nearby? I don't recall yhu sayin,' when I asked yesterdee'."

"Not here in Claysville." Angelica wiped her damped hands on the apron hugging her waist.

"Where yhu from then? When Jasion called to say he was drivin' down for a visit, he mentioned somthin' 'bout Augusta."

"I was born and raised in Augusta, Louisiana, just forty miles from here."

"Well, hush yhur mouth, chile," Aunt Claire shouted, slapping a hand against her soiled apron. "I might know som' of yhur folks. Bill and me go thera' som' weekends to visit friends."

Before the two women could finish their conversation, Jasion and the rest of the men came crashing through the back door with cooked meat in tow. Aunt Claire rose from the stool and kindly pointed them in the direction of the dining room.

"It never fails." One of the women entering the kitchen shouted. "Y'all, look who's driving up at the last minute, Philip and Terry. If you ask me, I believe they planned this. Them boys seem to know the exact time when dinner is served."

Another woman chimed in, "no way. See, that ain't right." She shook her head in a friendly protest.

"Go help them." Aunt Claire ordered the women, craning her neck toward the kitchen window. "Looks like they've got som' food in they's hands."

Aunt Claire turned her attention back to Angelica, signaling for her to help finish setting out the food. Angelica was grateful for the gesture, seeing as she didn't know anyone. She wasn't accustomed to being at a family gathering.

"Angelica, help me place the rest of the food over thera' on the tables while the others catch up on old times in the living room."

"Sure," Angelica said, relieved

"Suga', I see my nephew is quite smitten with yhu." I believe it's just a matter of time befo' he pops the big question."

Aunt Claire gave her a knowing wink, placing the silverware next to each plate.

"I don't know," she said, doubtfully.

"Chile, what don't yhu know? Yhu luv him, don't yhu'?" she asked. "I know he luvs yhu, just by the way he keeps sneakin' peaks at yhu when he thinks no one is lookin'. He's a good boy. Any woman that snags him gots herself somthin'."

"Yes, he is sweet and such a gentleman, but—"

"But whut?" Aunt Claire interrupted, looking at Angelica over the rim of her eyeglasses.

"It's complicated. Too complicated to discuss at the moment."

"Nuff said. I won't pry into yhur business." When they finished setting the tables, the two headed back into the kitchen to get the rest of the food. "Yhu did say yhu were from Augusta, right? Whut's yhu folks' name?"

"My dad passed away when I was twelve. His name was Maurice, and my mother's name is Gladys."

"Them names do seem to ring a bell. Whut's they last name?" Aunt Claire inquired, squinting suspiciously at her.

Angelica didn't like the turn of the conversation. Something told her to stop, but she continued. Her parents' names rolled off her tongue. "Maurice and Gladys Hope," Angelica said, hesitantly.

Aunt Claire eyes grew the size of saucers.

Angelica wished the older women would drop the subject, but she questioned her further.

"The couple I knew had two daughters. Their names were Fayth and Alycee."

Aunt Claire turned, and stared up at Angelica. "Lawd, I hope that hussy Gladys ain't your momma. She'd darn neared ruined my marriage."

The elderly woman's breathing had sped up. Jasion would never forgive her if she caused his beloved aunt to die of cardiac arrest. Nervously, she answered, "Ye-ss-ss, ma'am. I'm Fayth. Fayth Angelica Hope." Angelica squeezed her eyes shut, so she couldn't see what was about to come next.

Her scandalous mother had been the woman that nearly destroyed this sweet couple's marriage. Angelica didn't know whether to run or beg for mercy. Whatever the case, Aunt Claire was getting ready to lower the boom on her.

"Oh Lawd," Aunt Claire said, clutching her chest. "Look, I'ma say this as Christianfied as I can. I pray yhur not tryin' to run som' kinda sick game on my nephew?"

"No, I would never do anything to hurt Jasion. I love—," she stopped as tears formed in the corner of her eyes. "I love him, Aunt Claire. Whatever Gladys did to you have nothing to do with me. I haven't seen that woman since I was sixteen-years-old. Jasion and I are headed to Augusta because she's dying."

Angelica couldn't get her words out fast enough. She thought for sure when Jasion discovered that her mother almost destroyed his aunt and uncle's marriage, he would toss her out of their house on her behind.

She explained her abusive childhood and the importance of returning to Augusta to Aunt Claire. Both women sobbed bitterly, and then Aunt Claire held Angelica like a wounded child in her arms.

Jasion barged into the kitchen. "What's taking the two of you so..." Jasion's words trailed off when he found the women crying. Confused, he asked, "why are you two crying?"

"JC." A male voice yelled from the other room, "can we come in now? We're starving."

Angelica's head popped up from Aunt Claire's bosom. *Are my ears playing tricks on me?*

A tall, slender, and handsome young man, close to Jasion's age stepped into the kitchen. "Fayth, Fayth Hope. Is it really you? I haven't seen you since the eleventh grade. Everyone at school wondered what happened to you. It was as if you'd vanished into thin air."

"Who did you just call her, Philip?" Jasion asked, rushing toward Angelica and his aunt.

"Fayth," Philip responded, confused. "Why? What's wrong?" He shrugged his shoulders, tossing his hands in the air.

"Lord, is my mentally challenged cousin saying what I think he's saying?" Jasion nervously joked, praying this wasn't another one of Philip's sick pranks.

"JC. Man, are you all right? I thought she was your girl? Why are you looking at her as if it's your first time seeing her?" Philip asked, looking back and forth between the two.

Jasion never acknowledged his cousin's questions. He kept his focus on Angelica. He grabbed her up in his arms, stared into her eyes, and burst into tears. Jasion thought he was dreaming. All this time, the girl he'd fanaticized about for years had been with him all this time. He prayed that God wasn't playing some cruel joke on him and that this was indeed his Fayth standing in front of him.

"Are you JC?" Angelica finally asked. "Are you really the JC that I met at my father's funeral? Do you know how long I've waited for you to come and rescue me?" she cried, pounding on his chest as hard as she could.

He allowed her to use his body as her punching bag until she clasped into his arms from exhaustion.

"Is this yhur Fayth, Son?" Aunt Claire asked. "The girl yhu came searchin' fo' every summa'?"

"Yes. Yes, ma'am." He cried, trying hard to keep his composure. "God kept reassuring me that Fayth was near, but it just didn't make sense to me because I was falling in love with Angelica," Jasion explained, overcome with emotions. "Aunt Claire, she was with me all this time." Jasion gulped, wiping the tears of joy and disbelief from his face. "She was here all the time."

His aunt placed her arms around Angelica and Jasion, bowed her head, prayed and thanked God for the miracle He'd just performed. Then, her supplication began to take a more troubling turn. "Lawd, thera' be days of unrest ahead for this hea' youn' couple. They will be tried and tested by the evil one yhu call, Sa-ton. Please, Lawd, help them both to stand against his trickery."

Jasion pried open one eye and peeked down at the top of his aunt's head. His heart sank at her disturbing revelation. He'd hoped for a happy ending for him and Angelica, but with Aunt Claire announcing troubled days ahead for them, he closed his eye, adding a small petition of his own for strength and guidance.

Chapter Thirty Five

Unable to sleep, Jasion laid cramped in the same small bunk bed he'd slept in so many nights as a young boy at his aunt and uncle's home. The room where he'd spent each summer daydreaming about Fayth had now begun to close in on him. With his aunt and uncle policing the hallway, breaking into Fort Knox would have been easier than slipping into the room Fayth now occupied. The elderly couple went by the "Good Book," no hanky-panky under their roof before marriage, not that Jasion would ever consider doing such a thing.

After discovering that Angelica was Fayth, the girl he'd fallen in love with more than fifteen years ago, he couldn't sleep a wink. The reality of it still hadn't sunk in. Knowing she was just a few feet away made the mental agony that much worse.

With temptation sleeping in the room across the hall, Jasion knew being alone with his soul mate would put his promise to remain celibate in jeopardy. Thoughts of them being together intimately played repeatedly in his head. The pressure of wanting her mounted. To release the tension, he punched the pillow next to him. Having her so near and not being able to do anything about it agitated him to no end. How would he handle his raging hormones once he returned to Port City, with no chaperone? "Lord, have mercy," he whispered as beads of sweat trickled down the sides of his face

A mixture of excitement and anger tugged at Jasion's emotions. He worried that things might change once they arrived back home. Would he and Angelica's happy reunion survive the financial scandal at Spitzer Financial Firm? One thing he knew for certain, tomorrow, before daybreak, he'd propose marriage to his teenage love. The engagement would be short. He didn't want to run the risk of breaking his vow of abstinence.

The thought of tossing his blanket aside and going to her kept weighing heavily on his mind, but in doing so, he'd have to face the wrath of his aunt. No one broke Aunt Claire's house rules, not even her favorite nephew.

A grin stretched from ear to ear as he reflected on how blessed he was. God had fulfilled His promise. Not a day had passed without him thinking about Fayth. The woman he'd languished over for years. *Only a smooth God could pull off a move like this one*, Jasion thought, lying on his back, hands resting behind his head.

His family shared his enthusiasm. Questions flew from every corner of the room earlier today as he and Angelica tried making sense of it all. Their discovery tugged at every emotion. The girl he'd talked about incessantly as a young boy had materialized. He understood his family's inquiries and concerns, but it left little time for him and Angelica to process their miraculous reunion. His aunt followed them from room to room, like an over-protective parent who was afraid to leave two teenagers full of raging hormones alone.

She knew of his obsession to find Fayth, but never in a million years would he betray her trust by being intimate with Fayth under her roof, not if he wanted to live.

It amazed Jasion how God had kept them close. He made a mental note to thank his Cousin Philip, who'd been one of Fayth's classmates from high school. Because of him, God's master plan for reuniting them had come to pass. He would be indebted to Philip for the rest of his life.

Despite their joyous celebration, his aunt's haunting prayer resurfaced. It put a damper on his and Angelica's joyous reunion. With happiness within his grasp, her prophesy of trouble seemed to snatch it away. Turning on his side, he called it a night, but before he could, his cellphone hummed on the nightstand. The bright light from the device lit up the pitch-black room. He peeked at the screen. It displayed a Port City's area code. Immediately, he shot straight up in bed. An uneasy feeling erupted in his stomach. He didn't recognize the number, but the Port City area code caused alarm. "Hello," Jasion answered, cautiously.

"Well... hello to you too, J." A female voice purred through the receiver. "I remember how you loved hearing my voice just before falling asleep. I missed you, Boo. I finally realized that you were the best thing that ever happened to me."

"Who is this?" Jasion asked, alarmed. He removed the phone from his ear and looked at it, hoping he was dreaming. *This can't be who I think it is.* He put the phone back to his ear. "Nicole?"

She squealed like a hyena in his ear, "babe, you remembered my voice."

Jasion rolled his eyes. Who wouldn't remember the woman who almost destroyed his reputation as a minister? Hearing her irritating voice made him nauseous. "What do you want, Nicole?" he asked, sternly.

"Why are you taking that tone with me, Boo? Aren't you happy to hear from me?"

Was she serious? Heck no, I'm not happy to hear from her. He'd never thought that he could ever feel this way about another human being, but she made his skin crawl. "Nicole, I'm getting engaged. Please do not call me again," he ordered.

"Who is she?" Nicole yelled through the telephone. "How can you be engaged to someone else when you're still engaged to me?"

"Engaged!" He yelled back into the receiver. *What is she up to?* Jasion reached over, turning on the lamp beside his bed. She had turned his sleepless night into a living nightmare. He didn't give her a chance to refute, he said, "Good night, Nicole." He clicked the end button on his cellphone, shaking his head in disbelief.

A sharp, throbbing pain caused Jasion's head to ache. His aunt's troubling prayer resounded in his head. Nicole didn't fight fair or take no for an answer, a lesson he'd learned all too well when she'd strolled into his pastor's office, accusing him of sexually assaulting her. Was she the storm heading his and Angelica's way?

Nicole calling at this time of the night meant only one thing, trouble, he suspected.

*****

After struggling for what seemed like hours to find a comfortable spot in an unfamiliar bed, Angelica finally drifted off to sleep. The surge of adrenaline from the shocking news that Jasion was the young boy, JC, whom she'd met at her father's funeral years ago kept her wide awake.

Since rededicating her life to Christ, the horrible dreams of her childhood had vanished, until now. But this one was different. It wasn't about her mother. She and Jasion were in danger. What she couldn't understand was, why? An enormous black cloud, in the form of a man's hand, appeared out of nowhere. And, an eerie voice sounded from every direction. She and Jasion trembled when it said, "your days are numbered at Spitzer Financial Firm. You stole what's rightfully mine, and now you all will pay."

"What have I stolen from you?" Angelica cried out in the dream, begging the hand not to destroy them. When she'd turned, Jasion had disappeared from beside her. He was now standing in the lobby of SFF. The black cloud, resembling a man's hand, pointed in Jasion's direction. Gunshots rang out, and Jasion collapsed to the floor as she stood by helplessly, screaming for help.

The banging on her bedroom door woke her from the nightmare. She found herself screaming and fighting the covers. The knocks mimicked the gunfire in her dreams. Finally wide awake, she surveyed her surroundings and scrambled to compose herself. She thought for sure, Jasion's aunt and uncle would think she was some sort of nutcase. "Yes!" she yelled, sweating profusely. Her heart continued to pound out of control from the ghoulish nightmare.

Jasion barged into her bedroom within seconds. "Are you all right? I heard screaming." He rushed to her aide.

Without saying a word, Angelica wrapped her arms around his neck. She clung to him for dear life. She didn't want to release him for fear he'd disappear as he had in her dream.

"Whut's goin' on in hea'?" Aunt Claire limped into the room, giving the two a suspicious look. "I could hear yhu screamin' all the way down the hall, chile."

Angelica removed her arms from around Jasion's neck.

Aunt Claire stared at them again, skeptically and gave them both a knowing look. "The two of yhu betta not be doin' whut I think yhu were doin'."

The two never acknowledged Aunt Claire's comment.

"Is it another one of those dreams?" Jasion asked, wiping the sweat from her face with his pajama sleeve. "Could you give us some privacy, Aunt Claire?" He turned and gave his aunt a pleading look. His aunt laid down the law when it came to her beliefs. She'd told them both that she didn't approve of a single man and woman closed up in a bedroom alone, but she gave in to his plea.

"Is yhu okay, chile?" Aunt Claire asked, giving them another once over.

"Yes, ma'am. I'm alright," Angelica said, embarrassed. "Aunt Claire, nothing is going on. I would never disrespect you or Uncle Bill in that way."

"Well, Ima go on downstairs and prepare yhu kids some breakfast befo' y'all leave for Augusta." She turned to leave with reservation and then limped out of the room.

"Are you sure you're okay, Angelica?" Jasion asked again.

"I'm fine. It was just one of those crazy dreams. Probably from something I ate last night." She faked a half-smile, but knew Jasion wasn't buying it.

"Well, don't scare me like that again," he said, brushing the stray hair from her face.

She smiled.

Before she had a chance to protest, Jasion lifted the tiny cross resting on her chest. "Is this what you were hiding from me the day of our picnic?"

She nodded her head, yes, as he tried to compose himself. His hands trailed around the tarnished cross.

"I gave you this necklace at your father's funeral." Tears began to form in both their eyes.

The lump in her throat rendered her speechless.

"If you hadn't run off when I tried to take a peek at it, we would have discovered each other sooner." He wiped the tears from his face with the palm of his hand while holding the necklace in the other.

Like a mute, she wanted to speak, but couldn't. The dream was disturbing. Seeing Jasion lying on the floor in a pool of blood had terrified her. For now, she thought it best to keep quiet about it. She didn't want to alarm him about the unsettling nightmare.

Chapter Thirty Six

Jasion strolled downstairs to his aunt and uncle's living room. He found Angelica staring out of the window, seemingly deep in thought. He tiptoed behind her, wrapping his arms around her waist and pulling her body against his. She flinched at his touch. No doubt, he'd caught her by surprise. "Is everything okay, Babe?" Jasion inquired, kissing the nape of her neck. Her body began to relax against his.

"Yes. Much better," she sighed. "Sorry, I scared you guys this morning. It's nothing to be concerned about."

"Anything that involves you concerns me," he said, turning her to face him. "You can talk to me about anything. Please don't shut me out. If you're going to be Mrs. McCoy, you're going to have to learn to confide in me."

"Wha...t?" she gasped, struggling to catch her breath.

"Did I stutter?" Jasion pulled out an Amethyst fourteen-karat white-gold engagement ring from his shirt pocket. He dropped to one knee. "Fayth Angelica Hope, will you do me the honor of becoming my wife, lover, friend, and mother of my unborn children?"

"Are you serious?" she asked, nearly hyperventilating. With both hands covering her mouth and tears in her eyes, she knelt in front of him, overcome with joy. "I have just one question to ask you," she replied, holding his face between the palms of her tiny hands.

"All I want to hear is yes," Jasion said, smiling impatiently.

"I'll give you my answer once you answer my question." Angelica intertwined her hands with his as they knelt in the middle of the living room floor.

"Okay, ask away." He untangled one of his hands from hers, brushing back a stray curl blocking the view of her secretive, brown eyes. He just hoped she wasn't trying to think of a way to let him down easily. He was a big boy, but he hadn't prepared himself for rejection, so he held his breath, anticipating her answer.

"How did you purchase such an exquisite ring so quickly?"

A gust of air exited his windpipes. "Whew." He held a hand over his heart. "Is that your question?"

"Yes," she said, innocently. Her misty, brown eyes blinked incessantly from the sunbeams shining through the windows. The angelic look she possessed at that moment, made him fall in love with her all over again. His heart was doing double flips in his chest when he thought of how blessed he was.

"I purchased it the day we left Port City. I had planned to ask you the day at the Burger Pub, but we both know how that turned out." He lifted her delicate hand to his lips and kissed the back of it. Then, his lips trailed their way up to her ring finger. Jasion raised his head and asked, "so, are you going to marry me, woman?"

"Yes, I will marry you," she sang with joy. "I will be honored to be Mrs. JC McCoy."

"Now that's music to my ears."

Jasion placed the ring on Angelica's finger. Thrilled, he stood, bringing her up with him and took control of her lips. Time seemed to stand still as the two stood in the middle of his aunt and uncle's living room, holding and loving on each other. He held on to Angelica with all his strength, just in case it was all a dream like the ones he'd had of her throughout the years, quickly fading when he'd awaken. All sorts of crazy thoughts entered Jasion's mind at that moment. Maybe his obsession with Fayth had finally taken hold of his ability to think rationally. That was how surreal things were for him at that moment.

The sound of ringing coming from Jasion's pocket caused them to come up for air. "I'm not going to answer that," he said in a weak voice. "We've been separated for fifteen years. Whoever is on the other end will just have to wait. You don't know how long I've waited to ask you to marry me," he whispered while nibbling on her earlobe.

"I've waited for you as well," she said with her arms stretched around his neck. "But seriously, you need to answer that. What if it's someone calling about the case?"

"You're right," he agreed, half-heartedly. He fished the phone from his pocket. "Hello."

"Who is she, Jasion? I need to know the woman who's trying to move in on my territory," Nicole screamed through the phone.

The sound of his ex-fiancée's voice snatched the rug of happiness from beneath his feet. "Let me take this call in the other room, Sweetheart." He placed a hand over the receiver to keep Nicole from hearing his conversation with Angelica. Giving her a reassuring wink and a kiss on the lips, Jasion prepared himself to listen to Nicole's foolishness. He hoped that by taking the call, he would convince her to stop harassing him. Jasion had gone from being on cloud nine to falling from grace in a matter of seconds.

"I told you it was business." Angelica wiped her lip gloss from his lips and flashed him a supportive smile. "Go on. I'll be waiting for you outside on the porch." She rubbed her hand gently across his freshly shaven face.

He wanted to disconnect the call and hold Angelica prisoner in his arms when she touched him, but he didn't want to raise any red flags. She might become suspicious as to why he was trying to dodge the person on the other end. After all, she was an investigative reporter. Carefully, he searched the hallway for his aunt and uncle's location and then strolled into the dining room for privacy. He wanted to kick himself for getting involved with Nicole. She was going to be a problem, and threatened to ruin everything he'd worked hard to achieve.

"What do you want, Nicole?" Jasion said through clenched teeth. "I told you to stop calling me."

"Not until you're back in my arms, J," she growled.

Nicole sounded more delusional than she had before. "I'm trying desperately not to hurt your feelings. But move on with your life. I have." Knowing Nicole the way he did, he knew she was persistent and wasn't going to stop until she got what she wanted.

"No. Never. Not after all the intimate moments we've shared," she said with venom in her voice.

"You can't just toss me away like a piece of trash; we're in this together. Remember?"

"Nicole, have you been drinking?" he asked, stunned at her remarks.

"No, for your information. I'm quite sober, darling."

The cockiness in her voice made him nervous.

"You'll be sorry after I'm done with you."

Silence was all Jasion heard. Nicole had hung up. The dining room chair offered support for his weak legs. Slipping his cellphone back into his pocket, he didn't know what to make out of Nicole's threatening words. The squeaking sound of the porch swing put a smile back on his worried face. When he entered the living room, he saw the love of his life through an open window, swinging back and forth with a glow that covered her soft, dark features. The thought of Nicole's tirade quickly vanished.

Before Jasion could join Angelica outside, his uncle came out of nowhere, startling him. Uncle Bill grabbed one of his arms. "Son, I need to have a word with yhu." The look of concern etched his worn face. By that time, Aunt Claire wobbled in behind him.

"What is it, Unck? You seem agitated." Jasion turned to face the elderly couple.

"Me and yhur aunt overheard yhur conversation back thera in the dinin' room," Uncle Bill frowned, shuffling his feet. "Yhur not foolin' aroun' on that thera boo-ti-ful gal outside. Is yhu?"

If looks could kill, he'd be a dead man right about now. Aunt Claire shot him a look that made him wanted to run and take cover. "No, Sir. Why do you think that?" He was afraid to look in his aunt's direction. When she folded her arms around her thick waist, Jasion knew that she did so to keep from slapping him upside his head.

"Boy, we ain't crazy," Aunt Claire, scolded. "That wuz that evil woman, Nee-cole Sawaggut, yhu wuz talkin' to. And don't try lyin' yhur way out of it."

"But Aunt, you and Uncle Bill have it all wrong," Jasion pleaded. He thought he'd checked his surroundings thoroughly before talking to Nicole. He could kick himself for not being more careful. His aunt saw right through Nicole when Jasion introduced her to his family. She'd warned him in the past that hooking up with her would be his downfall. Her female intuition was on point. Nicole had become a thorn in his side. "She called me."

"We gon' say this one time, boy, and yhu betta listen. Out thera'; on the porch is the woman Gawd sent yhu. Now don't be no fool and mess it up."

His aunt scared him to death when she stepped toward him, chastising him with her words. She was a petite woman, but he knew not to sass her for fear of a frying pan finding its way upside his head.

"I swear to the both of you. Nothing is going on."

"Boy, don't yhu swear up in my house," Uncle Bill scolded.

"I'm sorry, Unck." Jasion humbled himself like a little child. "Give me a chance to explain—"

"We don't won't to hea' yo' excuses," Uncle Bill said, cutting him off. "Now thera's a boo-ti-ful young woman sittin' outside waitin' on yhu. I seegest yhu don't keep her waitin'. Now get."

Jasion walked outside with his head hung low as the elderly couple followed closely behind. He felt like a ten-year-old being escorted from the principal's office by his parents. Knowing the two, the parental advice wasn't over by a long shot.

"I thought I was going to have to come in and rescue you from that caller," Angelica joked as the three walked out on the porch.

Aunt Claire and Uncle Bill shot Jasion the evil eye.

"I was chatting with Unck in the living room when Aunt Claire joined in on the conversation." Swallowing hard on his words, he'd hoped that they wouldn't rat him out.

"Chile, we were just givin' him som' sound advice. So he can keep his head and other parts of his body in the right place." Aunt Claire gave Jasion a stern look from head to toe.

"Aunt Claire and Uncle Bill, thanks for making me feel so welcome in your home. I will never forget the love that you two have shown me," Angelica said.

The elderly woman took a seat next to Angelica on the swing. "Chile, yhur welcome. That's what family is fo." She reached for Angelica's hand and placed it inside hers. "Just don't forget to send us a weddin' in-vo-tay-ion. And thera's somethin' else I want yhu to do fo' me when yhu get to Augusta."

"What's that Aunt Claire?"

"Forgive yhur mother. Yhu'll never truly release the hurt and pain until yhu do. I forgave hur for almost destroyin' my marriage. No. I didn't go to hur and tell hur that I forgave hur, but I prayed to Gawd to help me to let go of the hatred that I carried in my heart against hur. Put it in Gawd's hands, chile. Let him carry this load yhu're carryin'. Until that happens, yhu'll never be able to go on with yhur life. Yhu hear me?" Aunt Claire advised, holding Angelica's face between the palms of her hands.

"Yes, ma'am. I understand." A lone tear trailed down the side of her face.

Jasion admired the way his aunt handled his future wife like a delicate flower. He just prayed when the time came, God would give Angelica the strength and the courage she needed to face and conquer her demons. He wanted this chapter in her life to come to an end. Their marital bliss depended on it.

Nicole was another problem he would have to take care of when he returned to Port City. Her annoying presence threatened to ruin his and Angelica's perfect life. And he wasn't going to allow that to happen, not by a longshot.

Chapter Thirty Seven

Augusta, Louisiana seemed foreign to Angelica. The small town she'd grown up in had changed. Trees that once spread as far as the eyes could see was now chopped down and replaced with fast food restaurants. It no longer had that country appeal. She and Jasion drove to Alycee's home. They relaxed, ate, and reminisced about old times, although the biggest portion of it wasn't so good. Angelica shared the miraculous story with her sister of how she and Jasion discovered each other.

Angelica noticed that Alycee resembled her father, Deacon Louis, more and more. Rumor had it that his family was Creole, which explained her sister's cream-colored complexion and jet-black hair. Her long waves now cut short into a pixie style. She was slender built, stood five-foot-ten and could grace the cover of any fashion magazine. When Angelica stood next to her baby sister, the two were as different as night and day. No one would have guessed the two had the same mother.

Why Angelica's father, Maurice had never questioned Alycee's paternity, was a mystery to her. She believed his love for her mother caused him to look passed her discretions. Whatever his reasons were, no man in his right mind would have ever stayed with a woman like Gladys, not after she brought another man's child into his home and tried to pass it off as his.

On their tour around Augusta, Angelica was amazed at the small-town's transformation. More importantly, she was surprised at how well Alycee had coped with knowing that her foster father was actually her birth father. Gladys' indiscretion had affected them both. However, Angelica found comfort in knowing that Maurice Hope was her biological father.

Angelica could feel Jasion's discomfort, but he didn't complain about being the third wheel. They soaked in the warmth of the spring sun while resting on a bench in the scenic area of downtown Augusta. The soothing sounds of a water fountain splashed in the background as she marveled over the town's city-like atmosphere. The sisters laughed and talked about the good times they'd shared together. Neither one wanted to spoil the mood by dredging up any bad memories. They had plenty of time for that.

After basking in the spring day's rays and inhaling the not-so-fresh country air, the three drove to the local hospice facility. Alycee had prepared Angelica for the sight she was about to witness. She'd told her how the cancer had ravaged their mother's body.

They parked in the facility's parking lot. Jasion offered to lead them in prayer before they went inside. As the three entered through the sliding doors, Jasion gave Angelica a reassuring nudge and kissed the top of her head.

Alycee grabbed her older sister's hand, and the two walked into the hospice center as Jasion followed closely behind. Everything appeared to happen in slow motion. She was finally going to see her mother after months of protesting against it.

As soon as the doors slid close, Death greeted them. Families sat grieving in the lobby. The smell of disinfectant filled the air. No matter how hard the staff tried to portray a homey atmosphere, death remained ever-present.

The more steps Angelica took down the hallway, the longer it appeared. Panic began to settle in. The three continued to march down the freshly waxed corridor in silence until Angelica shouted, "I can't do this!" Within seconds, she became the frightened twelve-year-old girl who feared her mother's wrath. She could hear Gladys' voice screaming at her for showing up unannounced.

"Babe, you've come too far to turn around now," Jasion said.

"Fay, he's right. You've come too far," Alycee encouraged. "When you open that door, the pain and hurt you've carried for all these years will dissipate."

"I can do this. I can do this," Angelica repeated, trying to convince herself as she took slow, methodical breaths. They were right. She had to face her demons. If she didn't do it now, tomorrow might be too late.

When they arrived at room number seven, which bore Gladys Hope's name, Angelica held Jasion's hand for support. They stood outside her mother's door for what seemed like hours. She braced herself, pushed the door open, and went inside to face her mother for the first time since the age of sixteen.

In the room were familiar faces. Faces she hadn't seen in years. Cousin Eunice, her husband Fred, Mrs. Bertha, and Mrs. Alice were gathered inside. If it weren't for all the contraptions connected to her mother, the room could actually pass for a suite. Cousin Eunice was the first to run and greet Angelica with her flabby arms waving out her floral, sleeveless lounge dress.

"Oh my, Lawd." Cousin Eunice blurted as if she'd seen a ghost. "Fayth. Is it really yhu?"

Angelica was reluctant to reciprocate the hug. She held a great amount of resentment toward her cousin. Eunice did nothing to protect her from Gladys' abuse. On more than one occasion, her cousin had witnessed the beatings Angelica had received from Gladys. When she'd gone to her for refuge, Eunice offered no safe haven.

Alycee introduced Jasion. He said his hellos but stayed close by Angelica's side.

Mrs. Alice, Bertha, and Fred were equally excited to see Angelica.

"Lil' Ms. Fayth has come back to us," Mrs. Alice sang. "It truly is good to see yhu darlin'. I thought I'd be dead and buried befo" yhu come back hea.' Yhu have grown into such a beautiful youn' lady."

Mrs. Alice, now in her eighties, wore a lopsided, bushy wig that didn't fit her tiny head. Word had it; she was still putting the fear of God in the members at Saint Gabriel Baptist Church. Alycee kept Angelica up-to-date on the latest gossip in

Augusta. Back in her heyday, Mrs. Alice was a force no one wanted to reckon with. She knew everybody's business and didn't mind spreading it. Back in the day, some even said that she believed in Voodoo. She carried a white, powdery substance in 'her purse, threatening to blow it on anyone that crossed her. Years later, Alycee informed her sister that it was only baby powder.

"Gal, whera' yhu been hidin'?" Fred asked in a deep, raspy voice.

The sound of Fred's voice terrified Angelica as a child. She hated when he'd come over for visits, especially at night. The sound of his creepy voice made her afraid to go to bed.

Fred still stuffed his pipe in the left pocket of his oversized shirt. He'd now gone completely bald in the center of his head, but someone needed to take a weed-whacker to cut down the sides of his overgrown gray mane. His advanced age caused him to slump over, which made him seem much shorter than Angelica remembered. He'd always been a small man, probably one-hundred and twenty pounds soaking wet. Standing five-foot-four to his wife's, six- foot frame made Fred afraid of her. When Eunice said jump, Fred asked how high, and nothing much seemed to have changed between the two.

"Don't be askin' nobody whera' they been." Cousin Eunice piped in, giving her husband the evil eye. "We're grateful that the chile's hea' now."

"That's right. Gawd has sent our lil' Fayth back to us, so don't go sayin' nothin' to run her off uhgin. Or we gon' run yhu off," Mrs. Bertha said, balling up her swollen fist at Fred.

Back in the day, friends and family referred to Mrs. Bertha as Peaches. Her skin was the shade of a smooth, ripe Dixie, Louisiana peach. Unlike Eunice, Mrs. Bertha had aged quite nicely for a woman in her early seventies. She was tall, poised, and her clothes always neatly adorned her slender figure. Mrs. Bertha corrected the young girls at church and throughout the neighborhood to cross their legs and to carry themselves as young ladies. With all of her self-proclaimed propriety and etiquette, she was downright mean, which made the kids run the other way when they saw her coming.

Nothing had changed much over the years. Angelica stood next to Jasion, smiling at the feuding friends. If memory served her right, the three had always bickered back and forth with one another. Their squabbling caused the others in the room to laugh. Eunice and Bertha always tag teamed up against Fred when he had something to say. Fred didn't know at times, whom he was married to, Eunice or Bertha, because they both bossed him around.

Alycee interrupted, clearing her throat to get their attention. "Are you ready to see, mama?"

Angelica's stomach somersaulted. Her nerves kicked into overdrive. Jasion squeezed her hand when she looked up at him. Her palms began to sweat. Everyone gathered around Gladys' bed. Angelica, Jasion, and Alycee stood over the sick woman. Angelica couldn't help but notice how frail her mother appeared. When she was a child, Gladys had towered over her like a giant. Now, as she stared down at her frail body, her mother appeared harmless. The cancer had ravaged her once full figure.

Everyone's eyes were glued on Angelica. True, she was scared, but suddenly the Holy Spirit calmed her fears. The silence broke when she asked, "is Gladys able to speak?"

"She goes in and out of consciousness," Alycee answered. "The doctors want us to keep her as comfortable as possible until—" Tearing up, she choked on her words.

"It's alright, Suga," Mrs. Alice comforted as she wobbled next to Alycee's side. "Gawd don't put no mo' on us than we can bear."

"I know that I'm not part of this family, yet," Jasion said, smiling down at Angelica. "But I'd like to pray for Mrs. Hope and the family. No matter what may have transpired in the past. God is still a loving and just God, who forgives us of all our transgressions."

"Who is this boy?" Fred questioned, looking Jasion up and down.

"Shut up fool," Cousin Eunice responded, slapping him on the shoulder.

"That's right. Hush up, yhu ole' fool." Mrs. Bertha shot him a threatening look. "Gon' on, son. We need all the prayers we can get. Cus only Gawd has the final say, not som' doc-ter."

They each joined hands around Gladys' bed. Jasion grabbed Angelica's hand in his. How she'd managed to make it to this point in her life was anyone's guess.

Months earlier, Angelica could have never seen herself praying or asking God for anything. With the spiritual guidance of Jasion and her best friend, Marissa, she had willingly renewed her faith in God.

Jasion prayed for God to give Fayth and Gladys the opportunity to repair their broken relationship. He asked the Heavenly Father to remove any pride or stubbornness that might stand in the way of their healing.

Before Jasion ended his prayer, a weak voice cried out. "Fay-yy-th... is that yhu?" Tears streamed down Gladys' sunken cheeks. "This medicine is causin' me to hallucinate ugain." She coughed and then ran her tongue over her dehydrated, cracked lips.

Gladys stared up at her daughter. Angelica's voice was caught in her throat. Her mouth opened, but no words came out. Jasion's firm grip secured her in his arms. He must have sensed her legs giving way from underneath her. Instantly, she

195

transformed into that fearful twelve-year-old girl who'd once ran and hidden from her abusive mother.

Alycee helped Jasion to steady Angelica's trembling body.

A nurse entering the room to change out her mother's empty I-V bag, saved her. It gave Angelica the time she needed to regroup. Her mother's teary eyes trailed her every move.

The eyes that once terrified her were non-threatening now. Angelica squared her shoulders, took a deep breath, and readied herself to speak with her mother.

"Mrs. Hope's vital signs are weak," The nurse informed. "Don't hesitate to buzz the nursing station if you need me." She placed her stethoscope around her neck and left the room.

"Thanks, Nurse Watkins, I will," Alycee said.

"Fayth. Fayth," Gladys called, pulling everyone's attention back in her direction.

"Chile, yhu mama is callin' for yhu," Mrs. Alice said.

Jasion guided Angelica as she took small steps towards her mother's bed. She'd repeatedly rehearsed in her mind what she'd say to her. Now that the time had come, the words she'd memorized quickly vanished. It was time for her to face her bully. The frail woman lying in bed couldn't swat a fly, even if she'd tried.

"Yes, it's me, Gla—dys," Angelica stuttered, trying to say her mother's name.

"My baby," Gladys said, reaching up with one of her bony, thin weak hand to touch the daughter she'd rejected years earlier. The loving act took Angelica aback. Her mother never showed her any affection, ever. With Gladys meeting her halfway, Angelica grabbed her frail hand. She wasn't the twelve-year-old girl anymore. The time had come to face her giant. Gladys wasn't Goliath anymore. Instead, she'd withered into a middle-aged skeleton.

"Don't strain to speak," Angelica stressed, trying to think of what to say next. Here she was — one of CBN News' top reporters — and she couldn't think of what to say to her dying mother. A hug and a kiss were out of the question. They had never had that type of relationship. Angelica often fantasized about all the mean and nasty things she'd say to her mother if their paths ever crossed, but what she possessed at that moment was compassion. The cancer had eaten her body to the core. It ripped Angelica's heart apart to watch her mother suffer such a fate. Gladys was a fragment of the woman she once was.

"I need to get som' things off my chest befo' the good Lawd calls me home. I know it wasn' easy for yhu to come hea'," Gladys gulped. "I'm not sho' if I was in yhur shoes, If I'da come.

"Now, Gladys, yhu don't have to do this," Cousin Eunice encouraged. "Som' things we just need to let be."

The others in the room watched in silence.

"No. No. No," Gladys protested, shaking her head. "I need to say this. I want to wipe my slate clean befo' I meet my maker. I'm sorry, chile, for hurting yhu, for making yhur childhood a living hell. I pray that one day yhu'll find in yhur heart to forgive me. I treated yhu less than human, like yhu didn't come from my womb. Thea're so many people that I hurt in my lifetime. Marriages I've destroyed, or almost destroyed, because of my evil, sinful ways." Gladys raised her baldhead off the pillow.

Jasion's aunt and uncle popped into Angelica's mind. They were one of the marriages Gladys had nearly destroyed. She noticed the tightening of Jasion's jawbone at her mother's confession when she'd glanced up at him.

"Gladys, please." Cousin Eunice begged. She clasped her chubby hands together as if to pray.

"What are the two of you hiding?" Alycee asked, moving closer to her mother's bed.

"Enough," Gladys whispered. "I don't know how much time I have hea' on Earth. I've treated this chile worse than an infidel. I owe her the truth. I have lived my entire life allowin' Satan to use me. I thought I was big, bad, and tough. I thought I was unstoppable, but God showed me who was in control. My wayward behavior affected many lives. No one stood in my way when it came to what I wanted. Young man, I know who yhu are." She looked up at Jasion. "Yhu're all grown up now, but they use to call yhu Lil' Preacher. Yhu used to preach at som' of the Youth Revivals around these parts durin' the summa.

Jasion nodded his head, yes.

Gladys continued, "Yhur Aunt Claire and Uncle Bill live over in Claysville. I did som' low-down, dirty things that almost split that couple up. I'm sorry. I recognized yhu the moment I opened my eyes. Yhu were the boy at the church talkin' to Fayth the day of my husband's funeral. I've seen yhu coming into town from time to time durin' the summa. I knew yhu were searchin' for Fayth. That's why I kept her hidden. But I see my meddlin' couldn't keep you two apart." Gladys let out a loud grunt when her eyes rolled up into the back of her eyelids.

Jasion's body jerked. No doubt, he was just as disturbed by Gladys' admission as Angelica. Her mother deliberately kept them apart. If it weren't for her renewed faith in God, she'd probably have exploded and given her mother a piece of her mind.

Mrs. Alice sat on the sofa, shaking her head, while the others stood by. Fred kept mumbling obscenities under his breath.

The tension in the room thickened. Everyone seemed to be holding their breath, waiting to learn what deep dark secrets Gladys had been hiding. Angelica believed that nothing her mother had to say could hurt anymore.

Her elderly relatives' eyes now focused on her, including Mrs. Alice and Bertha. She, Jasion, and Alycee were the only clueless ones in the room.

"Fayth—," Gladys called out.

"Don't. Please. I beg yhu in the name of Jeezus. Don't do this, Gladys," Cousin Eunice, interrupted.

"I have to, Eunice. I wasn't a good person when I was in good health. But at least I can try to regain som' sense of respect befo' my demise."

"Eunice, get out of Gladys face and let hur say hur peace to this hea gal," Fred demanded.

Fred's sudden outburst surprised himself as well as the others in the room. Angelica had never witnessed her cousin, ever, standing up to his overbearing wife. She just prayed the nurses wouldn't barge into the room with security after Cousin Eunice slapped the taste out of his mouth.

"Now yhu listen hea,' yhu old coot—," Eunice snapped.
Fred silenced his wife of forty years when he said, "No, yhu listen. I'm not backin' down this time from yhur crazy rantin' and ravin'." He pulled on his suspenders and stuck out his chest to assert his authority. "This chile has come back to us after all these yeas'. Now shut-up and don't interrupt Gladys no mo'."

Everyone stood at attention when Fred spoke out against his wife. Curiosity was getting the best of Angelica. What secret had these four been keeping from her all these years?

"Neitha' of us is innocent." Fred turned and eyed Eunice, Bertha, and Mrs. Alice. "I'ma shamed of the part I played in this hea' folly." And he dropped his head.

Chapter Thirty Eight

Fear swept over Angelica. Apparently, the four had pertinent information concerning her, and she didn't appreciate it one bit. She stared down at her mother and bluntly asked, "so what's the big secret?"

Eunice stood paralyzed by the bed.

Jasion wrapped his arm around Angelica's shoulders. She was coming unglued. Angelica had always held resentment against Eunice, but now she had to pray to keep from going off on her. If it hadn't been for Jasion encouraging her to stay calm, she might have told each of them where to go.

Gladys spoke in a tired, weak voice, "I'm not one-hundred percent sho' if Maurice is yhur father."

Angelica and Alycee stood beside their mother's bed shocked by her confession. Both sisters tried to speak, but their mother's admission silenced them both.

"Me and Maurice had only been dating a short time, but I had seduced him into sleeping with me." She stopped in mid-sentence to catch her breath. Mrs. Alice took some Kleenex from the table near Gladys bed and wiped the tears rolling down her sunken cheeks. She continued, "I kept flirting and throwing myself at him until he finally gave in. He wanted to wait until we got married, but—"

"Gladys," Mrs. Bertha interrupted. "You don't have to do this."

"No, Bertha, this need to be said." Gladys picked up where she left off. "I was at a local nightclub one Friday night, teasin' and flirtin' with a group of young men. I led them on. After the club had closed for the night, I thought the men had left. But they were waitin' for me outside in the alley next to the club. I was gang raped. The four of them had their way with me. Once they were finished doin' their business, they left me there like a piece of trash. I couldn't scream because one of the men duct taped my mouth shut." Gladys rubbed her tearful face against the pillow and let out a loud, contagious-sounding cough.

"Oh, my Lord," Angelica gasped, clutching her hands to her chest. Jasion steadied her. Knowing one of the rapists may possibly be her father sickened Angelica. The only good memories she had as a child, were those of her father—Maurice Hope. Now that was all a lie.

"I'm sorry, Fayth. I'm so sorry." Gladys wept bitterly.

"Did my father know about this?" She lashed out in anger. Angelica was determined not to let Gladys see her cry. She'd shed enough tears over her mother's behavior.

"Yes," Gladys answered.

The tears she'd fought so hard to hold back now came down like a liquid inferno. Angelica couldn't believe what she was hearing.

"He forced the truth out of me. After days of lying about the bruises on my body, I confessed. Eunice and Fred tried to give me an alibi. But Maurice wasn't stupid. He forced me to check into the county hospital. I was scared and ashamed. What happened to me was my doin'. I had no business throwin' myself at those men, knowin' full well I had no intentions of leavin' with them.

Alycee ran out of her mother's room in tears, and Mrs. Alice trailed closely behind. Jasion kept a firm hold on Angelica's trembling body.

"I hated yhu, Fayth," Gladys cried. "Each time I looked at yhu, it reminded me of that night. I had so many dreams and goals for my life. What happened that night destroyed everything. So, I wanted you to suffer the way I had. I never had any intention of marryin' Maurice. I just wanted to manipulate him out of a coupla' dollars to escape from this hick-town, but nine months later, you were born, and I was trapped."

"No, you dealt yo'self a dirty hand," Fred chimed in. I hate myself for not sayin' somethin' when yhu beat this chile black and blue. But no mo', it stops hea'." He nervously chewed on his bottom lip. "Eunice, I'ma tellin' yhu right now. If yhu want a dee-voce, then that's fine with me. Cus I'm old and I'm not goin' to stand befo' my Maker with this hea' on my record. Gawd don't like ugly and wee-ee-ave don' som' low-down, ugly thangs. Come clean now, we-ee-ave hurt this chile enough by not protectin' hur."

"Yhu're right, Fred," Gladys said.

Eunice set Gladys up on her pillow.

"Fayth, I pray that yhu'll find it in yhur heart to forgive me. I will go to my grave hatin' myself for everything that I put yhu through. Yhu turned out to be just what yhu said yhu would be; an investigative reporter. Alycee has been keepin' me informed with yhur career. No matter how hard I tried to destroy yhur dreams, God placed His protective hedge around yhu."

Alycee and Mrs. Alice returned to the room. It was apparent the news that Maurice may not be Angelica's father had shaken her up as well.

"I forgave you three months ago, Gladys," Angelica paused, trying to regain her composure after hearing the devastating news about her paternity. "Your hatred caused me to lose my way. I spent years wandering in darkness because of you, but God saw it fit to send me someone who truly loves me and sees the beauty within me, no matter how ugly you told me I was. Gladys, you hated yourself all those years you abused me, thinking it would ease your pain. The news you've just laid on me will never overshadow the fond memories I have of my father. Maurice Hope is my father. Your misery had nothing to do with me. I've returned to my faith and trust that God, along with this good man and others, will help me through this." She wrapped her arms around Jasion's waist.

"Yes, Gawd will, baby," Mrs. Alice said. She walked around to the other side of the bed where she and Jasion stood, placing her arms around them both.

Angelica leaned down, hugged, and kissed her mother. "I love you, mama. I forgive you. She broke down in tears. It was the first time she'd called Gladys, mama, without fear of the repercussion.

"Thank yhu, baby. Now I can go and be with the Lawd in peace. I love yhu, my beautiful flower." Gladys exhaled. Her vital sounds had flat-lined.

Alycee raced to the intercom to summon for help, but when the doctor and nurses arrived, it was too late. The physician informed the family that Gladys had signed a Living Will. Her last will and testament stated that if she coded, under no circumstances were they to resuscitate her. Angelica stood in a daze. Surely, she was in the middle of a nightmare. Her mother's lifeless body now lay inches away from her.

The hate for her mother that she'd held onto for years dissipated. Forgiveness was just the medicine Angelica needed. If she'd waited a day more, it would have been too late. She believed that God allowed Gladys to live long enough to make amends for her sins. The physician informed them that she didn't know how Gladys managed to survive as long as she had, but Angelica believed that it was God. The same God she'd rejected for so many years.

The doctor and nurses left the room, giving the family time to say their final goodbyes. One by one, they said their farewells in their own special way. There was not a dry eye in the room. It wasn't tears of sadness, but tears of joy — joy that mother and daughter had reconciled and that Gladys' painful bout with cancer had finally ended.

When it was Angelica's turn, Jasion gave her space and moved into the background. Her teary eyes stared down at her mother's lifeless body, and then she kissed Gladys on the forehead and whispered, "Goodbye, Mama, all is forgiven. You can finally be at peace now."

Chapter Thirty Nine

The trip to Augusta, Louisiana, no doubt was an emotional one, but Jasion and Angelica persevered through it. He'd never met a woman with such strength and courage. If the shoe were on the other foot, he didn't think he could have handled facing his estranged mother with such dignity and class. Angelica did exactly that. She forgave her dying mother, releasing Gladys from her guilt and shame.

Now back at home, Port City's investigators wasted no time turning up the heat at Spitzer Financial Firm. The president of SFF, Mr. Lexington, along with members of the board, voted to place Jasion on paid administrative leave until the case was resolved.

With nothing but time on his hands, Jasion had taken Angelica to meet his mother, Evelyn McCoy. His mother jumped for joy at the news of their engagement. He'd explained the details surrounding him finding his Fayth. His mother always expressed her concerns about him letting life pass him by. She'd wanted for years for him to settle down and give her a house full of grandbabies. Now, she would finally get her wish. Within a month, he and Angelica planned to walk down Bountiful Blessing Ministry aisle and exchange their wedding vows. His mother assumed that Angelica was in the family way, due to their rush to get married, but quickly, Jasion put her mind at ease when he'd told her that he and Angelica hadn't been intimate.

The beautiful woman, stirring in his arms on the sofa, made coping with the investigation tolerable. Jasion decided to use his downtime to learn all there was to know about his soon-to-be bride. She had three days left on her vacation before returning to CBN News. And they'd planned to spend everyone one of them together.

Jasion debated telling Angelica about Nicole Swaggart's harassing phone calls. Things were good between them, and he didn't want to ruin it by dredging up old drama from his past. He'd searched high and low to find his Fayth, and he wasn't about to do anything to risk losing her again. So, Jasion decided to extinguish the fire with Nicole as quietly and as quickly as possible.

"Cuddling up next to you is getting the better of me," Jasion moaned, squeezing Angelica into him with one arm. "I'm trying to channel my thoughts elsewhere, but making love to you is winning the battle in my mind."

She rubbed her long, sensual fingers up and down his clad chest until he grabbed hold of it. Her touch was pure torture.

"Just keep saying, one more month," Angelica reminded.

His hand caressed her long tresses as her words simmered in his mind. One more month until they consummated their union seemed like an eternity. He wanted her, and he wanted her now. Jasion tried praying silently for mercy, but no words came. Having her curled up in his arms was surely torment that had to end or else.

"That's easy for you to say, Babe."

"Jasion, I never dreamed I could be so happy." She shifted her body even closer to him, causing every hair on his body to stand on end.

"I feel the same way, beautiful." Jasion leaned down to kiss the most perfect set of lips he'd ever laid eyes on.

How could he be happy and sad at the same time? The case weighed heavily on his mind twenty-four-seven. He prayed that the investigators would move a little faster in bringing whoever was behind the missing money to justice. Surely, the perpetrator had to leave some type of clues behind.

Ending their kiss, Angelica changed the subjected. "I can't understand why Mr. Lexington put you on leave. Unless he knows something he's not telling."

Jasion relaxed his head back against the sofa's armrest and continued to run his hands through her hair. "He's just trying to protect the company's image. I'd probably have done the same if I were in his shoes."

"I've checked past financial records at the firm. You've made that company and investors a lot of money over the past five years," Angelica stressed. She brought his hand to her lips and delicately kissed it.

"Once the guilty party is apprehended, he or she will be faced with several charges," Jasion explained. "False accounting entries and illegal transactions to name a few. In a nutshell, it's a federal crime that comes with serving a lengthy prison sentence."

"Well, we better work harder to prove your innocence."

"Exactly."

"Just because Lance pulled me off the case when I told him we were engaged doesn't mean I can't continue to snoop around."

"What if your new case takes up most of your time?" They both sat up on the sofa when the conversation took a more serious turn. He wanted nothing more than for her to continue working on his case. He trusted her. The new investigator they assigned to take over lacked experience. He was fresh out of college.

Angelica swept her hair back with her hand and said, "this story is a piece of cake."

"Really. And what makes it so easy, beautiful?" Jasion loved watching her blush when he called her such names. She was beautiful; downright stunning. He remembered when they first met fifteen years ago, Jasion told her she looked like his sister's Barbie dolls and she still does.

"I am investigating a woman who broke out of a mental institution four months ago."

"That don't sound like a piece of cake to me, Babe." Now he was concerned. People with a mental health condition were potentially dangerous. His wife-to-be was no match for the criminally insane.

"The police report said that she took down two armed guards when she escaped Forest Oaks mental facility."

"Sounds like Catwoman. I wouldn't want to meet her in a dark alley." He leaned forward to get his bottled water off the coffee table. "So, Babe, what's the name of this mental patient you're investigating?" he asked, unscrewing the cap off the bottled water and taking a big gulp.

"Nicole Swaggart."

Water flew from his mouth at the sound of Nicole's name. Since arriving back in Port City, things weren't going as he'd planned. His company had placed him on administrative leave. And now his present fiancée was investigating his ex-fiancée. His day couldn't get any worse.

"Nicole Swaggart." He forced her name out after nearly strangling at the mention of it.

"Do you know her?" she asked puzzled. "The mention of her name caused you to choke and come unglued?"

"No, Babe. The water went down the wrong pipe," he lied. They hadn't tied the knot yet, and here he was lying. He felt like a heel, but he just couldn't risk telling her about Nicole, at least not yet. If Jasion wasn't scared of her, then he had every reason to be now. Nicole was crazy. That explained the fifty-something messages she'd left on his cellphone in Claysville, confessing her undying love for him. She wasn't operating with a full deck.

Jasion's life was playing out like a bad dream. If God was testing his patience, He sure was doing a great job. He didn't know how much more of this nightmare he could take. He'd found the woman of his dreams, the woman God had sent him, now his bad choices in women and impending imprisonment threatened to destroy it all.

He was a fighter and determined to see this through to the end. He'd waited for Angelica for fifteen years. Nothing and nobody was going to stand in their way of being together. His Aunt Claire had warned that trouble was ahead. Now he had to prepare himself because it had arrived.

"I've enjoyed lounging with you today, but I better get going," Angelica said, breaking his concentration.

"Don't leave just yet," he groaned. "I hate being in this huge house alone."

"I need to read up on some files Lance gave me on Nicole Swaggart before returning to work on Thursday."

Jasion stood with Angelica. She grabbed her purse off the coffee table and headed for the door. He pouted, trailing behind her. Who knew what she might find in Nicole's records? Jasion just hoped that nothing in her files linked her to him.

Changing the subject, Jasion asked, "when will the paternity clinic notify you about Maurice being your father?" He locked her in his arms from behind.

"Usually two to three business days. The clinic is waiting to receive my uncle's sample," she shrugged, turning around and burying her head into his chest.

"Well, that's great news, isn't it?" Jasion asked, caressing her back.

"My uncle doesn't trust sending the sample through the mail, and he has a fear of flying. So, I'll just have to wait until he arrives on the bus."

"How long will that take?"

"A week," she muffled in his chest. "He has to come from Portland, Oregon."

"Maurice is your father. The test will prove it."

"I hope so."

The two hugged, kissed, and said their goodbyes. Jasion walked Angelica to her vehicle parked in his driveway. He held her close, kissed her again, and watched as she drove off. Before he could head back inside, he noticed a suspicious car parked across the street from his home. He couldn't tell if the person was male or female. After hearing that Nicole had broken out of a mental institution, it might very well be her. Had she resulted to stalking? The thought of her calling him fifty times and sending him several text messages warned Jasion that Nicole was capable of anything. Whatever she was up to, he just hoped that Angelica didn't fall prey to any of her crazy tricks.

Chapter Forty

Since joining the Bountiful Blessing Ministry, sitting on the fourth row had become the norm for Angelica. After her spiritual conversion four months earlier, she'd been attending church regularly. She still hadn't become a member at BBM, stating that she preferred to wait until she and Jasion were officially husband and wife before taking such a huge step. If their relationship flopped, she'd have to change her membership. The thought of watching him date or marry another woman might send her over the edge. No, she'd play it safe and wait until the ink dried on their marriage license before joining BBM.

Something didn't set well in Angelica's spirit. Weeks earlier, when she'd mentioned Nicole Swaggart's name to Jasion, his eyes nearly bulged out of their sockets. She knew that look. Angelica had interviewed countless of suspects and could smell a lie a mile away. It came with the territory of being an investigative reporter. For now, she'd let it go, but she did intend to get to the bottom of it and soon. Jasion had explained his wayward past to her. If Nicole were one of those women from his past, she wouldn't hold it against him. She'd made some poor choices when it came to men as well. Who was she to judge him? However, to purposely lie about not knowing Nicole was another issue within itself, and she had no plans of starting off their marriage with lies and secrets.

The woman with her many assortments of hats arrived on cue. Angelica remembered the first time she and her best friend, Marissa, met Mrs. Ida Mae Howard. She gave them the evil eye for being disruptive during the church service. It was the same day Angelica renewed her faith. Mrs. Howard always arrived early to make sure that no one sat in her seat, two chairs down from hers.

Wearing a hat the size of a spaceship, Mrs. Howard squeezed her plus-sized body between the narrow pews and said with a huge smile, "good morning, love."

"Good morning, Mrs. Howard," Angelica said, standing to give her room to pass. "I was beginning to think you weren't going to make it to service today,"

"Baby, I wouldn't miss church for the world, especially today." She gave Angelica a suspicious smirk. "God has given me six days out of the week to do what I want. The least I can do is come and give Him two hours of my time on Sundays." She waved her hands in the air and then flopped down in her seat.

Angelica couldn't help but remember how she once was one of those people that found time for everything else, but God. Her Sunday mornings consisted of sleeping late and looking for the next high profile story to investigate. Now she looked forward to getting up early and worshipping with other believers. Church, along with her counseling sessions with Dr. Hawthorne was just the medicine she needed. Because of the joy and peace she'd found, her therapist had taken her off anti-depressants.

As praise and worship got underway, the ministers entered the platform behind the senior pastor. Jasion's eyes found her in the crowd. It wasn't hard to do because she always sat in the same seat when possible. Their eyes locked, and he gave her a smile that sent goose bumps up her arms.

Angelica clapped and sang along with the praise singers. If someone had told her that she'd be in church singing God's praises, she probably would have laughed in their face.

When the pastor dismissed the church service, Mrs. Howard grabbed Angelica by the arm, leading her in the opposite direction from the exit door. "Why are we going to the fellowship hall?" Angelica asked confused.

"All I know is that the pastor's wife wanted to see the women immediately after service," Mrs. Ida responded, wobbling next to Angelica down the spacious hallway. "And I'm just being obedient."

Angelica nodded her head in agreement and allowed her elderly friend to lead the way. She wondered why she hadn't heard the announcement before now.

When Angelica and Mrs. Howard entered through the doors, out of nowhere, everyone yelled, "surprise!" Her eyes lit up when she realized it was for her. The women at BBM had decorated the fellowship hall in her favorite color, lavender.

Marissa stepped from behind the door, giving Angelica a big hug and kiss on the cheek. "I'm at a loss for words." Angelica stood with tears in her eyes. She'd never thought that people could actually care about her enough to throw a surprise bridal shower. Strong, warm arms caged her in from behind. She knew his scent and the feel of his body anywhere. Jasion had come to share in her happiness.

"Surprise, my beautiful lady," Jasion said, giving her a quick peck on the check.

The women in the room sighed at his words and romantic gestures.

Just when Angelica thought her day couldn't get any better, her baby sister Alycee walked in. How Jasion managed to put together such a lovely gathering so quickly, was a mystery.

"Alycee!" Angelica screamed, moving out of Jasion's embrace and into her sister's. They hadn't seen each other since their mother's funeral two months ago.

"I wouldn't have missed this for the world, Fay." Alycee pulled back to look her sister in the eyes. "If anyone deserves to be happy, it's you." She tried hard to fight back the tears. "I love you, Sis."

All the people she cared about were present. She'd asked the question many times. Where was God? Now, she realized He'd been with her all the time. The choice to receive Him was always hers to make, and she was glad she'd made the right decision.

Jasion kissed her on the cheek, said his goodbyes, and then exited the room.

When the last guest drove off the church grounds after her bridal shower, Jasion rushed over to where Angelica stood. He planted a kiss on her lips. "I've wanted to do that all morning," he said, twirling her around like a ballerina.

The senior pastor and his wife cleared their throats, alerting the lovebirds that they weren't alone. Angelica and Jasion turned around and smiled as the couple waved and left them alone in the parking lot.

"That was embarrassing," Angelica said, burying her head in her favorite place, his chest.

"Why? It's not like we're doing anything wrong," Jasion replied. "You know lavender compliments your beautiful skin tone?" He trailed one of his fingers down her sleeveless arm.

"Oh, I see you're trying to change the subject. Besides, what do you know about colors?" Angelica asked, playfully punching him on the arm.

"I don't know the first thing about colors, but I know what looks good on you," Jasion responded, entwining his fingers between hers as they walked to his car. "So what do you have an appetite for, pretty lady?"

"Whatever my man has an appetite for." She bumped her hip against his body as they walked to his car.

"A woman after my own heart," Jasion joked, leaning down to kiss her again. But, before parting lips, a car sped in their direction. A female screamed obscenities and tossed a brick out of her car, barely missing Jasion's head.

Angelica screamed as Jasion pulled her down beside the car for protection. "Baby, are you alright?" she asked. Angelica held onto him. "Who drives on church property, cursing like a drunken sailor?"

With a quickness she'd never seen, Jasion hurried Angelica into the passenger's side of his BMW. He hopped into the driver's seat and sped off as if their lives depended on it. Taking long, deep breaths, Jasion finally spoke, "Angelica, wicked people could care less about God's house. The devil will strike anywhere; at any time."

*****

"Baby, what's wrong?" Angelica asked. "You've been playing with your food since the waitress placed it on the table thirty minutes ago."

"Nothing," Jasion lied, twirling the turnip greens on his plate with his fork. He knew it was Nicole. What other female would be brazen enough to throw a brick out of a moving vehicle, and in a church parking lot?

"Do you know her, Jasion?" she questioned with raised brows. "I know it was a female."

"No." Jasion felt sick to his stomach. Why was it hard for him to tell Angelica the truth about Nicole? He placed his fork on the table; eating was the least thing on his mind. Although she wore a wig to disguise her appearance, Jasion knew it was Nicole. A man doesn't spend two years of his life with a woman and not recognize her.

"If someone is after you, Jasion, the authorities need to know. What if it's the anonymous caller?"

"I hear you, Babe." He rubbed his hand across his face. "The thought of you getting hurt sickens me. The whole incident just put a damper on a perfect day."

"It didn't ruin my day," Angelica said, reaching for his hand across the table. "Like I told you before, Jasion, I'm here for the long haul, just don't shut me out. I've investigated and reported some of the most disturbing cases. I can handle myself."

"I'm sure you can, but I don't want you to get hurt because of me."

Jasion's appetite had finally returned. He took a bite out of his broiled catfish that was now cold. He contemplated

214

whether to tell Angelica about the threats he'd received from Nicole. Threats he didn't take seriously, until now. For the life of him, Jasion couldn't bring himself to do so. A part of him wanted to spit it all out, which he should have done, but he just couldn't go through with it. He feared that the reporter in her might go and confront his insane ex-fiancée. With Nicole's obsessive, violent behavior, who knew what she was capable of? So, for now, Jasion prayed that everything would work itself out. Realistically speaking, he knew nothing involving Nicole would be simple.

Chapter Forty One

Dressed in a disguise, Nicole drove downtown for a bite to eat at a local Waffle House. Having been cooped up in a stuffy motel room the entire morning, she needed some fresh air. The risk of the authorities or a trigger-happy civilian spotting her was always a possibility. Her face appeared on the front covers of newspapers and aired on local television stations, daily. Today, she threw caution to the wind. Being caged up like a wild animal, Nicole wasn't about to imprison herself in some cheap motel.

Out of nowhere, a hand rested on her shoulder, which caused fear to wash over her. Nicole slowly turned to put a face to the mysterious hand. "What are you doing here?" she asked, clutching her chest, and then slapped the man's hand off of her. "Are you trying to give me a heart attack?"

"I work across the street at Spitzer Financial Firm, darling, or have you forgotten." He pulled out a chair and took a seat beside her. "Besides, a man never forgets a woman like you. I'd recognized that body anywhere. No disguise can hide a figure like yours."

"I'm getting tired of you avoiding me, J. This hard-to-get act is beginning to wear on my nerves," Nicole snapped.

"Lower your voice," he whispered. "We have to lay low."

"What I'm saying is that you need to drop the attitude when I call. Remember you came crawling back to me for help, and since we share a common interest." She paused. "Money and a score to settle. I decided to hook up with you. So don't go thinking you're doing me any favors. You need me." She gave him a stern look to let him know she meant business.

"I know. I know. All I'm asking from you is to please stop with the calls before you slip up and get us caught," J pleaded. "Someone at the motel might get suspicious and call the cops."

"The room is in your name?" Nicole reminded him and gave him a look that he'd better think twice before double-crossing her. She knew when someone was trying to run a game on her. She grew up in the mean streets of New Orleans', Ninth Ward and learned a few tricks in the class of con-artistry 101 from the best.

"You better get your jealous rage under control," he scolded, taking a napkin off the table to wipe the sweat from his forehead. "That little stunt you pulled yesterday in the church parking lot has to stop. You're going to blow our cover."

"You're not the boss of me, J. I'm getting tired of you barking orders," she demanded. "I need that money just as bad as you. You better ditch your little girlfriend before we leave the country. I want you to listen and listen well. Don't try to double-cross me."

"This heist means more to me than just money, Nicole. My father gave his life to that firm and what did they do in return? They blackballed him from ever working at any local and national financial firms." He pounded his fist on the table, causing Nicole to jump. "So, you see, for me, it's about revenge. Taking their money only makes the payback that much sweeter."

"Well, you better not be playing me, or you'll regret it," Nicole warned. "You can have your revenge but not at my expense. I need that money."

He stood abruptly from the table and left, to Nicole's surprise. She got up and trailed him out of the door to a side alley. Away from the hustle and bustle of people on the walkway, J turned, pulled her close, and kissed her. She believed he only did it so that he could keep her under his control until the job was finished. Her instincts warned that he had no plans of taking her out of the country with him. But, it would be over her dead body before she allowed him to leave with all the money.

Nicole wrapped her arms around his neck, playing along with his acts of affection. He'd confessed his loyalty to her, but she knew differently. She'd been around the block enough to know when a man was lying. Nicole planned to let him continue his little charade for now. She had a few surprises as well. Where there were greed and revenge, someone was bound to get the short end of the stick, and it wasn't going to be her.

Chapter Forty Two

With their wedding day fast approaching, Angelica expressed to Jasion how she'd always wanted a large family. To her surprise, he'd planned a backyard barbecue at his home. He invited every cousin, aunt, uncle, and honorary relatives to welcome her into the McCoy's Clan. Her dreams of a real family had come true.

From the kitchen window, she watched the men playing football in the backyard. Jasion's athletic body moved with precision as the men tried tackling him. If it weren't against the law, she'd prefer to skip the wedding and go straight to the honeymoon. Thoughts of them together made her weak in the knees. The shorts and form-fitting t-shirt Jasion wore showed every muscle rippling through his toned body. Thank goodness, their big day was only a week away. They had known each other for six months, and Jasion had been the perfect gentleman, but fighting the urge of wanting him physically was wearing her down.

The women busied themselves in the kitchen, but Angelica couldn't pry herself away from the window. The reality that the handsome man outside belonged to her still hadn't sunk in. Jasion could have any woman he wanted, but he chose her. For months, she remained suspicious of his motives for dating her, but now, she realized that they were genuine.

In past conversations, Jasion had spoken to Angelica about avoiding moments that would cause them to give into temptation. He didn't want to dishonor God by having premarital sex. He wanted to wait until his wedding night to share himself completely with her. For that, she was grateful. He'd shared stories of his reckless past with sex and women, and she had expressed the same about her trying to find acceptance and love with all the wrong men.

Everyone seemed happy. His family's love for one another shone on their faces. *Yes, Jasion had the perfect family. Thank you God for blessing me to be a part of it,* she muttered under her breath, placing a pitcher of ice-cold lemonade on the picnic table.

Jasion made a touchdown and broke into a celebration dance. He looked over in Angelica's directions and blew her a kiss. As corny as it was, she reached her hand into the air and pretended to catch it.

*****

Later that evening, when the majority of his family had left, Jasion strolled over to where Angelica was cleaning up paper cups, plates, and napkins off the picnic table. The tiredness shown in her eyes, but she continued to keep a smile on her beautiful face. "Babe, you look exhausted," Jasion said. He removed the trash bag from her hand and sat her down and began massaging her tense shoulders.

"A little, but I'm okay," Angelica said, reaching back to pat his hand. "Jasion, you have a wonderful family. You can see and feel their love. This is one of the best days of my life."

"What's your best day before this one?" Jasion asked, fishing for compliments.

"You are something else, JC. You know that you're the second best thing, next to renewing my relationship with God," Angelica joked, lifting her head up to give him a kiss. "Satisfied."

"Now that's what I'm talking about." They both laughed. "Yes, I'm very satisfied now."

Jasion stopped massaging her shoulders and took a seat beside her. He felt it was time to come clean and lay all his cards out on the table. Nicole had become a thorn in his side. He would never forgive himself if something happened to Angelica because of him. Nicole wasn't playing with a full deck. He knew that now. Her violent acts on both their cars and the brick thrown at them on the church parking lot were evidence of how unstable she was.

He knew he needed to come clean, but the cookout wasn't the proper place to do it. There were still a few of his family members hanging out in the backyard, so he decided to cook dinner for her tomorrow. It would be their last dinner as a single couple.

He lifted her hand from her lap, held it inside his and said, "Angelica, I have something very important to discuss with you." Her eyelashes fluttered uncontrollably, which made him nervous. If Angelica found out that he lied about knowing Nicole, she might never forgive him.

"About what?" she asked, giving him a weary smile. "Is it about us being intimate before our wedding night? Baby, I can wait. We only have a short time to go. It's been a struggle for the both of us, but we're almost there." She brushed her hand to the side of his cheek.

"No. No. No… it's not that." Jasion wished it were that simple. He rubbed the side of his head with his free hand. Once he spilled his guts about Nicole, Angelica may never want to see or speak to him again, let alone sleep with him.

"Can you give me a hint?" Angelica inquired, yawning.

"Tomorrow." He kissed her as if it were his last time doing so, and afterwards said, "let's sit out here a while longer and enjoy the rest of this beautiful evening.

When the last family member left, Jasion and Angelica moved to the back porch. He took a quilt someone had left behind and draped it around Angelica's shivering body. The nights were cool in Port City. The lake surrounding the neighborhood made the evening spring breeze feel much cooler. The sounds of crickets and owls reminded Jasion of the short time they shared as kids. They'd steal away into the woods and listen to the birds and crickets serenading them or at least that was what he'd told himself.

Jasion felt that he was the luckiest man on earth. The woman leaning against his shoulders had come back to him, but what he had to say at dinner tomorrow might drive her away forever.

The couple held each other into the still of the night. They stared into space, admiring the canvas that God had painted just for them, each lost in their private thoughts.

Jasion had made mistakes along the way when it came to love, but believed it was worth the heartache and pain. God had shown His favor on him and he believed within his heart that things would work out for his good.

The soon-to-be married couple stared into the starlit skies, listening to the rhythm of the night.

Chapter Forty Three

Jasion and three of his closest friends from college met at a local sports bar for his bachelor party. A night out with the boys to watch the Los Angeles Lakers versus the Miami Heat in a playoff game was a much needed distraction to take his mind off his troubles. The dinner plans that he and his future bride had made didn't go as expected. She had to work late on a story. He'd just have to wait until tomorrow to discuss Nicole with her. Tonight, he intended to relax and enjoy an evening with the fellas.

The first of the three to get married, Jasion counted himself blessed to have found his soul mate. Two of his friends had come close, but cold feet kept them from walking down the aisle. Hail or high-water couldn't keep him from marrying the love of his life.

The four friends had been inseparable since college. They immediately jumped on board when Jasion pitched the idea of opening a youth center for at risk kids. Many of their childhood friends had given in to drugs and violence. Jasion and his friends thought they were lucky to have escaped the mean streets of Port City.

Each put up a share of their money and solicited donations from surrounding businesses. Jasion found a large vacant building in the heart of Port City's inner city. Offering a handsome bid to the owner, the four made a down payment towards ownership

Tonight, the restaurant appeared more crowded than usual. Every man in Port City seemed to be packed into the small establishment to watch the Lakers defeat the Heat. Jasion overheard a male patron joking about how he had to come to the sports bar to escape his nagging wife at home.

After an hour wait, the waitress finally took their orders, placing a basket of breadsticks in the center of their table. Rico took a bite of one of the breadsticks and said, "J, that's going to be you on lock-down soon, Bro. I guess it's just going to be the three Amigos from now on, because you will be out of commission." The other two agreed and laughed.

"No. I don't think so, Angelica's cool," Jasion said, stretching his neck in the direction of the flat screen television mounted on the wall.

"They all seem cool until the ring is on their finger," Brandon chided, "but seriously, if I was marrying a woman as beautiful as Angelica, I wouldn't want to leave her at home just to hang-out with a bunch of musty dudes."

"All I know is, he better treat her right. A woman like her doesn't come along every day. In case, you start having any second thoughts coming up to the wedding, just think about whom you almost married. Thank goodness, you dumped that chick before it was too late. Man, Nicole Swaggart had some major issues," John said, grabbing a breadstick from the basket.

"Look, we're here to celebrate. What kind of bachelor party is this?" Jasion asked. As soon as John brought up Nicole's name, his mood had changed. "I just hope the police catch her before someone gets hurt. The quicker she's off the streets, the less I'll have to worry about. Now, let's order because I'm starving and I want to watch the game."

The friends ate, talked, laughed, and watched the game. It was like old times, freshmen hanging out in the student union to catch the basketball playoffs. This was the first time in months that Jasion was able to relax and be one of the guys. They reminisced about loves they'd lost, and some they hoped stayed lost.

The Lakers were leading the game by twenty points and the night couldn't get any better. Until his deceased father's advice came and invaded his good time. Jasion's dad had tried to warn him about the dangers of getting involved with the wrong women, among other things. His father had constantly reminded him that he had a bright future ahead of him and warned him about the pitfalls in life. Jasion had heard how gifted and anointed he was since the age of five. He went against his father's words of wisdom and tested the waters, and nearly drowned in his disobedience.

He did exactly what his father advised him against. He had Bible knowledge but lacked common sense when it came to the opposite sex and life. His father had warned him to keep his spiritual eyes open when choosing a mate, stating that most women would chase after him for what he could financially provide.

Nicole Swaggart was far worse than any woman he'd ever known or dated. She was very conning, which Jasion blindly ignored. Caught up by her physical beauty, he nearly let her destroy him. Nicole was rotten to the core. She only showed him what she wanted him to see. Once she had Jasion wrapped around her fingers, the claws came out. It was as if she had direct orders from Satan to destroy him.

Jasion thought about the time Nicole approached the senior pastor's study at BBM and demanded he gave Jasion more Sunday's to preach. She'd told the pastor that Jasion was the most gifted son of the house and the others failed in comparison.

Her cutthroat tactics also offended many of the ministers' wives as well, expressing that the program committee should put her over the church's women's conference after she and Jasion wed. Nicole believed that their decorating skills and ideas were tacky and lacked style. She'd continued issuing demands when she was asked to march out on the platform that was strictly for ministers. She thought that she was just as important and needed to stand by her husband's side.

A patron, who'd gone outside the sports bar to smoke, ran back inside shouting about a crazed woman in the parking lot. The man's deep, frantic voice snapped Jasion's mind back to the present. The man claimed that a woman was waving a handgun in the air, screaming obscenities. He shouted for the owner to call the police.

As soon as the four friends heard what all the commotion was about, their eyes bulged and they shouted in unison, "NICOLE!" They rushed to a nearby window and witnessed her circling the parking lot, cursing like a drunken sailor.

The owner stood at the door with his cellphone in hand to call the cops. The screeching sounds from her tires led Jasion to believe that she had fled the scene, but not before screaming at the top of her lungs, "you can run J, but you can't hide. I'll never allow you to walk down that aisle and marry another woman." Nicole sped off into the night like a deranged lunatic.

Jasion knew he had no choice but to tell Angelica everything before Nicole struck again. If there were ever a time he needed the Lord, it was now. He was shaking in his shoes.

A man shouted from across the room, "whoever J is up in here, you better watch your back. That woman means business. I wouldn't want to be in your shoes."

The other patrons laughed, except for Jasion and his friends. They were terrified. Jasion the most because of what Nicole might do to Angelica. He knew he had to go to her and fast.

Chapter Forty Four

"Why do you insist on making a fool of yourself, Nicole? That fiasco last night at the sports bar takes the cake. In case you have forgotten, our freedom is at stake, while you're out parading around town, pulling your crazy stunts. I think it is best we go our separate ways," Caleb scolded, pacing back and forth in Nicole's motel room. Images of his hands wrapped around her throat brought a smile to his face, but he quickly tossed the idea out of his head. Murder wasn't his forte.

"I've warned you about following me, J!" Nicole snapped. She quickly sat up across the bed and let him have it. "Don't get it twisted, you're not my man. Remember, we only have two things in common — money and revenge. Once this gig is up, I'm outta here. So don't go questioning my whereabouts."

Caleb hated when Nicole called him J, taken from his first name, Joseph. The night he and Nicole met, he knew she might be trouble. They had both sat next to each other at a local bar, nursing their wounds. Nicole had confessed escaping from Forest Oaks mental institution after she has had too many drinks, so he'd told her his first name.

A name he seldom used. Her admission would be just the admonition he needed to blackmail her later. But, her calling him J had reached its limit. She did so because of her obsession with Jasion, a man he loathed.

"I was at the sports bar with friends, trying to have a relaxing evening. But, guess who showed up, waving a gun and acting like a raving lunatic in the parking lot? You know the cops are looking for you. And yet you continue to go out and do something stupid to draw attention to yourself." Caleb rubbed his head out of sheer frustration and dropped down into a chair next to the bed.

Dealing with Nicole's unpredictable behavior made him realize that he'd made a mistake in hooking up with her. Hindsight being twenty-twenty, he should have left her on the bar stool where he'd found her. But he needed her.

The master keys Caleb stole from Ms. Kennedy's purse after their first date had gained him access to Jasion and Mr. Lexington's office. Nicole would handle business on the outside, while he worked from the inside. Now, it seemed like a bad idea. Her behavior was growing increasingly erratic.

Nicole's greed made her easy prey. Upon completing the job, Caleb planned to notify the authorities of her whereabouts. He was already planting evidence that would point towards her and Jasion. Neither would see it coming. Caleb learned about her and Jasion's past relationship the night they met at the bar. In her drunken state, Nicole had confided many dark secrets. Admitting her undying love for Jasion McCoy would prove to be her first downfall.

The night that Caleb met Nicole, she had passed the stage of tipsy. She was downright intoxicated. She revealed the reasons for her bitter break up with Jasion. Nicole vowed to destroy Jasion's life the way he'd ruined hers. From her admission of juvenile delinquency to wounding a security guard while trying to escape a mental institution, it was all like music to Caleb's ears. He kept the drinks coming as she spat out information about her criminal past. He had hit the jackpot in meeting her. Her hate for Jasion ran deep, which meant he didn't have to twist her arm when it came to framing her ex-fiancé.

Nicole's nagging voice faded in the background as Caleb sat, wondering how he'd dug such a deep hole for himself. He'd tried working his charm on Jasion's secretary, Patricia Kennedy, but her jealous and clingy nature kept him at bay. Patricia would go berserk whenever she caught him flirting or talking to other female employees. Caleb fed her his celibate line. It worked for a while until another female employee exposed him to make her jealous. He was young and had no plans of hooking up with just one woman, so Patricia served him his walking papers, but not before he'd stolen and made copies of her keys to every SFF office door.

He needed someone on the inside to watch his back while he hacked into Spitzer Financial Firm computers. Patricia apparently wasn't the one. Her straight-laced attitude would get him caught for sure.

He knew that Nicole would eventually need money because she was an escaped convict. Caleb fished her telephone number out of his wallet and called her. She had expensive taste; he could tell that night, even in her drunkenness. Once he'd laid out his plans to steal millions, he knew it would be just a matter of time before she wanted in.

Nicole had all sorts of shady friends. She'd paid handsomely to make fake identification cards for her and Caleb. They'd opened up several bank accounts in different states and countries to ensure they wouldn't raise any red flags while transferring the stolen money. The bogus identification cards could fool even a trained eye.

Caleb thought his worries were over when Nicole became his accomplice. It was as if a higher power had answered his prayers. He needed her criminal instincts. But his days as a free man might end if she didn't stay focused on the job at hand. Her revenge against Jasion stood in the way of them planning the perfect crime.

He'd moved the electronic device which altered his voice to Nicole's motel room. Caleb carefully wiped his fingerprints off the equipment. The device was like a new toy for Nicole. She loved calling and making threats to Angelica, knowing that detectives couldn't trace her calls. Instead of investigators believing he was the unidentified caller, they would accuse her. Months earlier, he'd led Angelica on a wild goose chase by calling and giving her false leads on the case. Now he had no use to continue his charade. He'd tried his best, convincing her of Jasion's guilt, but his scheme to rip them apart had only brought them closer.

The job is almost complete. While Nicole is having her revenge, the money and I will be long gone. Caleb grunted under his breath.

Jasion's discernment of people made it harder to con him. But his co-worker Ian was clueless. If it weren't for his father, Mr. Lexington, a brilliant entrepreneur, Ian probably would be a bum on the streets, begging for bread. *The saying, "Like father, like son, is farthest from the truth when it comes to those two."* Ian was nothing like his father. He lacked business sense. Caleb never bothered to hack into his computer. Mr. Lexington only allowed him to handle small accounts and entrusted Jasion to handle the major ones.

Caleb pretended to make small talk with Jasion at the firm to gain his trust. For reasons unbeknownst to him, Jasion would brush him off, which infuriated him. He hated Jasion because the position he held once belonged to his father. Mr. Lexington accused Caleb's dad of misappropriating funds. He'd always known his father to be an honest man, but SFF fired him after years of dedicated service on suspicion of theft. Someone had to pay for his father's injustice, and Jasion would be the first to taste his wrath. Mr. Lexington replaced his father with Jasion and for that reason alone, he hated him.

His father died, trying to prove his innocence. When the verdict came back guilty with a life sentence, he committed suicide. Caleb vowed to drain Spitzer Financial Firm dry because of their heartless attitudes. They showed his father no mercy. In return, he had no compassion for them.

"So, Nicole, have you given any thought as to how you're going to frame Jasion?" Caleb asked with raised brows.

"Yes. And it's going to be the ending of all endings. If I can't be happy, why should he?" Nicole replied, licking her ruby red lips with a wicked grin.

"Care to share?" Caleb got up from his chair and sat next to her on the bed where they'd had many intimate rendezvous. Nicole's wickedness turned him on, which was why he'd tolerated her foolishness for months.

"No. I don't," she snapped, slapping his hands off her thigh. "You just take care of your part of the job and let me handle mine."

"Fine. Just don't screw it up, because if you do, both of us will be behind bars for the rest of our lives."

Chapter Forty Five

Angelica whipped her vehicle into Jasion's two-car garage that he'd conveniently left open for her. She stepped out and unlocked the side door with the key he'd given her. Strolling through the spacious washroom, she smelt the mouth-watery aroma of home cooking.

Angelica stopped in the kitchen and peeked inside the pots simmering on top of the stove. Grabbing a bottle of sparkling water from the refrigerator, she took a big gulp, and then called out to let Jasion know that she had arrived, "babe, I'm here."

"I'll be out soon. I'm headed to the shower," he announced. "Make yourself comfortable."

As she left the kitchen, Jasion's cellphone rang. Being nosey by nature, Angelica picked the phone up off the countertop. Unknown caller lit up the screen. She wasn't about to invade his privacy by answering it, so she placed it back and went into the living room.

When she entered the living room, she'd spotted documents sprawled across his coffee table. Before she could peek at them, the house telephone rang. *Now who could that be?* she thought. Since it wasn't her home, she had no right to take his calls. The answering machine picked up. A woman's seductive voice caught Angelica by surprise, drawing her attention away from the documents.

"Hey, Babe, I've missed you. Call me when you get this message."

"Who-in-the-Sam Hill is that?" Angelica's jaw dropped as she stared at the telephone, believing she'd heard wrong. She listened as the woman continued to talk. *Has Jasion been having an affair behind my back?*

"I'm not going to hold any grudges against you for trying to make me jealous with that reporter chick," the female caller

232

expressed. "The money we stole from Spitzer Financial Firm is enough to help me get over your little deception."

Angelica was now sick to her stomach.

"Get rid of her tonight, so we can be together as planned. I let you get away before. But, I'll be damned if I'll sit by and let some other woman below your standards steal you away from me." The caller's sultry voice turned threatening, and then she hung up.

After the shock had worn off, Angelica stumbled over to the telephone. The sight of Nicole Swaggart's name on Jasion's Caller ID seemed to cause the room to spin. She became infuriated. Her mind went back to the day she'd ask Jasion about ever knowing Nicole. His face told her he was lying, but she had let it go. All this time, Nicole had been the one sabotaging their cars and the one who assaulted them on the church ground with a brick. Angelica's blood had passed boiling point. It had erupted. If she'd stayed focused on the case, instead of blinded by love, she would have seen the warning signs. Jasion had been playing her for a fool. And the dinner he'd planned might be her last meal.

After all, what did she really know about him? A person could change tremendously in fifteen years, and apparently, Jasion had. He'd turned into a heartless, money hungry, two-timing liar.

She calmed herself down long enough to try and think straight. Angelica called her boss, Lance and asked that he send detectives over to Jasion's home. She'd explained the message Nicole left on his answering machine and that she was his accomplice at Spitzer Financial Firm. In turn, Lance informed her that detectives already had a warrant out for Jasion's arrest and that he'd explain all the details later. She hung up and anxiously waited for Jasion in the living room.

At that pivotal moment, her heart felt as if someone had yanked it off her chest. Angelica was disappointed in herself for falling head over heels in love with Jasion, and that she couldn't see his deception until now. Who was this man she'd professed her undying love to? He sure wasn't the boy she'd met fifteen years ago. JC was kind and thoughtful of others, especially of her. The man he'd grown into was a coward who had stolen from innocent people.

She wanted to cry, but no tears would come. She refused to play the weak little victim again. To channel her energy elsewhere, Angelica returned her attention back to the mess of papers on the coffee table she'd seen a few seconds ago. She saw a weird looking electronic device that sat next to the files. She bent down to read the inscription on the side of it, "Voice Altering Device." Her legs buckled, causing her to collapse into Jasion's favorite recliner.

He's been professing his love for me while sleeping with some tramp behind my back, she thought. *Now everything is so much clearer. I see why he could resist me sexually. He's sleeping with another woman. I bought into his celibacy lie. What twenty-eight-year-old man, full of raging hormones, is celibate in today's time?* Angelica buried her face in her hands. Being blinded by love had caused her to miss the warning signs. And for Jasion to take the Lord's name in vain, pretending to be a minister was just downright blasphemy.

Angelica pulled herself together. She had a job to do, and she planned to do it. Her broken heart had to take a backseat to doing the right thing. She forced herself from the chair and began thumbing through the files. They were the same ones Jasion reported missing from his office. How did he manage to get his hands on them? The voice-altering machine helped him to disguise his identity. What Angelica couldn't understand was how he could be so stupid. He had left everything out in the open, knowing she'd be coming over for dinner. His rush to get home had caused him to slip up. *As the saying goes, "there's no such thing as a perfect crime."*

"Dammit, Jasion, how could you?" She tossed the folders across the carpeted floor. The tears she'd tried to keep from forming earlier had a mind of their own. She thought someone had taken a knife and ripped out her heart. The pain was overwhelming. The tough reporter had to take a backseat to the vulnerable woman she had now become. She'd given her heart and soul to a man that turned and crushed it in a matter of seconds. "How could you do this to me... to us?" She wanted to leave, but her feet were heavy as cement blocks.

Her old demons began to resurface. "Gladys was right when she'd said that I was an abomination. She'd told me that no one would ever love me because I was a cursed child. I should have listened, but I believed that You, oh Holy and just God, had finally sent someone to love me. But, I see that the joke was on me. Ha. Ha. Ha. God, You get the last laugh. I've heard that You have a sense of humor. Too bad it came at my expense. Why did you create me, only to treat me so cruelly? What did I do, God what was so wrong?"

Angelica took her fist and pounded it on the table, causing the remaining files to fall onto the floor with the rest of the documents. She picked up the contraption Jasion used to disguise his voice and tossed it out of her sight.

He had this planned from the start. Pretend to fall for the love-starved reporter. Save her lost soul. Propose to her, so she'd take herself off the case, and then leave without warning, Angelica assumed, just the thought of it all made her ill.

Surely, he couldn't have orchestrated a job of this magnitude with just Nicole's help. His friends, Rico, Brandon, and John may possibly be involved. They all work at the center together, she thought, trying to keep her wits about her.

Lights from a vehicle beamed through the window. She peeked out, signaling to detectives that she was okay. The last thing she needed or wanted was to have them kick down Jasion's front door, alerting him of what was about to go down. She didn't want him to escape.

I remember Jasion saying that he needed to discuss something important with me.

She peeked out of the window again, and noticed lights from a car, slowing down as it passed Jasion's house. She'd seen the same car earlier. Maybe it was a coincident, or maybe it was his accomplices.

Angelica pulled her cellphone from her jacket pocket and called Detective Lewis. She wanted to be the one who ousts Jasion about his dirty dealings and see his face once he'd been caught red-handed. Detective Lewis warned that it wasn't a good idea, but it was something she had to do. She wasn't running from her problems anymore. She had to face them head on. Angelica closed the curtain and waited for Jasion to come out of the bedroom.

An alluring smile curled up on Jasion's chiseled face as he strolled into the living room. He pulled her off the sofa. Catching her off guard, he leaned her back into his arms and took her breath away with a mind-blowing kiss. She wanted to protest, but his lips transported her back into happier times in their relationship, or what she thought were happier times. Sadness crept into her heart. This wasn't how she imagined their lives would end. The tough girl in her wanted to reach out and slap the taste out of his mouth. But the woman who'd fallen in love with him wanted to stay in his strong arms forever. Their forever had ended because of greed, lies, and lust.

When their lips parted, Angelica looked up into his hopeful brown eyes, and cried. "How could you do this, Jasion? I loved you with all my heart, and you go and hurt me this way."

"Baby, slow down, what you're saying isn't making sense. What are you talking about?" Jasion asked, confused.

"I can't marry a man like you. A man with no conscious and could steal from innocent people that trusted you with their hard earned money. I never knew you... the real you," Angelica spat out venom in each word she spoke.

"What in the world are you talking about? I would never do anything knowingly to hurt you or anyone else, for that matter."

"Stop acting like you're innocent." She folded her hands across her chest to keep him at bay. "And oh, by the way, one of your accomplices or should I say, girlfriend, Nicole Swaggart left you a message."

"Wh… What… Who?" he stuttered.

"You heard me loud and clear." She raised her voice, something she hadn't done since they'd been dating. "The woman you've been cheating with behind my back. The woman you said you didn't know. Remember?"

"God, why is she trying to ruin my life?" Jasion cried out. "Don't believe what you've heard."

Angelica looked at him as if he were crazy and said, "do you expect me to believe that lie. I wasn't born yesterday, you know. I'm getting outta here."

Jasion grabbed her by the arm. "Let me explain. I invited you over to dinner to tell you about Nicole."

"Then what? Kill me after your confession, Minister McCoy?"

"Kill you. Are you crazy? Woman, I love you. I wouldn't harm a hair on your beautiful head. But you are going to sit down, and you're going to listen to what I have to say," he demanded.

"Explain what? That you're a two-timing, lying thief," she screamed at the top of her lungs.

He pulled her into his arms. Angelica tried to wiggle and worm her way out his grasp, but his strength had overpowered her.

"No. Stop saying that. You know me." Jasion said forcibly.

"Do I?" she asked, giving up the struggle of freeing herself from his strong hold.

Jasion told Angelica the story about his ex-fiancée, and all the problems she'd caused since escaping from the mental institution. He explained that he came through the garage door, put dinner on to warm up, and headed straight to the bathroom to shower. That he had no knowledge of how the electronic device or his clients' confidential records got into his home.

His pleading words meant nothing to her because the incriminating evidence was staring her right in their face. It was hard for her to keep up with his lies. With all her heart, she wanted to believe him. Angelica couldn't bear looking into his eyes without bursting into tears. Even after Nicole's telephone call and the proof staring her in the face, she couldn't make her heart stop loving him.

A knock at the door startled them both. Jasion released Angelica from his arms and opened the door to detectives with handcuffs, who read him his rights. She watched as they hauled him away, like a thief in the night.

Chapter Forty Six

Undercover officers surrounded Spitzer Financial Firm the next morning. A security guard, working the graveyard shift, reported seeing Jasion in the building last night. He stated to authorities that a man close to Jasion's height and build ran down the emergency stairwell when he'd called out to him. But Jasion had been in jail, awaiting bail.

Officers took their positions. All entrance and exits at SFF remain blocked off. The employees stayed in the conference room for their safety. A man like Caleb Michaels, who'd gone to great lengths to hide his identity, could very well be carrying a loaded weapon. The last thing officers wanted was to have employees caught in the middle of a shootout.

Thanks to Jasion's arrest and extensive months of surveillance, officers were able to connect Joseph Caleb Michaels to the crime. Records showed that Caleb had received two years' probation for writing hot checks but other than that, nothing major until now. When investigators dug into his past, they discovered that his father was an employee at SFF, fired for embezzling money from the firm.
Caleb's father also sold his stocks in the company to pay off his outstanding gambling debts.

Caleb used his mother's maiden name, Michaels, to land a position at SFF. Mr. Lexington hadn't seen Him since the age of ten. His father had shipped him off to a military school.

When Jasion's boss, Mr. Lexington paid his bail last night, he asked Jasion to report to work the next business day. He informed Jasion on what was about to take place at the firm, and he apologized for doubting his innocence.

Jasion stayed in his office while detectives continued to gather employees in the conference room. He wanted to witness Caleb's arrest. The man had brought nothing but heartache and pain in his life. The thought that he and Nicole hooked up to destroy him still angered him.

As he stared out his office window, reporters and television crews lined the sidewalk to get Port City's biggest story of the year.

Relieved that the nightmare was about to end, he and Angelica could continue their wedding plans. Jasion was thankful that his arrest last night wasn't going to prevent them from tying the knot. He smiled, knowing that he and the woman he loved would be together soon.

He immediately called Angelica after he'd made bail, giving her every sordid detail of Caleb and Nicole's embezzlement scheme. He informed her that the firm would be on lockdown and Caleb had zero chance of escaping. Jasion left the window and peeked out of his office door. Plain clothed cops stood by the exit stairwell and elevator.

"Okay, men, this is it. I've been briefed that our suspect is heading down the hallway." Jasion overheard one officer relaying the message to another one on his walkie-talkie. He continued to listen to the officer giving orders. "We'll wait until he approaches the conference room, and then take him down. There's only one way in and one way out."

"I wouldn't want to be in Caleb's shoes," Jasion exhaled, closing his door. He was now able to breathe a sigh of relief after months of uncertainty.

Just when Jasion headed to his desk, his cellphone rang. Angelica's number appeared on the screen. Before he could speak, she overloaded him with a series of questions. "Are you okay? What's going on? Someone reported that there was gunfire in the building and hostages taken."

"Slow down," he chuckled, trying to sound calm, but his nerves were on edge as well. "I'm fine, sweetheart, and no, there aren't any hostages."

"Are you sure? You're not just saying that so I won't worry. Are you?"

"No, babe, we've been through too much for me to lie to you." All he could think of at that moment was pushing his way past the barricades, finding Angelica, and scooping her up into his arms. He wanted to carry her far away from this place. They had been through hell and back in the last couple of months, and needed some peace. "Where are you?"

"Downstairs in the lobby. Detectives refuse to let me up to see you."

"Stay there until Caleb is escorted out of the building. He is being arrested as we speak," he pleaded. "I'll feel much better if you do."

"No, Jasion, I have to see for myself that you're okay," she insisted. "What about Nicole Swaggart? Have officers located her yet?"

A pain shot through his heart at the mention of Nicole's name. "No, they haven't a clue of her location."

"I'm on my way up to see you, bye."

"Angelica, don't—"

She'd hung up.

Knowing her, that meant only one thing; she was going to find a way upstairs. Jasion tossed his cellphone down, sprinted out of his office to head off Angelica. On his way out, he'd noticed officers scattering throughout the building.

"Mr. Michaels has escaped." One detective yelled out to the others, and they split up and went in different directions.

"Angelica!" he shouted. Jasion darted down the emergency stairwell, praying that she didn't cross Caleb's path. God only knew what he was capable of, especially now that the police were after him.

Jasion didn't bother to take the last three steps down the emergency stairwell. He leaped over them, pushing open the door leading into the lobby. Caleb blindsided him with a sucker punch to the ribcage, then grabbed him by the collar and held a gun to the back of his head.

Jasion staggered, trying to gain his footing. Here, he thought his life was finally getting back to normal, only to end up in the clutches of a psychopath.

News stations were filming Port City's most exciting story in months. Jasion, Caleb, and the detectives, every move was being filmed. It looked as if the circus had come to town.

Jasion's life might possibly end at any given moment, but he was thankful it was him, instead of Angelica. He would have lost his mind if Caleb had taken her hostage, instead of him. With so many cops patrolling the building, how could they let one man slip through their grasp?

An older officer pleaded with Caleb, "son, you don't want to go down this road."

"And what road is that?" Caleb asked, pressing the pistol deeper against the back of Jasion's head.

"Son, let the gentleman go." The officer beckoned for the gun with his hand, but Caleb wasn't buying it.

It felt as if his heart had stopped. His future with Angelica and babies they would never have crossed his mind. Then he thought about the dream Angelica shared with him. A dream she'd kept from him for weeks. That a gun went off, and he was lying in a pool of blood, and at that critical moment, he realized that his life could possibly end. What if the dream, depicted his death?

His heart ached at the thought of never knowing her intimately. He braced himself, made peace with his maker, and prepared to die. If this were his final moment on Earth, he would use it thinking about the love he and Angelica shared, and thank the Lord above for blessing them to meet again, even if it was fleeting.

"Jasion," Angelica screamed at the top of her lungs as officers escorted her out of the elevator.

Jasion never felt more helpless as a man, than at that moment. He didn't want Angelica to see him with a pistol aimed at his skull. "Babe, get out of here," Jasion yelled.

"You let him go," she cried, as an officer tried forcing her outside. "He hasn't done anything to you."

"I will blow his brains out if you utter one more word," Caleb threatened.

Jasion noticed Caleb's hand beginning to shake and prayed that Angelica would do as the officer commanded, but he knew she was just too stubborn to follow orders.

"If you shoot him, you will never walk out of these doors alive."

"Angelica. Sweetheart, please do as the officer requested, and leave," Jasion begged.

"I'm not leaving you, JC," she yelled, choking on her tears. "We've spent fifteen years apart, and I promised myself after last night's fiasco, never to leave you again."

Jasion knew if he were going to get out of this mess alive, he'd have to come up with a plan and fast. He prayed for a miracle from above. "I love you, Angelica, never forget that." He waited for the perfect opportunity to make his move. It was do or die for Jasion and he had no plans of dying without a fight.

The officer began to plead with Caleb again, and when Caleb aimed the gun at him, Jasion elbowed him in the stomach with all his might, but Caleb never dropped the gun. Jasion tried prying the weapon out of his hands, with no such luck.

Caleb managed to push Jasion away and aimed the gun back at him with hands trembling.

Angelica broke through the barricade and launched her body in front of Jasion. Gunfire rang throughout the lobby of Spitzer Financial Firm. When the firing ceased, Angelica and Caleb lay motionless on the freshly waxed marble floor.

"Somebody... call 911," Jasion shouted, dropping to his knees beside Angelica. He rocked her limp body close to his chest and wondered how a day that started out with so much promise ended with so much grief.

Epilogue

"You may kiss the bride." The pastor of Bountiful Blessing Ministry announced to the happy groom. Everyone in the congregation stood and clapped for the newlyweds.

Just three days ago, Jasion thought he'd lost the love of his life. When the paramedics arrived, they informed him that Angelica had fainted and would be fine. After waving an ampule of smelling salts underneath her nose, she awakened. Tears of joy ran down Jasion's exhausted face when the most beautiful set of brown eyes stared up at him.

A sharp shooter, hiding inside the lobby vents at Spitzer Financial Firm, killed Caleb. Although he wasn't one of Jasion's favorite people, he'd never wished death on him.

Later that day, detectives apprehended Nicole Swaggart at Caleb's home. They confiscated a Duffel bag filled with money, passports, fake ID's, and a flash drive containing Jasion's clients' financial records. Surprisingly, she'd admitted to planting the evidence in Jasion's home and conspiring with Caleb to milk millions from SFF.

"Church, I introduce to you, Mr. and Mrs. Jasion McCoy," the pastor announced.

The newlyweds entered the beautifully decorated reception hall, where festive music played. Oohs and ahhs filtered throughout the room as they took their seats at the head of the wedding party's table. Everyone was having a good time. Kids were running. Some danced, as cameras flashed from every corner of the room.

The DJ requested that the bride and groom come to the middle of the floor for their first dance as husband and wife. Jasion happily obliged. He took hold of his beautiful bride's hand and led the way. As they passed their family and friends' tables, smiles and tears of joy were seen on their faces.

Jasion felt the warmth from his wife's body as they swayed to the music. He was caught up in the rapture of her love. His life was empty, and his future bleak before Angelica entered it, but fifteen years later, here he was, married to the girl that he'd fallen in love with at the age of thirteen.

Angelica was floating on cloud nine as she nestled her tired body against her husband's strong chest. Her life had never been a bed of roses, until now.

She planned to counsel young teens at his youth center once they settled into their new life together. Angelica believed it was time for her story to be told. Her testimony might help other abused teens to learn to forgive their abusers. When she was a child, Angelica believed that she was the only abused kid in the world. But God had seen it fit to bring a strong man into her life, to help to bear her infirmities. Angelica learned that she had become stronger because of Jasion and her new-found faith. Learning that Maurice was her father also helped to put her in a better state of mind. The DNA test came back ninety-nine-point-nine percent positive, which boosted her confidence even higher.

The newlyweds continued to dance long after the music had ended. Each of them, lost in their thoughts as the rhythm from their heartbeats kept them in sync. No one bothered to interrupt them, so the DJ replayed their favorite song, *Ribbon In The Sky*, by Stevie Wonder.

The couple said their goodbyes to their wedding guests. A stretch limousine was parked outside, waiting to take them to the airport where a private plane awaited to whisk them off to the Caribbean. It was a wedding gift from Mr. Lexington.

Jasion and Angelica drove off into the night to enjoy their first night as husband and wife.

*****

The limo driver drove as if he was leading a funeral procession. Jasion wanted him to step on the gas and get them to their hotel. The Caribbean scenery was breathtaking. But the only site he cared to see at that moment was his curvaceous wife. The wait had been long enough. He didn't want to waste another precious second. For months, he had to pray to God for strength whenever he was alone with her. Now that they were married, he could be with the woman he'd pined over for years and love her without restraints.

When the bride and groom arrived at their hotel, they stood in the doorway of their suite like two nervous virgins. Jasion took a deep gulp and asked, "Mrs. McCoy, will you grant me the honor of carrying you over the threshold?"

"Yes, you may kind Sir," she said, tossing back her long tresses. "Just promise, that you won't drop me."

Jasion lifted her into his arms, carried her into the room, and then ran back into the hallway to retrieve their luggage. He rushed back inside and grabbed his wife around the waist. "Have I told you how beautiful you are today?" he asked, planting butterfly kisses along her neck.

"Yes, a million times," she giggled. "But I will never get tired of hearing it from someone as handsome and sexy as you, darling."

"Fayth Angelica McCoy, I will spend the rest of my life trying to make up for the lost time we've spent apart. You mean everything to me, lady."

He engulfed her mouth without worrying about restraining himself. On numerous occasions, he wanted to break his vows of celibacy but was thankful he'd waited until their wedding night.

His manly touch made her warm and tingly inside. His hands possessed great physical strength, yet his caresses were soft and electrifying. She'd never met a man that made her feel the way Jasion had. He was everything she'd dreamed he'd be. He wasn't forceful like the men in her past. He had a heart for God and was comfortable with who he was as a man.

When their lips parted, Angelica knew she couldn't wait any longer. The look in his eyes told her he felt the same. The smile on his face revealed to her that the moment they'd both waited for had come. Their first night together as man and wife, a night she would never forget. Their bodies would be a gift to each other.

"Let me go and freshen up," she said, unlocking her arms from around his neck.

"Don't take too long, or I'm coming in after you. I have waited for you fifteen years, six months, twelve hours, and nine minutes to be exact," he joked. He rocked her in his arms before releasing her.

Angelica emerged from the bedroom, wearing a sheer lavender negligee that left nothing to the imagination. "Looks like someone needs to pick their tongue up off the floor." She stood nervously with both hands folded in front of her.

Jasion was speechless.

"So... how do I look?"

Jasion didn't say a word. He walked over to where she stood, picked her up in his arms and carried her to the bed and consummated their marriage.

If you enjoyed reading, *Where Was God?* Please leave a review at the bookseller where you purchased the book. You can find other books by Sheila L. Jackson at www.sheilaljackson2.com or any online site where books are sold.

Contact Information

To contact Sheila L. Jackson for book signings/workshops/ speaking engagements, you can email her at: SJ@comcast.net or visit her website, www.sheilaljackson2.com

Discussion Questions

1. When Fayth told her Aunt Beatrice at her father's funeral that her mother didn't care about her. Do you think the aunt should have delved deeper into Fayth's claim? Kids are abused at an alarming rate in our society because we miss important clues right in front of us.

2. Fayth abuse began at the age of twelve when her father died. At that moment, her faith in God died also. She believed that He had abandoned her to her mother's harsh brutality. When tragedies or bad experiences happen in our lives, why do we turn away from God rather than to Him? Why does it seem easier to blame Him than the persons that are afflicting us?

3. At the age of twenty-seven, Angelica severs ties with her first name, Fayth. Parting ways with a name that had more curses attached to it than blessings, she thought it would give her a fresh new start. Oftentimes, we feel as though we can run from our past, but sooner or later it catches up to us. When help is not sought, how can unresolved issues hurt or destroy us later in life?

4. When it comes to Jasion and his past relationship with a women like Nicole, as a minister, should he had

been wiser when yoking up with a women like her in the first place? Or is he like most men of the cloth, a pretty face and nice body rules their better judgment?

5. Do you feel that Angelica is like most women, who play the tough girl role only to mask their hurt and insecurities? Like her, many are hurting on the inside but to strong willed to allow a God fearing man to rescue them.

6. The villain, Nicole Swaggart suffers from mental illness, which millions of Americans do. How important do you, the reader feel, like Angelica, Nicole is a victim too? And how would you explain her being a victim?

7. As a man of God and one who made many bad choices when it came to women. Jasion thought it best to live celibate even after he and Angelica became in a committed relationship. When he found out that she was Fayth, his childhood love, practicing abstinence became a mental/physical battle. Do you believe that remaining celibate until marriage strengthens a person physical and spiritual relationship?

8. Satan planted the seed of doubt in Angelica's head when she heard a message left on Jasion's answering machine from Nicole. She believed that Jasion was able to resist her physically because he was sleeping with Nicole. Do we find ourselves doubting the good that God has placed in our lives?

9. Jasion sermon, Where was God, was a power packed message that we have all asked at one point in time in our lives. As a reader, how would you describe Angelica's breakthrough moment after hearing the answers that she'd often asked throughout her life?

10. Would you say we sometimes jump to conclusions like Angelica and Marissa did at the restaurant when they say Jasion with a woman and young girl, who they later found out, was his sister and niece?

11. As a reader, how did you feel after reading Fayth Angelica Hope story of abuse and turning her back on what she needed the most, God? What emotions did it evoke in you?